BAD COMPANY ON CORONATION CLOSE

LIZZIE LANE

Boldwood

First published in Great Britain in 2026 by Boldwood Books Ltd.

Copyright © Lizzie Lane, 2026

Cover Design by Colin Thomas

Cover Images: Colin Thomas

Every effort has been made to obtain the necessary permissions with reference to copyright material, both illustrative and quoted. We apologise for any omissions in this respect and will be pleased to make the appropriate acknowledgements in any future edition.

A CIP catalogue record for this book is available from the British Library.

Paperback ISBN 978-1-83656-417-1

Large Print ISBN 978-1-83656-416-4

Hardback ISBN 978-1-83656-415-7

Trade Paperback ISBN 978-1-80656-209-1

Ebook ISBN 978-1-83656-418-8

Kindle ISBN 978-1-83656-419-5

Audio CD ISBN 978-1-83656-410-2

MP3 CD ISBN 978-1-83656-411-9

Digital audio download ISBN 978-1-83656-413-3

This book is printed on certified sustainable paper. Boldwood Books is dedicated to putting sustainability at the heart of our business. For more information please visit https://www.boldwoodbooks.com/about-us/sustainability/

Boldwood Books Ltd, 23 Bowerdean Street, London, SW6 3TN

www.boldwoodbooks.com

PROLOGUE

The coal hole was dark. There was no point in crying, no point in pleading with him to let her out. She had been a few minutes late putting his dinner on the table. No matter whether he was on the day or night shift, he was fastidious about what time he ate his meals – to the minute, if not the second.

And when she was late...

There was also the pig bin inspection. Every bone had to be cleanly picked of meat. Vegetable peelings must be boiled to get the last bit of goodness out of them before being thrown in the pig bin. The pig bin itself had to be scrubbed after every emptying. Newspapers had to be properly tied up – or she would be.

She tried to remember if she'd done everything she should have done that day, but it seemed that she hadn't.

Ever since she was a little girl she'd hated the dark. Percy knew that, knew how to make her suffer. And here they were with a coal hole off the kitchen beneath the stairs that led to the first floor. The dream of a happy married life had been a nightmare, the coal hole revisited in the darkest, deepest time of the night.

1

MAY 1942

Margaret Routledge who lived at number five Coronation Close, was putting on her 'warpaint' downstairs in the house she'd once shared with her policeman husband Percy and their three children. Percy was gone and so was Albert, her youngest son. Her angelic little boy Albert had died from diphtheria around the same time as her husband. The pain of losing Albert was still there, like a knife forever twisting in her heart. Her husband was another matter. She was glad he was gone.

It was just the three of them now, her, seventeen-year-old daughter Judith and fourteen-year-old son, Howard.

A smile flickering on her lips, she pulled on the silky stockings given her by some Yank soldier, an exciting man of the type she was attracted to. A type totally the opposite to her late husband.

Once they were smoothed into place, she tucked her hair into a sequined snood, humming along to the song she'd heard the night before. Her life was fun, fun, fun all the way, and why not?

She didn't care that her behaviour was the talk of Coronation

Close. She didn't care that they called her a tart, and frequented places where women sold their bodies, mostly because they had nothing else to sell.

People would find it difficult to understand why she had changed so much since her husband had died. To her, it was quite simple. Some people indulged in drink or drugs. Margaret had decided she would indulge in sin.

A powdered face looked back at her from the mirror hanging on the chimney breast. Stretching her lips into a perfect 'O', she ran a bright red lipstick from top to bottom, end to end, pouted, brought the top lip onto the bottom one to set it.

The result was pleasing. There was no trace of the cowed wife that used to be, the wife who had lived in fear of saying the wrong thing, making the wrong move.

She smiled at her reflection. 'If only you could see me now,' she breathed, her eyes sparkling. 'I've become everything you didn't want me to be.'

People had been shocked by the death of a seemingly respectable man and there'd been sympathy for the widow. Not that Margaret had need of sympathy from anyone – and that included the minister and congregation of the church they'd attended.

Eyeshadow next then mascara. Like a vamp from the silver screen. Sensual. Alluring. Happy?

'You bet,' she hissed. Not as some had expected her to be. Not now and not back when it had first happened.

Margaret Routledge recalled very well the expression on the sanctimonious face of the Reverend Maurice Grinder when he'd visited her immediately following the death of her husband. Two years ago, but the reverend's pudding face, his oily voice and his total ignorance of the nature of their marriage still set her teeth on edge.

'The pain of losing your husband will cut deep, but regular prayer and church attendance may go some way to soothing the pain of your tragic loss. Everyone at the church has pledged their support.'

He could not possibly comprehend what joy she'd felt on determining that she would never again go to church or adhere to any of the rules her husband had laid down. He couldn't know. He couldn't possibly know.

When her icy countenance had failed to thaw, he'd suggested she keep a journal where she could record her happy memories. The fool wasn't to know that there were none, not latterly in the marriage anyway. As for the early years immediately before and after the wedding, well, viewed from a distance she should have recognised the signs that Percy was a man who needed to control other people. A wife was ideal. She had spent years in purgatory – or hell.

She grimaced at the thought of another memory from that time when she'd first realised that she was free.

A beatific smile had remained fixed on the reverend's face. He'd thought he knew Percy but didn't know him at all. Neither did he know her; in fact, she'd barely known herself.

That was when she'd exploded. Not fiercely like a fire, but coldly like the ice on windowpanes.

'Get out.'

Her voice had been sharp. Her look even sharper.

'Mrs Routledge...' That condescending voice. Even now, after the passing of time, it unlocked something deep within her. Something obstinate and at variance with the life she'd had, and the woman Percy had moulded her to be.

A good woman. An obedient woman. A woman with no life outside the family home. That was what Percy had ordered her to be. Not to talk back, not to make decisions, always to obey and present a saintly figure wherever she might be. Sin was anything not ordained or approved of by him. Sin was perfume, make-up, looking anything but a dowdy church mouse. That's how she had lived. And now?

Remembering the clergyman scurrying from her house followed by a barrage of expletives made her laugh out loud.

'I'm going to be everything my husband didn't want me to be. I'm going to be a sinner, Reverend Grinder. Do you hear that? I'm going to be a sinner!'

Before sliding her feet into a pair of high-heeled court shoes, she crossed the bedroom and looked out of the window.

Her lips curled in a surly smile. 'There they are,' she murmured, her eyes raking the women assembled around the garden gate of number two Coronation Close. 'Ready to pass judgement.'

It was an ingrained need to retaliate that caused Margaret to push open the window and shout down at them, 'Yes, I'm off out again tonight. And I won't be back until late.'

They looked up, then looked away again, engrossed in a conversation that was likely about her.

Smiling to herself, Margaret slammed the window shut.

* * *

Jenny Crawford lived at number two Coronation Close with her daughters, Tilly who was nineteen and Gloria who had lately celebrated her seventeenth birthday. Roy, her husband, had been with them when they'd first moved from slums in Bristol's medieval city centre to the council house where they had the luxury of an indoor bathroom and a cold water tap over the sink.

From the very first, she'd struck up a friendship with Thelma

Dawson who lived opposite in the crescent-shaped close at number twelve. Her son George and daughters Mary and Alice lived with her – or did at first. Like a lot of other people, and despite their youth, they were now engaged in the war effort. George was at sea with the navy. Mary had married rather hurriedly and was living up north. Alice was training to be a nurse.

Although it was easy to feel lonely, Thelma had the luxury of having daughter-in-law Maria and three grandchildren living just around the corner.

It had been Jenny's suggestion to forgo a cup of tea and go to the pub, citing the undeniable fact that Thelma looked as though she could do with something stronger.

'Are you all right?'

Thelma twisted her lips as though chewing on something bitter. 'I've got to be all right. What choice do I have? What choice does he have for that matter?'

Jenny felt for her. Peter van Luntzen had come into Thelma's life on a Sunday afternoon. A pilot officer with the Dutch Air Force stationed at Bristol's Whitchurch Airport. He'd been stationed there a while, but that had changed about two months ago. He'd been restationed, called away for extra training, the details of which he'd kept close to his chest.

'I can't help thinking he's going back there – to Holland, that is. But he wouldn't say. Told me not to worry. Pah!' she exclaimed, tossing her head. 'How can I not worry? Tell me that. How can I not?'

Jenny had no answer to that. Her dear friend had led a colourful life – if the fact that her children had been fathered by three different men could be called that. Not that she shared her secret with just anyone. It was safe with Jenny. As far as the rest of Coronation Close was concerned, she was a widow like Jenny, and there were plenty of those around after the Great War of 1914 to 1918.

Having finished their first drinks, Jenny asked if she'd like another.

'My shout,' offered Thelma.

'No. It was my suggestion we come here. There'll no doubt be another time when I'm in need of you treating me, but for now... Another port and lemon?'

Thelma didn't argue.

Jenny picked her way to the bar, the empty glasses held close at shoulder height. A port and lemon was a bit pricey, but Thelma looked as though she could do with it. Not being a big drinker, Jenny had settled for half a shandy. After handing over a pile of coppers and two sixpenny bits, she put her purse back into her brown leather shoulder bag. The table they occupied was tucked into a corner behind a screen; a private place where they could discuss their concerns without being overheard.

Conversation hummed in the smoky atmosphere, working men and women out to grab a moment of pleasure following long hours of work.

Jenny eyed her friend over the rim of her glass. She took in the strained expression, the fear haunting her eyes. Despite being in her forties, Thelma was still a good-looking woman. A few strands of grey showed in her glossy dark hair, and her curvy figure was much the same as it had always been, the kind called Rubenesque that featured in old paintings.

When she'd first known her, Thelma had been involved with the senior rent collector, a chap called Cuthbert Throgmorton. He too must have seen the similarity between Thelma and the models in old pictures because he'd painted and sculpted her himself. It had always struck Jenny as strange that Bert, as he was more commonly known, hadn't fulfilled his promise to marry her. She suspected the loss of his mother, with whom he lived, might have affected his judgement and that was why he'd joined up. He'd not been the most exciting of men but had seemed dependable. It turned out they'd been wrong. The last they'd heard of him, he was serving as a wages clerk in the army.

Peter van Luntzen had come along and picked up the shattered pieces Bert had left behind – though being the trooper she was, it hadn't taken Thelma long to brush herself off and find herself hopelessly in love. 'At my age,' she'd exclaimed to Jenny, her face flooded with colour.

'Age has got nothing to do with it, not in my opinion.'

And now here they were, sitting across from each other in the bar, Thelma rigid with worry.

Jenny decided that getting it out in the open might help. To that end, she asked, 'What did he say in his letter?'

Thelma winced in such a painful manner that Jenny regretted she'd asked.

A swallow of the spicily flavoured drink was swigged before Thelma managed to answer.

'Nothing much more than he said whilst he was here.'

It wasn't entirely true. She glanced at Jenny. For goodness' sake, if she couldn't trust her dearest friend, who could she trust?

'I'm frightened. He's being so secretive.' Her eyes widened. 'I can't help thinking he's heading into danger. That's why he wouldn't be drawn.' Thelma began running a finger around her glass. She looked thoughtful. 'I wish I could go with him.'

'Into Holland?'

Thelma shrugged. 'I know it's daft. I suppose it's my mothering instinct, wanting to take care of him – as if I could.'

Jenny couldn't help looking bemused. 'He's not a child, Thelma.'

'I know that!'

'No need to snap.'

'Sorry.' She shook her head. 'I just can't help myself. I think of him in the morning and in the evening.'

'It's only natural. After all, you two were talking about getting married.'

Absorbed in her own thoughts, Thelma did not respond.

Jenny eyed her sadly. In her mind, she pictured the handsome man who they hadn't seen for some weeks, his hair the colour of wheat and a roguish, merry look in his blue eyes. No wonder Thelma had fallen for him. Good-looking, affable, a man of depth. If only she could find someone like that.

There was Robin of course. They'd known each other since their youth, but she'd heard nothing of him since he'd joined up. He'd gone away following his second-hand shop going up in flames. The worst part about it was that his son was responsible for the blaze and he'd had trouble facing up to it. There was an element of shame, in fact, and difficulty in accepting that Simon was the culprit.

He was his son and our children are precious to us, she thought. *What would I have done? Would I have run away?*

The answer never came, but more questions did. Where was he? How did she know whether he was alive or dead?

'Let's hope it won't be long until he gets back.' It was Peter, Thelma's love who she was referring to, but could also be applied to Robin.

Thelma looked thoughtfully at what remained of her drink as though hoping she could see something in it – her future perhaps, like a fairground fortune-teller.

Seeming to come to a decision, she picked the drink up and downed the lot. 'I needed that. Thanks, Jenny.'

Jenny smiled. 'It's my pleasure.'

She didn't go on to say that Peter was not only a brave man, but he was also clever. For both Peter and Thelma's sakes, she prayed he would come back safely.

'And your girls, son and all the family,' Jenny said brightly, thinking it a good move to change the subject. 'How are they?'

Although Thelma's expression didn't alter, a smile twitched at her lips. 'Our George's on the Mediterranean run on a mine-sweeper. They're running supplies to Malta, but he says it's not so dangerous an area as it was. Maria misses him but keeps herself occupied with the youngsters. As for my Mary, well, she's enjoying married life up north, although there is talk that Gerald might be transferred to London. An office job no less! Clever clogs that bloke. Our Alice is happy enough.' She shook her head, her expression one of disbelief. 'Who would ever have thought that she'd become a nurse.' A warm, cosy look came to her face as her thoughts transferred away from Peter and onto her children.

Glad to see her smiling again, Jenny asked if she would like another drink.

'Might as well make a night of it.'

Thelma's hand quickly covered that of Jenny's who had been about to rise from the table.

'No. Let me.'

She had a strong hand, which matched her strong character. Seeing as she only had two shillings left in her purse, Jenny conceded that it was her turn.

Jenny followed her progress to the bar, a saucy smile lifting her dour expression. How long it might last was anyone's guess, but if there was one thing Thelma was good at it was socialis-ing. There were risqué comments and laughter – both from her and the men she barged through on her way to the bar and back.

Thelma had always had a way with men. They laughed with

her rather than at her and rarely got the better of her sharp wit. She was a force of nature, thought Jenny, and of womanhood.

'I've got you the same as me,' she said when she came back carrying two measures of port and lemon.

Laughingly, Jenny remarked that Thelma might need to carry her home. 'You should know by now that I can't hold my drink.'

'It's only one. Half a shandy doesn't count. Now tell me about your girls. Heard much from Tilly?'

Pride shone on Jenny's face at mention of her eldest daughter. 'She's loving being in the Land Army.' Her smile vanished as a worrying thought came to mind. 'I sometimes wonder if she'll ever come back to Coronation Close.'

'Of course she will. You're here.'

Jenny didn't voice what she was thinking. Thelma loved having her family around, especially her son and Italian daughter-in-law. It was hard, but Jenny had prepared herself for the time when her girls would fly the nest. The war had been brutal but had also opened wider horizons for women. Would the younger generation go back to the old way of life, marry, have children and keep house? They might do, but in a different country. Many young women had taken up with the handsome young men who looked smart and had money. Women had been liberated from the old life. Men were about to be shocked at the changes that had occurred.

'And your Gloria is growing up.'

Jenny held back a threatening grimace. 'Gloria will always be Gloria.' The fact was that Gloria was the wild one, although carefree and wilful might be a better description.

'They all go through a phase. Look at my Mary. In love with a Canadian one minute – who, by the sound of it, was of Indian descent – and next minute marrying a steady Eddie and settling down like a turtle dove to married life. I never would have thought it.'

'You miss her.'

Thelma nodded, her eyes downcast.

Jenny bit her lip. She hated seeing Thelma looking down. It just wasn't her, but what with worrying about Peter, she could understand it and sympathised.

They were both lost in their own thoughts when someone began playing the piano and singing in a voice that grated on the nerves.

Thelma broke out from her thoughts and frowned in the culprit's direction. 'That bloke's got sausages for fingers and the voice of a blocked drain! Time we went, I think.'

Jenny agreed with her. 'Look at the time. Gone nine o'clock.'

The stick-thin legs of the wooden chairs grated across floorboards dark with spilled beer accumulated over many years.

As their slightly pink faces hit the evening air, Thelma laughed. 'It's not that late. It's not midnight, when you're likely to lose your glass slipper and be chased by a handsome prince.'

The fresh air smelled of late wallflowers, most welcome after the fug that pervaded the public bar. They would have been more comfortable in the saloon bar, where most women congregated, but Jenny had judged that Thelma needed a bit of noise to help drown the turmoil she felt inside.

Absorbed with her own problems, she failed to notice the faint glimmer of concern in Jenny's eyes.

A trio of aeroplanes flew overhead just as they turned into Coronation Close.

Thelma followed their progress with a worried frown.

'They're ours,' Jenny said reassuringly. 'On their way to the airfield.'

Thelma heaved a huge sigh. 'I wish I could believe that Peter is on one of them, but I've a worrying feeling that he isn't even in this country. It scares me to think about.'

'Where do you think he is?'

Thelma dropped her gaze from overhead, her expression tense.

'I know he went for parachute training. You don't do that unless you're going to be dropped somewhere. And it certainly won't be Victoria Park,' she said with an attempt at humour.

2

The summer twilight of late evening was awash with swarms of insects beneath the trees on the green that divided the crescent of houses in Coronation Close.

Children not yet called into bed ran through the midges beneath the trees, uncaring that they might have swallowed a few in the process.

The call went out from parents – mothers mostly – for them to come into bed.

'Get in yur or I'll give you a clip 'round the ear.'

A reluctant tide, they drifted to their front gates, heads bowed and hands over their ears just in case the threat was carried out.

Thelma had been about to ask Jenny if she had heard from Robin, what did Tilly have to say and when was she coming home. On seeing her front gate hanging open, she stopped, rested her clenched fists on her hips and tutted in annoyance.

'I'm sure I didn't leave that gate open. Them kids will get a clip around their ears from me if they're to blame.'

Jenny suggested that the kids might not be to blame. The

gate open might be due to a stray dog. Despite a lot of dogs being destroyed prior to the beginning of the war, the odd stray did wander into the street and houses scavenging for scraps.

'They might have done.' She slammed it shut behind her. 'Never mind. It's shut now.'

'Goodnight then.'

'Goodnight.'

Like all the residents of Coronation Close, Thelma's habit was to access her house via the side path and then through the back door into the kitchen. The latter was usually left unlocked. All it required to open it was a firm push, though not tonight.

At half past nine, the path that ran between the side wall of the house and a tall hedge was already pitch-black. Because of that she got out her front door key.

Jenny left her to it, heading for home, a cup of cocoa, a book and an early night. Strong drink made her feel a bit woozy.

Aware that Thelma had already put her key in the lock and pushed the door open, she was about to do the same. Unlike Thelma, she had not left her back door open. When she heard Thelma shout for her to come quickly she turned and looked across the road.

The front door was still open, an oblong of light falling out onto the front garden. There was no sign of Thelma.

Taking her key from the lock, Jenny retraced her steps to the front gate and crossed over to number twelve.

On reaching the doorstep, she called out, 'Thelma. Is anything wrong?'

Her first thought was that she might have had an accident.

The patch of light from the front door became larger as Thelma appeared and opened the door wider. Even in the encroaching darkness, Jenny perceived the shocked look on her friend's face, the dropped jaw, the wide-open eyes.

A swift intake of breath was accompanied with, 'Someone's been in here.' The firm voice Jenny knew so well sounded sharp with shock.

'What? Are you sure?'

Brusque, chin set square, Thelma stepped to one side of the doorway. 'Take a look for yourself.'

Thelma was house-proud. Nothing was ever out of place. Pride of place was her collection of coronation crockery displayed on the built-in dresser at one end of the living room.

'Just look! Just look!'

Jenny covered her lower face with both hands. Even then, her gasp was audible through her spread fingers.

It seemed that every single cup and saucer, mug, bowl, jug or plate had been thrown onto the floor. Most were in pieces, handles without cups, plates broken into jagged shapes that no amount of glue could ever put back together.

Thelma too looked shattered, shocked to the core.

Jenny found her voice. 'Who would do such a thing?'

Thelma picked up a few of the broken pieces, then let them drop again. Never in a million years could any of it be put back together.

Her eyes were dark anyway, but now they turned darker. 'Kids.'

Jenny thought of the children running around on the green, all gone into bed now. Was it possible that they were the culprits?

After thinking about it, Jenny suggested it might be one of the gangs that robbed bombed, deserted houses. There were a few of them around. They'd even given themselves names like the Scallywags or the Marauders. Most of them were school age, though not all.

'If I get my hands on them...'

Although Thelma clenched her fists as though ready to land a few punches, it sounded to Jenny as though she was on the verge of tears. Thelma was tough, thanks in most part to the life she'd led. Brought up in a children's home. Three children by three different fathers. Her collection of coronation memorabilia and her fondness for the royal family was somewhere she retreated to that helped her rise above what her life was and had been.

Words were sought that Jenny couldn't utter. These broken bits of crockery represented so much in Thelma's life. Who could have been so cruel? Surely either of the local gangs of lads little more than children couldn't do such an awful thing?

Thinking along those lines brought Simon, Robin's son, to mind. He'd been so hating of his father's relationship with her that he'd set fire to his business premises. All that Robin had worked for had been lost.

Jenny lowered herself as close to the floor as she dared, the jagged pieces likely to tear her stockings. Stockings were expensive – and rare.

Jaw set firm, Thelma remained standing, her tall shadow falling over her.

Jenny picked up a large shard of broken plate depicting Queen Mary, one half of the coronation of King George the Fifth and his queen. At least it was a half, she thought. The king's half of the plate was smashed into at least six pieces.

Keeping her eyes on Thelma, Jenny rose slowly to her feet. Was that despair she saw on Thelma's face or resignation that there was no chance of gluing any of the splinters and jagged remnants back together?

So, what else could be done?

'Do you want me to fetch the constable?'

The police constable who had replaced Percy Routledge was

a dependable sort. He'd been pensioned off at the outbreak of war, then called back in once half the local police force had been called up to serve their country.

Thelma appeared not to have heard. For a moment, it seemed as though Jenny could have poked her friend hard enough for her to fall over. She was that stiff, that unseeing.

She tried again. 'Thelma. Would you like me to go to the telephone box and phone the police?'

Thelma narrowed her eyes and pursed her lips, a sure sign that she was thinking very deeply indeed.

'I would be grateful if you could help me clear up the mess.'

Thelma's response had surprised Jenny. 'Just that?'

Thelma eyed her sidelong. 'At this moment in time, I've got more serious things to worry about than a load of broken china.'

'Yes. I suppose you do.'

Jenny headed for the kitchen and the back of the coal house door where the dustpan and brush hung from a nail. The coal house was off the kitchen, a narrow, dark place beneath the stairs. The stairs ran up from the hall at the front of the house. It had always struck Jenny that keeping the coal in a cupboard off the kitchen was not an ideal situation. Still, Bristol Corporation must have had a good reason for doing so.

'Won't be a moment.'

With that, Thelma was gone.

Jenny heard her voice blaring out at the kids on the green, from the front door.

'Was it any of you lot? Come on tell me, or I'll beat you with that cricket bat you've got there.'

The small figures were no more than black smudges against the indistinct background of grass and trees.

'We didn't do it.'

'Nothing to do with us.'

'Any other kids from around? Did you see any of them go into my house?'

'No, missus. Honest, missus. No other kids have been around.'

'Anyone else?'

'Air-raid warden might have been.'

'You saw the air-raid warden? Did he go into my house?'

The kid who'd suggested it shrugged. 'Don't know. It was my turn to bowl.'

'How do you know it was an air-raid warden?'

'He was wearing a tin hat of course.' The boy said it as though she really should have known better.

Air-raid wardens wore tin hats. So did a few other people.

Back in Thelma's living room, Jenny was sweeping bits of broken china into the dustpan and from there into the dustbin.

Thelma followed her out through the kitchen to the back-yard. 'I'm going to call in at the air-raid post. God help them if one of them is responsible.'

Jenny shook her head. 'But why would they be?'

'Could have been an accident. Thought they'd heard an intruder or something.'

Holding the dustbin lid in one hand, dustpan in the other, Jenny looked solemnly down into the bin, which was barely distinguishable in the diminished light.

Thelma's face was solemn. 'That broken crockery represents the best part of my life. Now look at it. Just rubbish in the bottom of the bin.'

'It's just stuff, not you, Thelma. Your life isn't over yet. And there's something much more exciting on the horizon. You and Peter are getting married. You know he wants to. I'm already thinking about my outfit. A pair of brocade curtains should make a decent jacket and skirt, don't you think? I'll expect you to help me cut it out and sew it up.'

Thelma looked at her incredulously, her dark, perfectly formed eyebrows arched and hinting at humour.

Thelma gave the bin a kick, which resulted in the broken china rattling like a bucket of chains. 'You're right. It's the past in that bin.'

They went back into the kitchen. Thelma held her head to one side as she automatically filled the kettle and lit the gas.

'I'm going to stick my neck out and make a promise. No more gathering of coronation crockery until I know that Peter is safe and well.'

Jenny recalled seeing Thelma's collection for the first time back in 1936 – the year of three kings. First King George the fifth, who had died to be replaced by his eldest son, King Edward the Eighth, the king who was never crowned. Edward had abdicated so he could marry the twice divorced American, Wallis Simpson. He'd been replaced by his brother, King George the Sixth. All in all, it had been quite a year. The most important thing in Jenny's life had been moving into Coronation Close and meeting Thelma. She'd never regretted it.

'Do you mean that?'

Thelma threw back her head and laughed. 'You bet I do!'

It gladdened Jenny's heart to see Thelma laugh.

Thankful that Thelma was holding up, Jenny did as she intended that night: a cup of cocoa, some music on the wireless, then a book that she'd begun to read.

Although, really, she sat in the armchair staring off into the distance, not really seeing anything at all.

Why hadn't she mentioned to Thelma that she had something of her own to worry about?

There was no answer, except it seemed that by voicing it the problem would take on a life of its own, it would be accepted and therefore real.

Leaving the cocoa half finished, the book flung to one side, she headed for bed.

For a moment, she stood at the bedroom door, staring at the double bed where she'd once slept with her husband, Roy, a long time ago, before he'd joined the army, a career soldier who loved being with other men. A sick man when he'd come home, never to recover or go back to the life he'd loved so well.

She'd been alone ever since, except for Robin. She'd worked for him at his second-hand furniture business and had hoped that they might end up together. What she'd hoped for and reality had not been on the same track.

Flinging off her slippers, Jenny walked barefoot across the bedroom and began to undress. Before removing her underwear, she slid her cotton nightgown over her head. So attired, she picked up her hairbrush and kept brushing until her hair began to crackle. Her hair gleamed, and although she was in her forties, there were few grey hairs. She supposed that this was down to the fact that grey – or white – blended easily with fair hair.

Her deep-set eyes scrutinised the reflection looking back at her from the dressing table mirror. She was oddly surprised to find that she looked as she always looked. Nothing had altered. Or so it seemed.

Was it still there?

Wishing against hope, she ran her hand down onto the soft firmness of a breast that had fed children, acted as their cushion, lured her husband's eyes.

Her fingers delved down between her breasts, divining further over and beneath the curve of her left breast.

All felt silky smooth, soft as a feather cushion, as it always had – except at the very bottom of the curve, her fingers found the hard lump that she was trying to pretend did not exist.

It could have been that I hit it when I was taking the bin out. Bruised it. That's what she told herself as she climbed into bed.

Imagining a future with her daughters married and presenting her with grandchildren was a pleasant diversion and helped her sleep. So too did telling herself that it would be gone by the morning. It wouldn't be the first time she'd told herself that. The lump remained.

The best way to fall asleep was to fix visions of Tilly and Gloria in her mind. Thinking of them made her smile. Jenny closed her eyes.

3

MERRYWEATHER FARM, SUFFOLK

Tilly Crawford, Jenny Crawford's daughter, was dreaming that she was on a tropical island, just like the one described in *Desert Island Discs* on the wireless. The blue sky joined seamlessly with the sea, which continually tossed surf-crested waves onto a sandy beach that blazed white beneath the incredibly white sunshine.

It was somewhat disappointing to open her eyes and see only a thin strip of pale grey daylight. The faded green curtains, that might once have been deep green, didn't meet in the middle, thanks to age and shrinkage after being boiled in the wash.

She groaned and buried her face into the pillow. Mrs Forester, the farmer's wife, never failed to shout up the stairs half an hour or so after the farmyard rooster had crowed.

'And cockle doodle to you too,' Tilly muttered, her voice muffled by the pillow.

Mrs Forester's foghorn voice shouted again. 'Miss Crawford. If you wants yer breakfast, you'd better shake a leg and get down here.'

Not keen to shake a leg or anything else for that matter, Tilly blinked, groaned and buried her nose further into the pillow in the hope of obliterating the smell of fried bread. Always and forever, she would refuse bread deep fried in beef fat.

Mrs Forester was not one to give up easily.

'Did you hear me, young lady?'

A thud from a heavy boot vibrated the first tread of the bare wooden stairs. Mrs Forester meant business.

There was nothing genteel or ladylike about the farmer's wife. She wore heavy boots most of the time, indoors as well as out.

Summer it might be, but dawn had only just broken. That's how it was on Merryweather Farm. The moment it was light, everyone was turfed out of bed, fed a breakfast of fatty bacon, an egg, two if the hens had been generous, and the ubiquitous fried bread, cut thick enough to be termed a doorstep.

There being a long day's work ahead, there was no way she could possibly go without breakfast. Despite the hard work and the fatty breakfast, Tilly did not regret joining the Land Army. She even loved the uniform. And the fresh air, even the earthy smell of damp fields and always animals.

Flinging the bedclothes aside, she swung her legs out of bed and reached for her green jumper, white shirt, brown hat and jodhpurs, plus the thick socks. The latter looked quite incongruous when at this moment worn with her zip-up slippers. She'd left her muddy boots downstairs, knowing very well that Mrs Forester would have scraped the mud off and readied them for her to wear for another day. Boots were acceptable downstairs, but not upstairs – unless you were Mr and Mrs Forester.

On arrival in the warm farmhouse kitchen Christine, her fellow land girl, was already at the table, her face greasy with fat from the piece of fried bread she was halfway through eating.

Christine had the sort of face that reminded Tilly of cream

and red apples: creamy complexion and apple-red cheeks. Her eyes were blue and her hair the colour of straw and when she opened her mouth, you knew beyond doubt that she was from London.

Thinking of cream brought the apple pie and cream Tilly had consumed the night before to mind. Mrs Forester had skimmed the cream from the top of that day's milking. The pie had been made three days ago, big enough for everyone to have large portions for each day. Tilly had to admit that food in the country was superior to that in the city. Ration books were used for tinned things, soap, washing flakes and suchlike, things that the farm could not produce.

'Get that breakfast down you, Tilly,' exclaimed a grinning Christine. 'Don't want to faint away in the field from lack of nourishment, now do you.' A merry chortling accompanied by a saucy wink left Tilly in no doubt that the jovial London girl was taking the mick out of Mrs Forester, who said the same thing every morning and tended to repeat the same sentence more than once.

'Get that breakfast down you, Tilly, my girl, or you'll be fainting away in the field...'

Tilly exchanged a cheeky grin with Christine and said, 'Yes, Mrs Forester.'

Back turned to them, Mrs Forester had put on her horn-rimmed glasses, her hand searching behind one of the ugly ornamental urns at either side of the mantelpiece.

'I got a letter for you, Tilly. It got delivered to the post office yesterday. Mr Bedlow gave it to our Johnnie in the pub last night. It was too late to hand it to you. I expect it's from your mother.'

Tilly's eyes lit up as she took it. Although she loved the farm and the Foresters had made her very welcome, there were times when she missed her mother and Coronation Close. Sometimes she even missed her sister, Gloria. They were chalk and cheese, but blood was perhaps thicker than water. Tilly was the self-possessed and thoughtful one. Gloria tended to be full of herself. It could be downright annoying.

'Eat your breakfast before opening it.'

Tilly slid the envelope into her pocket and attacked the plate placed in front of her. She would prefer to be alone when she read the letter – just in case she was tearful – which might be likely.

Two cups of tea later, she was ready for the fresh air and hard work of the farming day.

'Gonna read it now then?'

Tilly was already on her feet. 'Must get on. I'll read it later when I eat my lunch. Is it cheese and chutney sandwiches?'

She refrained from adding the word 'again'. It was Mrs Forester's habit to provide them with cheese sandwiches made with her own bread, own churned butter and home-made cheese. Sometimes it came with chutney lathered on so thickly that it oozed onto her fingers. Licking off the excess was a delicious experience. A filling of cheese coupled with tomatoes or salad was not so messy but just as delicious. The main variation from cheese sandwiches was thickly sliced ham, but then only after a pig had been slaughtered, salted and hung from the rafters in the old smokehouse. A slice of pork pie was set aside as an evening meal and often followed by stewed fruit picked straight from the orchard.

She knew she'd guessed wrong and it wasn't cheese today when Mrs Forester waggled her head from side to side as one of the horses did when Tilly had given him a carrot: a sign of plea-sure – for the giver and the receiver.

'No. I've sliced some ham,' she exclaimed, her meaty fists resting on her equally meaty hips. 'There's still plenty left.

Though as it's been hanging there a time, we might have to eat it more quickly. Might even have to sell some if the weather gets warmer. Luckily, the old dairy is cool. Them walls are two feet thick. Thanks be to Mr Forester's great-great-grandfather.' Her eyes looked up at the ceiling as she reconsidered what she'd just said. 'Or was it his great-grandfather?' She laughed. 'No matter. Whoever it was had his head screwed on. I've never known anything go off in there.'

Ham sandwiches, the leg of ham home cured, hung up in the smokehouse for a few months until it was succulent and very, very tasty. Even though she'd just had breakfast, Tilly's mouth watered at the thought.

Mrs Forester followed them out to the door.

'Tell your mother that you're being well fed here. Wouldn't want her to think you're missing home too much. Don't go telling her that. It would only worry her. Eat your sandwiches all up. Don't want you fainting off in the field.'

In other words, she was aching to know the contents of the letter once Tilly had read it.

The two girls reined in their laughter. Mrs Forester was a good sort and Tilly for sure didn't want her to think they were making fun.

They were still laughing when they were outside, their wellingtons splashing through the sloppy mud.

Milking the cows was their first job of the day. The grey of dawn was giving place to early morning. The milking sheds were lit by just three electric light bulbs, which did not quite reach the further corners. The farmhouse was still gas lit, the meagre glow boosted by strategically placed oil lamps. A candle carried by each of them lit their way up the stairs to the attic, two single beds, a chest of drawers, washbasin and jug. Nails were positioned along one wall to take their clothes. Payment for their accommodation was sixteen shillings per week, half of the thirty-two shillings wages.

Yes, if she'd stayed in Bristol, Tilly could have been paid more, and she would have had all the advantages of shops, friends, family and access to everything a city could offer. At first, she'd wondered if she would ever get used to doing without all she'd been accustomed to, but the countryside gradually grew on her.

'What will you do once the war is over?' asked Christine.

Tilly, whose shoulder was thrust into a cow's side, face warmed by its flank as she pulled the teats, thought before she answered.

'I haven't given it much thought. I suppose it depends what's on offer.' The last squeeze and the bucket was full to within five inches of the brim. More than that and it would be slopping out. 'How about you?'

Christine laughed. 'Let's put it this way, there's more going on back in London than here. If you know what I mean,' she added with a grin.

'You'll miss the dances at the air base.'

Christine loved the young Americans from the air base: 'They got more going for them than the local lads.'

'Such as stockings and chocolate?' Tilly questioned.

'There's that.' Christine tilted her head and drew on a cigarette. 'But I won't be staying around 'ere. Once the war's over, the only dances will be at the village hall and not a Yank in sight.' She pulled a face. 'All farm labourers with rough hands and smelling of oil or manure. Yuk.' She shook her head vehemently. 'No bloody thank you!'

After they'd chivvied the cows out into the fields, their next task would be to wash the floor of the milking parlour. After that, John, Mrs Forester's oldest son, would start up the tractor and take them out into the fields. This was the bit Tilly liked most, being out in the fresh air and looking west from the farm in the general area of the city of Bristol and imagining what was going on there.

Her mother's letter would tell her more of the comings and goings in Coronation Close. There hadn't been an air raid for a long while now and she lived in hope that there wouldn't be. If there had been, she'd feel a bit guilty not being there. London was the only place being attacked from the air, the menacing V1 rockets, termed doodlebugs by the populace and the press.

A cool breeze caressed her cheeks as she scrutinised the barns, milking shed and lean-tos built of rough stone a few centuries ago. The slurpy mud mixed with the cow droppings; the ducks and chickens puddling around the edge where grass heads drooped heavy with seeds.

The stone buildings had a mellow, warm look when the sun was shining like today. Sad-looking and oddly haunting when grey Suffolk skies hung like a blanket over the flat, fertile acres.

I like it here.

The thought came as something of a surprise and made Tilly ask, 'What will you do when the war ends?'

Christine stopped tumbling potatoes into sacks, glad to take the opportunity of a short rest. One hand swiped across her brow where sweat trickled into her eyebrows. She groaned as she fisted the other hand into her aching back. 'There's more than one choice back home – if I'm lucky. A demobbed bloke from me own neck of the woods, though I'd prefer to nab meself a Yank before they all disappear. Become a GI bride and shove off to America.' The saucy wink was followed by a jerk of her head.

They headed out of the barn to where John was standing on the back of the cart, hauling aboard the sacks of potatoes once they were filled.

Tilly saw him glower in Christine's direction. No doubt the reference to Christine's feelings about other men had hit home. Occasionally a truck full of Americans attended a dance at the village hall and Christine was in her element.

'Not so loud. You've upset John,' Tilly whispered.

Christine tossed her head. 'That's his problem. I want a Yank. I definitely want a Yank.'

Poor John, thought Tilly. Right from the moment she'd arrived, it had been apparent that John was sweet on Christine. Hopelessly smitten. Even when she gave him the brush-off, he kept coming back.

'And what if you don't nab yourself a Yank?'

Christine heaved her mighty bosom – of which she was very proud – and took a deep breath. 'As I've already said, if that's the case I might 'ave to settle for something home-grown. Something as ordinary as one of these potatoes.' She held up a particularly misshapen specimen that looked to have lumpy legs and two bumps where arms might be.

Not wishing to upset Johnnie, who was forking silage into mangers, Tilly hid her smile.

Boots caked with mud and a far from amused expression on his rugged face, he strode over and barked out, 'Less chatter and get on with yer work.'

'Rules and regulations! That's you, Johnnie Forester. You would have made a good sergeant major.'

Tilly knew that John had been obliged to stay on the farm. Food was needed as much as fighting men. She felt for him.

'What about you, John? What will you do after the war?'

'Farming. What else would I be doing?'

'And married with more cows and half a dozen brats,' laughed Christine.

Tilly flinched. Christine's laughter was mocking and to Tilly's ears somewhat cruel.

'I don't blame you for carrying on with the farm. It's peaceful here. What more could anyone want?'

Christine began singing a children's song. 'The farmer wants a wife, the farmer wants a wife, hey ho cheerio, the farmer wants a wife.'

Johnnie stalked off, Christine's song following him out into the farmyard.

Tilly did not join in.

'Leave him alone, Christine. Can't you see he's upset?'

'So what?'

Once he'd started the tractor up, he came striding back like an avenging angel.

'It ain't lunchtime yet. You've got time to drive the cows already there in Hope Meadow into Brook Meadow. Do you know the one I mean?'

'Great,' said a beaming Christine. 'We can eat our sandwiches there.'

'Not you,' he shouted at Christine. 'You can clean out the milking shed. There're droppings in the corners that you missed. After that, you can eat your sandwiches and then shovel the muck out of the pigsty.'

Christine opened her mouth to protest, but a glowering John beat her to it.

'Get on with it. Now!'

Keen to get away whilst luck was on her side, Tilly waved her hands in surrender. 'I'm going. I can manage to move the cows by myself.'

Her feet sped over the muck-strewed cobbles. Taking her lunch with her in a canvas knapsack, off she went. She also took a long stick for twitching at the rears of the more reluctant animals.

Sandwiches, Thermos flask of unsweetened tea, then her mother's letter. What could be better!

She'd also had the foresight to pack a notepad and pen into her haversack, which turned out to be a good idea.

Once she'd done all she had to do and had finished eating her lunch, she turned her attention to writing a letter back.

Resting the pad on her bent knees, she firstly considered what she was going to write about. She'd already written some basic stuff about life on the farm. What next?

Tapping the pen against her teeth, she stared at the trees on the horizon. People in the city believed that nothing happened in the country. What if she told them of gossip and happenings here? They would see then that people were not that different wherever they lived.

Having made up her mind, she took the pen firmly in hand, rebalanced the notepad and began to write.

Dear Mum,

Your writing about home makes it seem as though I'm back there. It doesn't seem to have altered that much.

Things are happening here too. Christine, the other land girl, is aiming to catch herself a Yank. She's keen on living in the United States. In the meantime, John Forester, the farmer's son, used to be keen on her, but I think he's got over that. She's pretty but can be a bit mean at times.

The US base is holding a dance on the last Saturday of the month. There's one at the village hall on the following Saturday. Both are quite fun, although the one at the base provides beer and suchlike. The village hall does not. The vicar isn't in favour of young people drinking. Dancing and music are acceptable, but not strong drink.

However, the local young men are not in agreement with that, and neither are the American servicemen. The locals smuggle in strong cider and pour it into the lemonade. The Americans bring Scotch.

One of the elderly ladies in charge of flower arranging at the church was very thirsty one night and drank THREE of what she thought was straightforward lemonade. They had to carry her home, but only after she'd danced herself to a standstill before falling onto the vicar's lap. She was quite mortified afterwards. Her dress was all awry, not that there was much to see. Her bloomers reached to her knees.

I'm sat here on a grassy bank. There's lots of bees and butterflies and a warm smell of cow manure and wildflowers. Quite a mix, you must agree.

We're a long way from the nightlife of the sort you get in Bristol, but that doesn't mean there's no scandal here. There's a lot of gossip about local girls going with the American airmen and getting into trouble. An old lady told me she wasn't shocked by it. Told me there's more goes on behind a haystack amongst country folk than most people realise. Also told me that not as many as you'd think got married in church – not of her generation anyway. Nature in the raw, you might say. Said something about jumping over a broomstick.

Bye for now, Mum. I'm missing you lots. Won't be long now before I get a third-class train ticket home. No more than a month. It will be a nice break.

4

A warm breeze disturbed the bedroom curtains bringing with it the smell of roses and carnations, plus the less attractive smell of dusty privet hedges.

Bleary-eyed, Jenny Crawford watched the fragile fluttering of the flowered fabric, breathed in the subtle draught of air. In her mind, she sang 'Greensleeves', a soft melody with ancient words. Such gentle music and words were usually enough to send her off to sleep. But not tonight. Like other recent nights, she slept for only a couple of hours, then woke. When had she first noticed the lump? Was it anything to worry about?

Go to the doctor. Let him sort it out. But what if he told her what she suspected? Ignoring it, pretending she was only imagining it was her way of coping. If she didn't acknowledge its existence, it couldn't be there – could it?

Sleep still elusive, she threw back the bedclothes, uncaring that her feet missed the rag rug at the side of the bed and landed on the linoleum. It was cool beneath her feet and jolted her awake.

Blackout restrictions meant not turning on the light, but she could see well enough without it.

Pushing open the casement, she took deep gulps of air, anything to help her sleep. It didn't matter what time she got up tomorrow. She had no work until the afternoon. The job at the Broadway Picture House was only part-time but suited for now. It was a totally different job to the one she'd had with Robin at his second-hand furniture shop, which had ended when it had gone up in flames. He'd been mortified that his son had been to blame for the conflagration. In that moment, their relationship as well as his business had fallen apart. He'd been left stunned that his son could do such a thing.

She'd always had an inkling that if it came to the crunch, he would choose his children, right or wrong. When the fire had occurred, his opinion of his son Simon had shattered and he'd run away, joined the army, leaving her high and dry, without a job and without him even saying goodbye as though he was sorry to go. She'd heard nothing from him. It hurt, but perhaps time and space would bring both to a greater understanding of their position.

Knowing him, she surmised that he'd retreated into self-loathing, blaming himself for the blaze that had destroyed everything he'd owned. Never blaming his son, the person truly responsible. But that was Robin. His kids came first and, to Jenny's mind, always would. A little time might heal, resurrect or bury whatever feelings they shared, but for now their relationship seemed beyond repair.

The air hung heavy. Her skin felt hot beneath the neckline of her nightgown and the hand that pushed aside the material held no coolness.

Coronation Close was shrouded in night. Something – perhaps a cat or a fox – scampered over the green around which the houses were gathered. The only movement. Even the leaves on the trees hung immobile in the still air. None of her neighbours were out and about, most exhausted after coping with long hours of work. Some were still at work, manning searchlights or other part-time jobs required by the war.

A figure came into sight at the confluence of Coronation Close and Leinster Avenue. The figure was no more than a silhouette weaving along the pavement from one side to the other. The glow of a cigarette temporarily lit a small patch of darkness. A loud hiccup was followed by a female voice swearing as she suddenly toppled to one side, a sure sign that her heel had caught in the gap between paving slabs.

Jenny shifted so that she was hidden by the curtain. Her keen eyes recognised Margaret Routledge as she tottered down the street to number five.

It was a good job Mrs Frogmore, the local gossip, was not around at this time of night. Jenny could imagine her gravelly voice shouting out, *Out on the town again, Margaret?*

She smiled as she imagined the response.

Mind yer own bleedin' business! I can do what I bloody well want. Nosy old cow.

Jenny sighed and hugged herself. Life had certainly taken many turns since she'd moved out of Blue Bowl Alley in the heart of the city of Bristol and to number two Coronation Close. The lives of many of her neighbours had also changed. The old Margaret Routledge would not have said boo to a goose.

She's on the game. That was the consensus, though nobody condemned her out loud – not to her face.

Jenny preferred to be open-minded. Margaret, now a widow, had been through a lot. She surmised, but didn't know for sure, that Percy had hardly been the most loving of husbands. As a police officer, he'd been excessively overbearing to the general public and his neighbours, so it didn't take much to think he might be even worse behind his own front door.

On public view was a different matter. Every Sunday, she'd watched as the small family had made their way to the Methodist church or sometimes St Barnabas. They seemed to pick and choose which suited them, as though they were hedging their bets. Jenny had noticed that Margaret no longer attended church. Neither did her son. She wasn't quite sure about the daughter, a silent girl who rarely acknowledged anyone, as aloof as her father had once been.

She knew very well what it was like living with a difficult man. Her own husband had not been easy, so she thought she knew what Margaret might have endured.

Without caring about waking the neighbours, the garden gate, then the door of number five slammed shut and Margaret was gone. It occurred to Jenny that she did it on purpose as if to make a point or give further fuel to the gossip that abounded about her.

The night returned to its ongoing quiet.

Jenny had known Margaret dance around the green, her arms waving and singing at the top of her voice, not a very melodious voice, and it wasn't the first time she'd snapped a heel. On one occasion, she'd seen her throw her broken shoe against someone's front door. Comments had been made the following day that she was a disgrace.

But it was funny, Jenny thought to herself.

There were many more who'd been changed by this war. No longer housewives, but widows and working women who had never worked in peacetime. And once alone? Jenny sighed. Before the war few married women had gone out to work. Fewer still had entered a pub without their husbands. It had been their life's work to care for the family whatever their circumstances.

But now? It wasn't only single women who got led astray by strapping military men missing home and female company. They were taking the opportunity to snatch at a little happiness whilst they still could, whatever the consequences.

Jenny jerked the curtains back across, the flowered ones first, and then the blackout curtains. Perhaps if the room was in total darkness, she might fall asleep and stay asleep.

After giving the pillow a good pummelling, she closed her eyes. Back to thinking about her daughters: Tilly the responsible one, and Gloria, the wild child who had very definite ideas regarding the direction of her life.

'I'm going to be a film star and drink champagne and eat caviar.'

Her pronouncement had made her mother smile. She doubted whether Gloria knew that caviar was fish eggs and Gloria never ate fish. As for champagne, she'd never tasted it herself but did know it was very expensive.

Gloria had done surprisingly well in her last year at school, attaining the School Certificate. Right from the first, she had categorically stated that she would not work behind a shop counter or in a factory. Luckily, she'd landed a job in an office.

The firm she worked for had been a high-class electrical shop before the war but like many of its ilk had turned to manufacturing grommets and gaskets for military use.

Jenny smiled at her daughter's determination. Working in an office was far from being a film star, but around here it meant something. Gloria was one step above the rest of the girls, who, if they hadn't joined the services, were working in the shops and factories she so despised. If anyone thought she was a bit hoity-toity, then they didn't say it to her face. They would have got a mouthful of home truths if they had, she thought. Gloria could stand up for herself, a trait she'd inherited from her father.

It was something of a relief to have one daughter still at home, though there were times she wished she had both. Tilly had been called up and chose to become a land girl. It was usual for land girls to be found work close to home, but it couldn't always be managed. In Tilly's case, she'd ended up working on a farm in Suffolk. The other side of the country. She'd sent her a card with a picture of two horses – Suffolk punches, she said they were called – pulling a plough. 'I hitch up the two we have to the plough, just like this.'

Thinking of the card reminded Jenny of the unfinished letter on the dresser downstairs. Tilly had asked her to keep her informed of the happenings in Coronation Close – 'I miss it,' she'd said. That fact alone gave Jenny the encouragement to write about almost anything that happened. Perhaps Coronation Close was more vibrant and colourful than those living here imagined!

Yes. If you can't sleep, write a letter. Make a cup of tea. Tire yourself out. After doing that you're liable to fall asleep more easily.

The low-wattage bulb in the bedside lamp threw shadows as much as it did light. Electricity was precious. Low-wattage bulbs were encouraged, but goodness, she thought, what with the blackout curtains, her bedroom resembled a cave.

A flickering candle would have done better, although, like the lamp, would have done nothing to enhance her reflection in the wardrobe mirror. Was it merely the dull light or was there a new gauntness to her features, dark lines beneath her eyes? Her breasts thrust against the cotton nightgown, reminding her that this was not the first night she hadn't been able to sleep.

Seeking a reassuring diversion, she tiptoed from the bedroom and across the landing to Gloria's room. Softly, not wishing to disturb, she peered in at her daughter. Gloria was sound asleep, her breathing soft and even. Jenny was immediately filled with love. Both daughters were on the threshold of life.

They were the reason she was reluctant to accept that anything was seriously wrong, the problem pushed determinedly to the back of her mind. Eventually, she would tell them, but not yet. After seeing the doctor and him telling her she had nothing to worry about. She imagined all three of them laughing about it, calling her a silly goose for not going to the doctor sooner.

Yes. All would be well.

Resisting the urge to turn the landing light on, she felt her way down the stairs and into the living room.

Once she had the half-completed letter accompanied by a cup of tea, she sat down at the kitchen table and read through what she'd written. The wording was a bit ambiguous and might make Tilly think that something was wrong. She didn't want that.

Ripped to pieces, the letter flared into flames on the gas ring. Now how best to detract from conveying her personal fear?

It was strange that Margaret came to mind. But that was it. Talk about other people and what they were up to. A tale of someone everyone was gossiping about. She would tell it like a serial in a magazine, one episode leading onto another in a 'guess what happens next' kind of way.

A plan in mind, she began to write.

Dear Tilly,

I'm missing you very much and do hope everything is still going well at the farm. The horses look amazing. I can't believe that someone as slender as you can cope with such large animals, but there, you're no longer a child. You most definitely have hidden strengths.

Everything around here is much the same as it was before you left, though I will try to keep you informed of the small events in our lives, the things that have developed, shall we say. Who is up to what and how everyone is generally faring – and more besides.

The biggest shock was finding Thelma's collection of coronation ware smashed to bits. Why anyone would want to smash it all up rather than stealing it is lost on me. I suggested she report it to the police, but she declined. She doesn't set such great store on her collection as she used to. She's worrying about Peter. He's gone off for special training and won't be around for a while. She's very worried of course.

There's gossip galore in Coronation Close and it all concerns Margaret Routledge. You may recall that her husband was found dead some time back, not long after the death of her little son, Albert.

Back then, you may recall she was a dowdy sort, kept herself to herself, her husband not allowing her to mix with the likes of me and Thelma – or anyone else in the street. She even had to shop between certain hours, so she was at home before him with a meal waiting on the table.

Anyway, the worm has turned. Not that Margaret looks anything like a worm nowadays. She wears make-up, paints her nails and dresses like a film star, though a bit of a down-market one, the clothing ration being the way it is.

Rumour has it that she goes to the pubs frequented by Americans. I don't know that for sure, but what I do know is that she doesn't come home until after midnight. She's usually a bit the worse for wear. I'm not sure whether she drinks at home, but some around here believe that she does. I give her the benefit of the doubt.

At present, she doesn't bother with anyone in Coronation Close but tosses her head and blows raspberries at those who comment on her lifestyle. It's quite funny to see.

I believe I've already told you that I work part-time at The Broadway. That way, I get to see a lot of films for free, the newsreels too. News about the war used to make me shiver, but I've got used to it now, especially now we appear to be winning.

Gloria is doing well in her job, although she still insists that she wants to be a film star. I had to tell her that I didn't know quite how anyone goes about getting into that kind of job. Knowing your sister, she already has her own plan in place as to how to go about it! She always was a sparky one! Not that you're not. You are my dependable and dearly loved eldest daughter and will always have a special place in my heart.

It's early in the morning and quite warm. I just couldn't sleep. My first thought was to write to you.

I hope you enjoy reading this as much as I've enjoyed writing it.

Love too from your sister (sound asleep at present).

Warm greetings from your ever-loving mother.

5

After three or four sherries in merry company, Margaret Routledge couldn't give a fig about the opinion of her neighbours in Coronation Close. If they wanted to pass judgement, that was up to them.

Her coat hung off one shoulder and the top button of her blouse was undone. Her cheeks were pink, her laughter raucous and her legs felt as if they no longer belonged to her.

Because of her unwieldy gait, her drink, the colour of burnt caramel, slopped in her glass. 'Whoops!' Clasping it with both hands saved too much being spilled as, like an errant dodgem car at the fairground, she bounced against strangers, laughed at jokes she didn't really understand and sang along with whatever was being bashed out on the old Joanna! To her, it was a piano, but wanting to fit in with the ribald, noisy company, she followed their lead and called it a Joanna. It rhymed, she noticed, too far gone with drink to realise that was the whole point of calling it that.

Drinking had become something of a hobby, as was wearing

shoes with high heels that her husband would have termed 'tarty'.

'You wouldn't have liked my face paint either,' she muttered.

The combination of high heels and drink made her legs feel like they might buckle under her. Such a thing had never happened in the days when she wore the ugly flat shoes that Percy had insisted on, the high-necked dresses and long sleeves that had hidden her body – and a lot more besides. Bruises. There had always been bruises. As far as Percy was concerned, she'd always been a sinner and in need of punishment.

Lipstick smudged and laughter harsh enough to scratch her throat, she raised her glass to the latest man who'd stood her the cost of the schooner of rich, dark sherry wobbling in her hand.

'Cheers, love.' She slugged it back. She'd never enjoyed a drink in the days of her marriage. Never drank in fact. Percy had frowned on women drinking or entering pubs. Didn't approve of men going in pubs either, come to that.

As for make-up, well, if he could see her now!

'Hello, gorgeous.'

She tittered. 'Gorgeous? Do you think so?'

The man leaned in closer. 'Yeah. You look a treat. Bet you're married.'

'Widowed!'

'Sorry to hear that, love.'

'It's of no account. He didn't appreciate me, you know.'

'Is that so?'

'Never let me doll myself up. Do my hair. Put on make-up.'

'He must have been daft. It's good to see a woman taking care of herself. Makes a man feel proud.'

'Not my husband. I like wearing make-up. Like making myself look glamorous. Percy did not approve,' she said with an aloof pout of her lips as she recalled and regurgitated what he used to say. 'The warpaint of Jezebels! That's what my husband used to say.' Shouting it out gave her a thrill.

The man she was talking to stepped back, not that she cared much about that. Her loud statement went sailing over the heads of the clientele, mixing with the hubbub of conversation, singing and laughter. It didn't really matter that nobody was taking much notice. In her mind, she could see Percy as he used to be, like a fire-and-brimstone minister, shouting hell and damnation from the pulpit.

In his youth, he'd entertained the possibility of entering the church but had settled on becoming a policeman instead. Someone had once told her it was because there was no empathy in him – possibly her late mother or perhaps Bill Lockhart, her brother-in-law, Cath's husband. A minister of the church needed to be able to put themselves in the shoes of the congregation at large. Percy couldn't see that. In his eyes, everything was his version of black and white and therefore becoming a policeman seemed the next best thing.

Man should abide by God's law first and man's law second.

She laughed at his pronouncement because she could, because it was only in her head and no longer a scripture in her life.

He'd ended up with his second choice and wouldn't have liked her laughing at him, but there, he wasn't around to make comment. Percy was dead now at the hands of a shady character who had eventually been carted off by the authorities. She presumed he too was dead now, executed for spying, but didn't know for sure. Neither did she care.

'Here. I bought you another. Won't say no, will you?'

The man who had bought her the drink raised his glass too. She eyed him speculatively over the rim of her glass. She'd met his sort before.

'A few drinks and they think they own you' was the advice from one of the new friends she'd met at the Hatchet. The Hatchet was a pub in the centre of Bristol where sailors had gathered for centuries, the city docks being close by. 'After that, they want you to be nice to them.'

Margaret hadn't understood at first but wasn't long in cottoning on. Men wanted what they wanted without recourse to marriage and once that was taken, they were gone. In a way, she wished Percy had been like that, selfishly sexual but not violent. She'd met with a few men since being widowed. None of them had treated her as badly as Percy.

She looked up into the man's eyes and smiled. Behind that smile, her mind was considering how she would play this. Love and affection had been missing from her life and for a while she chose to indulge to receive what she had so craved.

One nicotine-stained finger doodled in the little bit of cleavage exposed by the undone button. Her eyes followed the finger as it circled the soft crescents of her bosoms. She awaited the suggestion she sensed was coming.

It came.

'Bloody 'ot in yur,' he said as he leaned close, the smell of tobacco and beer on his breath. 'How about we go outside and get some fresh air?'

Margaret laughed. 'Going outside can wait. It's getting hot that makes you thirsty. And I am very thirsty. How about another?'

Her teeth flashed in an almost white smile. She followed that by wiggling the tumbler in front of his face, a signal that she wanted it filled whilst she contemplated his motive.

Usually, she only had three drinks before accepting a man's invitation. Perhaps it was her encounter with her neighbours that had made her throw caution to the wind and drink more.

She was too drunk to take on board the hardening of his eyes, the clenching of his chin. Instead of answering, he flattened the stub of his cigarette in the ashtray beside him on the bar.

The pub was crowded, a fug of cigarette smoke fouling the air, stinging her eyes so much that her mascara ran.

A woman with a drink in one hand and a smouldering cigarette in the other was belting out a Vera Lynn number, aided by a chorus of drunken customers, all singing off-key.

Her life before becoming a widow had been grey. Life now was filled with colour.

The man leaned closer, so that the brim of his trilby skimmed her forehead. 'You're a nice-looking woman. Looks like a film star's.'

She thanked him and chose to believe that his eyesight was one hundred percent.

Snatching the tumbler from her hand and slamming it down on the bar, he said, 'Time to go.'

She opened her mouth to protest that she didn't want to go. Not with this bloke and in the state she was.

His big square fingers gripped her upper arm so tightly it was painful.

'Ouch. You're hurting me.'

She wriggled, tried to get out of his grasp. Laughter was all around her. Nobody noticed that her face was screwed up and her hat had tipped over one eye.

'I don't want—'

'You've 'ad too much drink, me love,' said a glossy-faced woman, laughed and shook her head. 'Off to bed for you, me duck. Your wife, is she?'

The man who gripped her arm nodded and said, 'She never could hold 'er drink.'

The laughter followed them out beyond the blackout curtain and the double doors he dragged her through.

Outside it was cooler.

Margaret had been having fun. Being treated like this scared her, but he was a man and stronger than her. She resorted to the wheedling request for him to buy her a drink.

Some bought the girls drinks straight away. Margaret had held back at first but didn't now. The only thing she'd drawn the line at was when payment was asked for. Not payment in money, but in intimacy. A quick grope in one of the dark alleys off the street and in the bushes on College Green. Those with a car insisted on driving up to Durdham Down where the professional girls walked up and down the straight road running through it, the area commonly called Ladies Mile. Though they were far from that.

So far, she'd been lucky and hadn't had to give in to the groping of a man she didn't know but had been warned by the girls that she couldn't hold out forever.

'If some bloke gets you in a tight corner and there's no going back, tell 'im you don't do things for nothing. None of us do.' The girl who said this to her was named Ethel.

At first, Margaret had been so naive about these girls and hadn't realised that they were paid for sex. The same old excuse everyone used for everything came to mind. There was a war on. People did whatever it took to survive.

The women who frequented the Hatchet had laughed at her naivety. At first, she'd been embarrassed, but she had ended up enjoying their company. Some, like her, had been widowed. Others were single mothers, left high and dry with a kid, the father going absent the moment he was cornered.

'If you don't want to get fruity, don't get drunk.'

That was the warning they'd given her. Up until tonight, she had more or less followed their advice.

The man was still dragging her along.

Fear led to panic, an attempt to do anything to stop him and save herself. She dragged her heels and tried to wrench her arm out of his grasp.

'I don't want to go with you. Let me go. I'm a married woman with children. My husband's a policeman.'

The fact that Percy was dead was neither here nor there. Just mention of a policeman should have put the wind up him. Unfortunately it didn't.

The alley he dragged her into stank of drains and dampness. A single gas light hung from a bracket high on the wall. After that it was all darkness.

'Come on. I bought you drinks.'

'That doesn't mean you've bought me!'

Using both arms, she tried pushing him away, but the heat of his body was clamped against her.

Gripping her wrist, he placed her hand on the stiff bulge at the front of his trousers. 'Come on. 'Ave a feel of what I'm giving you. Undo the buttons. Go on. Stop messing about.'

He did it himself and, despite her protests, her shouts and her pushing, shoved her hand inside.

'I'll give you a five bob.'

It shouldn't have mattered, but although she had her freedom, she wanted to see her children educated, well dressed and fed.

She thought of her widow's pension from the police. It wasn't as big as Percy had told her. Money didn't go far with two children – it would have gone less far if young Albert had not died from diphtheria. But it was still hard. And she didn't want to make up the shortfall with work.

It was hard to see his expression in the mouldering gloom where the smell of drains and dust, beer and other sickly smells combined.

He had a strong grip. She touched the hard throbbing at the front of his trousers without gagging. She wasn't so naive that she didn't perceive him beyond the point of no return. He wasn't going to give up now. He wanted what she was offering him.

'A fiver,' she said.

'Ten bob,' he said, his voice breathless, his pleasure coming quickly.

'No.'

She began to withdraw her hand.

'Two pounds,' he said, his voice shaking as his end came near.

His breathing was husky. She wondered whether he might renege on the deal once he'd finished.

Perhaps he sensed what she was thinking. In one quick movement, his free hand dived into his trouser pocket. Out came two one-pound notes.

She snatched them quickly and shoved them into her cleavage with her free hand. Her brassiere was as safe a place as any.

Once it was over, she ran away as fast as she could.

'Fancy another drink,' he shouted after her.

She ran faster. How could she have done this?

The answer was obvious. Deep down, she'd feared what he might have done if she'd been less than willing. She didn't want to be one of those women found strangled up on the downs.

Despite the drink sloshing around inside her and a bit tottery, she was still upright and didn't look back, fear giving wings to her feet.

6

Morning came and the kettle was boiled for a single cup of tea, but Thelma couldn't face breakfast, hadn't done ever since Peter had gone away.

She slipped her fingers into the waistband of her skirt. No problem doing that up this morning.

'Go on like this, Thelma Dawson, and you'll need to put a tuck in this skirt!'

Before leaving home, she eyed the pathetic remnants of a collection that had once been so treasured. A stout mug bearing the likeness of King Edward the Seventh had survived unscathed, a jug lacked its handle, another sported a crack running right through the visage of Her Majesty, Queen Victoria. And on her diamond jubilee too!

Feeling oddly unmoved, she put it back on the shelf and headed out. Her collection of coronation items had once been her pride and joy. Losing them should have affected her more than it did. Living through these dangerous years might have been the reason why they were no longer quite so important. It was people that were important, some more important to her than others.

The air was balmy, and everyone seemed in high spirits on the bus into work, not just because May was warmer than usual. Summertime was sure to lift tired spirits.

A woman was talking about going to the seaside.

'A beach where there ain't any barbed wire.'

'Might take you a while finding one of those.'

'Not Weymouth. Clevedon should be all right. Or Weston-super-Mare.'

'You should be all right. Jerry would have to wait for the tide if he wanted to come ashore there!'

A few old stagers insisting that a warm May meant a wet June didn't dampen the atmosphere of apprehension that something fantastic was about to happen.

Others remarked that as long as there were no more air raids, it could bucket down with rain for all they cared.

The bus was crowded. The Easter air raid on the twelfth of April 1941, had destroyed the tramway system. There was no tram to Knowle West, but as the bus wound through the central area, passengers who would have caught the tram in the past piled on.

I've a lot to be thankful for, Thelma thought as the bus passed damaged buildings and piles of sandbags, air-raid posts and public information posters about gas masks, rationing or enlisting in the services.

Looking out the window at the damaged buildings assured her that she was one of the lucky ones. Her home, her family and her job were what mattered. Her family were alive and well. Her priority at present was that Peter would keep out of trouble and hadn't volunteered for anything dangerous. Knowing him, her greatest fear was that he had.

* * *

Bertrams Modes, the shop that sold ladies fashion, was an oasis. The mannequins in the windows smiled the same enigmatic smile they had done for years. Time had not tarnished them to any great extent.

The swing doors still made the same swishing sound they'd always done. The interior still smelled of polish and a vase of silk flowers stood on each counter. In front of each counter was a stool upholstered in red velvet for the benefit of the customer. None for sales personnel who out of common courtesy were required to remain standing despite their aching feet.

Nothing much had changed since the outbreak of war except for the half of the shop that dealt with second-hand items. There was less stock than pre-war, but that was only to be expected, thanks to the shortage of fabric. Seamstresses too were in short supply, their skills applied to making uniforms for the armed forces.

But Bertrams was the same. Thelma sighed with relief, sure that nothing would change here for a long time to come. That was still her belief one hour later after she'd swallowed her nerves, did a bit of tidying up and served ladies in pursuit of silk underwear and a rubber corset. Thanks to keeping busy, the minutes flew by. She checked the Roman numerals on the wall clock. Five minutes to go before she was scheduled to report to Mr Bertram. No more customers, she studied her surroundings. How long had she loved this place? How long had she thought it the very height of glamour? The years had passed leaving the plaster mannequins, the silk flowers, and the velvet-covered stools with an air of shabby vulnerability.

Their customers tended to be the wives of professional men who could afford to indulge their spouses in the latest fashion.

They lived in opulent houses in places like Clifton and Redland. Their children went to the best schools, and they employed a cook and at least one maid. A gardener too. If their husbands had been called up to serve in the forces, they all seemed to end up as officers. The wives, although still able to buy better than most people, did voluntary work for the WVS or any other good works that didn't spoil their soft hands.

Living as she did on the Knowle West council estate to the south of the city, Thelma had always felt very privileged to work in such a swish shop, serving women with cut-glass accents. To that end, she had upgraded her way of speaking, putting on a posh accent almost on a par with the customers.

Her neighbours envied her being sales manageress, having made her way up from being a lowly sales assistant. Not for her wearing an overall in a factory or behind the counter at Woolworths or indeed a shop of any description. Bertrams, she reminded anyone who termed it a shop, was a purveyor of expensive fashion.

It had changed a bit since war was declared, one half of the store given over to a facility where women could exchange garments no longer needed for clothes they could make better use of. The other half had retained the pre-war atmosphere of privilege and money, ladies of means perusing what stock they managed to get hold of. There wasn't as much choice as before the war and the women of means, keen to still look good and with an eye on value for money – or coupons – did on occasion peruse the exchange rails in the other part of the store.

A smile twitched at Thelma's red lips when she thought of the melee of working-class housewives and wealthy women in competition for the pick of the bunch. One specific attraction was that all items were donated and free to those who wanted them.

Her first task every morning was greeting her sales team, which nowadays consisted of the demure Rosie Ball and Anne Lewis. She looked them over as she always did, checking that they were well turned out and that their black dresses – the unofficial uniform of Bertrams Modes – were of a standard and cleanliness expected by both management and clients.

Rosie rubbed a bit of spit on one small stain that was pointed out to her and Anne flicked at a speck of dandruff on her right shoulder.

Thelma sighed but let it go.

'I would suggest mixing a tablespoonful of vinegar in with your shampoo,' she suggested to Anne.

Barbara, the trainee, was perfectly turned out, not even having a single ladder in her stockings. In fact, they looked as if they'd come straight out of the packet, which led Thelma to suspect that she was walking out with a Yank on her arm. Not that she could hold that against her. A lot of women were doing that. Make do and mend could also be interpreted as getting what you could from where you could. The Yanks were complicit in providing – though mostly if it was to mutual advantage.

Thelma beamed at the girl who wasn't much older than her youngest daughter, Alice. 'I can find no fault with you, Barbara. I wish we could all look so perfect in these turbulent times.'

'Thank you, Mrs Dawson.'

Mrs Dawson. Little do you know, she thought to herself.

Despite having three children, she'd never been married. On top of that, her children had three different fathers. Anyone who did suspect her true status would never dare bring it up for fear of getting a piece of her mind. Her children were the most precious thing in her life, and she would defend them to the death.

After dealing with her staff, Rosie going off to tidy up the clothes exchange, and Anne whisking a feather duster over the clothes rails, Thelma turned her attention to the glass-topped counter containing women's underwear and foundation garments. The vase of silk flowers looking a bit askew, she straightened it firmly.

Just as she judged it perfect, Mr Bertram appeared. His smile was oddly hesitant, and she judged his manner a little furtive. As for the bags beneath his eyes, well, was it her imagination or were they puffier than usual?

He stopped on the other side of the lingerie cabinet and replied good morning to her good morning before adding, 'Mrs Dawson. If you could spare a minute, I'd like a word with you in my office.'

'Right now, Mr Bertram?'

'Right now, if you please. If you can spare the time,' he added. His tone was almost apologetic, as though it had come to him that he was rudely interrupting what she was doing.

Telling herself there was nothing to worry about, she followed in his footsteps.

His office had a male atmosphere, the sort that comes with dark wood and the smell of pipe tobacco.

He sat down with obvious relief, the silver chain of a pocket watch dangled across the taut stretch of his waistcoat and an unlit pipe quivered at the corner of his mouth.

He indicated the beechwood chair on the other side of his desk. 'Do sit down.'

Thelma tried to think what this might be about. She knew his son had been shot down in a dogfight over the south-east coast – one of the Battle of Britain air crew that had not returned. But it wouldn't be about that. Like everyone else who'd lost a loved one, he had a stiff upper lip.

Clearing his throat, eyes downcast, he tapped his empty pipe on the edge of a green glazed ashtray. On realising it was already empty, he let it fall, before intertwining his fingers across his midriff.

'It's like this,' he began, eyes still averted, one entwined finger tapping against the others. 'I've always had great enthusiasm for this business. My wife said that I loved it more than I did her.'

He chuckled at his little joke, but the lightness ended as quickly as it had begun.

Sensing that something about his mood was a little off-kilter, Thelma tensed and looked tellingly at the smart wristwatch Peter had given her.

'I am rather busy, Mr Bertram,' she stated hesitantly, impatient to know what he had on his mind.

'Of course. Of course.'

Two nods, one closely following the first before he found his voice.

'The thing is that... what with everything that's happened...'

She heard the note of sadness in his voice.

'The truth is that it's aged me. I no longer have the enthusiasm for business. The war hasn't helped.'

Thelma felt a yawning chasm open inside. Once before she'd thought he was drawing out of the business, but it had turned out he'd wanted to open the exchange clothes shop on part of the premises.

'I've decided to sell the business. My wife, Ethel, and I, have decided to move to our cottage in Cornwall. We need time to heal after losing Thomas. We also want a few precious years to ourselves. Peace and quiet and the simple life. Time to reflect...' His voice trailed away.

Thelma was speechless. All the joy she'd ever felt working here crumbled to dust.

'Really.' She said it abruptly and not without rancour. She'd given her life to this place. And now, at her age, what else was she going to do?

Apology was in the pale eyes that glanced up at her. 'I'm sorry. You've been a stalwart support and much appreciated.'

'I'm sorry too.' The truth was she was angry enough to spit pips. 'So, I'm out of a job.'

'It might not necessarily be so bad...' His voice was apologetic, almost timid.

Thelma erupted. 'Oh no? And how do you work that out?' Her chair was sent clattering as she sprang to her feet and slammed her palms down flat on his desk. 'So that's what I get for my loyalty,' she hissed, barely able to take breath. 'Well, thank you very much!'

Head in the air, she stalked out, leaving the door ajar and swinging behind her. All she could think of was the possibility of working somewhere she didn't want to work. She adored her job and had envisaged working up until she retired.

Tears stung her eyes, but she brushed them away.

Regardless of what anyone else thought, she wanted to retain the freedom her job at Bertrams had given her. In latter years, she'd been involved in ordering stock, dressing the models in the shop window and hanging clothes on rails and the mannequins inside the store. To some extent, they had seemed as much her workmates as the flesh and blood people she worked with. And now?

She ground her teeth as one thought after another careered through her head like a line of runaway buses. A future by herself in an empty house was unthinkable. Maria, her daughter-in-law, did call in at the weekends for afternoon tea, and of course there was Peter, who had swept her off her feet – in more ways than one. They'd first met when she was hanging onto a barrage balloon to which a young boy was entangled. Even now, in dark moments, it made her laugh and his passion for her made her blush.

But what next? Her world had suddenly come crashing down.

* * *

Behind the closed office door, Mr Bertram was holding his head in his hands. Thelma storming out was not the scenario he'd envisaged. She hadn't given him time to discuss the possibilities – and there were certainly plenty of those.

Unable to think straight, he sought more sage advice about handling the situation and reached for the telephone. He'd married his wife at the end of the Great War. They shared everything and when it seemed that he had no solution to a problem, it was her who offered him a conclusion.

Ethel answered after about the sixth ring.

'Darling, it's me.'

He explained to her that he'd carried out what he'd had to carry out but was having trouble living with it.

'I feel I need to do more. Mrs Dawson has always been such a loyal employee. I didn't think she'd take things so badly.'

'Then you don't know her well enough. She loves the shop just as much as you do, my darling, perhaps more so. She's every right to be upset and you really should have known that. I do believe I did warn you, my darling.'

Mr Bertram realised that his wife was right. Mrs Dawson threw herself into the daily routine with vigour and even pleasure.

'What can I do?'

There was a minute's silence before Ethel, his love and strongest support, stated, 'Think more deeply. Bertrams is Mrs

Dawson, and Mrs Dawson is Bertrams. If you look close enough at the matter, amongst all the nutty slack, you might find a golden nugget.'

He smiled at her response. Ethel was from Lancashire and had a colourful and matter-of-fact wisdom.

Once their phone call had ended, he thought on what she had said and smiled. In his mind, he could see heaps of coal and a single golden nugget. As yet, he couldn't quite make out what it was. A little thinking was needed and another look at the healthy balance sheet. Perhaps that might trigger a clearer and better prospect to the dilemma.

7

Another day taking the cows to the field. Knapsack slung around her shoulder as usual, Tilly swung the thick stick and whistled as she drove the cows across the field.

The sun was warm on her back, the field was dry, and the cows were more than willing to move from the field of grass chewed down to the stubble to one of verdant green.

Swallows were diving across a blue sky. As she watched them chasing the insects, she couldn't help comparing them to Spitfire and Hurricane fighter planes swooping and diving in much the same manner.

After shutting the gate on Hope Meadow behind her, she surveyed Brook Meadow which sloped downhill to the brook it was named after.

Grass interested the cows and once they were chomping at its lush succulence, they forgot that she was there. This, she decided, was the ideal time to take a break.

Shielding her eyes with one hand, she sought out the best spot and decided on a grassy hillock perched against a stone wall. Slightly elevated from the rest of the pasture, it seemed a pretty spot. Speedwells and campions sheltered at its base and bees dipped in and out of the dainty flowers.

She sighed with satisfaction as she shifted herself into place, thick grass beneath her bottom and sun-kissed stone warm against her back.

The green meadow sloped away from her to a band of trees immediately opposite her luncheon spot. To her right, the land sloped down to the far end, where the brook ran between this meadow and the next one. A tumbledown cottage nestled beneath a mighty elm tree, throwing shade over its crumbling stone and mossy roof tiles.

The heads of gigantically sized cow parsley fluttered like ripped lace along its facade so that only the top of the windows and lopsided shutters showed.

Although hungry, she opened her mother's latest letter before reaching for her lunch.

To my darling Tilly,

I hope you are well. I am missing you very much. Please give my best wishes and thanks to Mrs Forester for the offer of fresh farm produce when you next come home.

It sounds indeed as though the countryside is far from dull. I liked your story about the doctored lemonade and the elderly lady showing her bloomers!

Despite the ongoing shortages and feeling that everything is grey, Coronation Close is not without its excitement.

Anyway, that's it for now. Can't wait to see you. The house seems so empty with only me and Gloria in it. She's at work during the day and off out at night. I can't blame her. Might as well enjoy yourselves whilst you can. Just take care of yourself.

Love, Mum

Returning the letter to the rucksack, she reached for her lunch.

Leaning her head back against the wall reminded her of just how tired she was. The early start and exertions of that morning caught up with her. What with the drone of bees and the soft soughing of the breeze, her eyelids began to flutter and finally close.

It must have been only minutes – a very pleasant few minutes – when something caused her to wake up. Was it her imagination or had a shadow fallen over her?

Alarmed, she blinked her eyes open and sat up straight.

It might only have been a cloud passing over, nothing alarming at all.

Gripping the gritty roughness of the stone wall, she hauled herself to her feet and looked around. Tall feathery heads of grass moved like waves upon the sea, driven by the warm wind. Her gaze fixed on movement in the far right-hand corner of the field. The cow parsley was still there. So too were the swifts and swallows soaring high in the sky.

Her gaze fixed on the tumbledown cottage. A thin ribbon of smoke now arose from a broken chimney reduced to half its height; the upper half heaped in a pile on the ground.

Standing on a raised hillock, she could see a line of laundry billowing in the breeze outside the cottage.

She recalled Mrs Forester telling her that a cowherd and his family had once lived there but it hadn't been used for years.

'Well, it is now,' she whispered as she watched the washing blow.

A murky yellow cloud spread in the air above the mouldy thatch and tiles that constituted the roof.

Tucking the detritus of her meal inside her knapsack, she

brushed the crumbs from her dark green jumper and prepared to investigate.

Curiosity roused, she threaded her way along a narrow winding path where feet had beaten the earth hard between the long grass.

Overgrown bushes obscured the view between broken bits of wooden fence. Within the curtilage, yellow rattle, purple foxgloves, daisies and thorny rose bushes jostled for space. A swift movement led her eyes to the nests of busy swallows bulging with life beneath the eaves.

She listened for voices. If there was anyone inside, they either had not heard her approach or preferred to stay hidden.

Just as she was about to call out, she sensed she was not alone, that someone had come up behind her.

The grass whipped around her legs as she turned to see the presence she had felt.

The woman looked as surprised as she was, wrapping her arms around the enamel jug she was carrying as though it would protect or make her invisible.

Her eyes were huge in a thin face, the cheekbones sharp angles with hollows beneath them.

At sight of Tilly, she hugged the jug closer and began to shake.

'Please. My boy needs the milk. I'll pay for it if you like, only don't turn us out. We've got nowhere else to go.'

Tilly looked at the jug she was clasping to her breasts. 'Did you milk one of the cows?'

The woman nodded.

'Now you've got it, you might as well have it. It would take some skill indeed to put it back into the udders. As for identifying the right cow, don't they all look the same to you? They do to me.' It was hard not to laugh, but now was not the time for hilarity. The woman looked in dire straits.

The woman did not laugh. Her expression was full of pleading. 'I will pay. I've got a farthing somewhere...'

Tilly shook her head. 'If that's all you've got, then keep it.'

Misconstruing what was being said, the woman held the jug of milk out in front of her.

'You milked one of the cows, and you didn't get kicked?' Tilly herself had been kicked and learned how not to.

A shaking of head.

Tilly managed a reassuring smile. 'I'm sure Farmer Forester can afford to give you a pint of milk.' She held her head sideways. 'Hold on a minute.'

The weight of her canvas rucksack seemed suddenly to weigh heavily on her shoulder.

Whilst she was in the act of swinging it forward and searching inside, the woman had disappeared inside the low front door, reappearing again and holding out a single farthing.

Tilly shook her head. 'No. I told you. Keep it. And the milk.' She rummaged more deeply in her bag. 'I've got a ham sandwich left, a piece of cheese and an apple.' She took in the woman's thin form and held out the bag. 'I'm not hungry, though I would like the bag back.'

A head of white-blonde curls appeared behind her, a small boy of about three or four years old rubbing his eyes with one hand as children do when they've just woken up. He held a tin cup in the other.

The woman, suddenly protective, stepped in front of him. 'Go back in, Jack. There's a good boy.'

The boy began to grizzle. His chubby hands clung to his mother's skirt which was close fitting and grey checked. A motherly hand cupped the boy's head against her side.

'Please,' she said through cracked lips, her gaze fixed on Tilly. 'Let us stay here. You don't need to give me your food.'

Tilly nodded at her lunch bag. 'You look as though you could do with this more so than me.' She jerked her chin at a place where a grassy mound intersected the broken fence. 'Let's sit here and eat. And whilst we're at it, why don't you pour your boy a cup of milk? My name's Tilly Crawford by the way. What's yours?'

There was a pause born of nervousness before she replied. 'Sybil.'

It was noticeable that she did not offer a surname.

Her long thin frame folded against the wall.

Tilly handed her the bag. Mrs Forester was generous with her food portions despite the rationing.

She watched as they ate, the little boy ravenously, the woman wary and slow.

Once the food was finished, Sybil got up. 'I'd better get Jack more milk. He's finished that one.'

Tilly wasn't sure that he had, but sensed Sybil did not want to be prodded for more information.

'Let me,' said Tilly to Sybil. To Jack, she said, 'How about we get you some more milk, Jack. Just you and me.'

The truth was, it seemed a good idea to give Sybil breathing space. She was also curious to see the inside of the cottage.

Reluctantly, Sybil agreed.

The interior was gloomy, the smell of damp tingling her nostrils to the extent that she was in danger of sneezing. Little daylight found its way through the small square windows. A blouse formed a curtain of sorts at one window, a skirt at the other. Clothes airing whilst serving a dual purpose.

The enamel jug containing the milk sat in the stone window ledge covered by a piece of muslin to keep the flies at bay. A wooden pine chair sat to one side of what remained of the fire, lit only long enough to boil the kettle that hung over it. A three-legged stool occupied the other side of the fireplace and benefitting from the warmth of what fire there was, a small iron saucepan and a slightly larger one hung from nails hammered into the wooden mantelshelf. There was little else, except for a photograph, curling at the edges, of a young man in battledress.

Tilly smiled down at the little boy patiently waiting for more milk, then studied the photograph.

'Is this your daddy?' she asked.

The boy looked at it questioningly and smiled.

She presumed the answer was yes, though failed to see much of a likeness between them.

The photo was returned to its rightful place.

Sybil was chewing her bottom lip as she scrutinised the apple she had in her hand. 'I think you'd better have this,' she said, offering it to Tilly, who shook her head. 'No. You have it. I had a big breakfast.'

You look as though you're starving.

She kept the words inside. There was no doubting mother and son were hungry, but remarking as such would only dent Sybil's pride. Looking at her, Tilly sensed there was a grim story to tell, a tragedy relating to the young man in the photo perhaps.

She thought of the larder back at the farm, the sacks of potatoes, the hens and ducks scavenging around the yard, the smell of home-made bread. It wouldn't hurt to share some of it. Mrs Forester needn't know, and even if she did, Tilly doubted she'd notice.

'I can make us a cup of tea,' Sybil offered, breaking into her saintly thoughts.

Tilly was about to refuse. After all, there was more work to do back at the farm and victory depended on everyone doing their bit.

'Yes, please. I'd love one.' She nodded and smiled appreciatively, and, she hoped, with reassurance.

Whilst his mother was inside occupied making tea, Jack picked dandelions and Tilly watched him. There was something familiar about him, but she couldn't tell what.

Sybil came out with two cups proudly borne on mismatched saucers.

'I'm sorry, but I've run out of sugar,' she said apologetically.

'That's fine. I don't take sugar anyway,' said Tilly. She took a sip. 'That's good,' she sighed.

Her new companion also took a sip before they both looked further down the field to where the brook shone like silver in the sunlight as it gurgled and frolicked over its pebble and rock bed.

'How long have you lived here?' asked Tilly.

Sybil gulped back her tea. 'Not long. About three weeks. It's so peaceful here. No bombs. No noise except for the cows and I don't mind that.'

To Tilly's ears, she sounded a little terse, like someone who didn't want to divulge too much.

'And your husband. Will he be joining you?'

Sybil's eyes were downcast when she answered. 'No. He won't be coming.'

Tilly's frown was hidden by the wide brim of her land girl hat. 'Do you have any relatives? Anyone who might be worried about you and want to know how you were getting on. Might they want to see you?'

Alarm flashed in Sybil's eyes. 'Nobody. I have no one.' She sucked in her breath and, still showing alarm, said, 'You won't tell anyone I'm here, will you?'

'What about the Foresters? The farmer and his wife?'

'Please! No. No.' Sybil shook her head and turned away. Her gaze followed Jack chasing after a blue fritillary, its butterfly wings like flower petals. The little boy was laughing, waving his hands and kicking his spindly legs behind him. 'I need to stay here. I must. I've nowhere else to go. The farmer might not want me here.' Her thin face was creased with concern. Her fingers were tightly interlaced enough to make her knuckles glow white.

Tilly felt for her.

'I won't say a word. You might want to keep the smoke to a minimum, especially during the day, or someone will see you.'

Sybil sighed and closed her eyes. Her head drooped low, her chin closing on her chest.

'If Mr Forester does find out, you may have to leave, unless...' A lightning thought came to Tilly's mind, such a good idea that she couldn't help but voice it out loud. 'Unless he can find a job for you.' She jerked her head over her shoulder at the grazing herd. 'You can obviously milk a cow. He might even be able to find you a better place to live in town. Better than this draughty old place. You wouldn't be isolated as you are here.'

Sybil went white. She shook her head adamantly. 'No. No. I can't do that.'

There were two-pound notes in Tilly's purse. She had been saving up for a decent pair of dancing shoes and a pretty lace blouse she'd seen in Bertrams Modes back home. With a bit of luck, her mother's close friend, Thelma Dawson, might be able to get her a discount. A bargain outfit would be like a dream come true, but it wasn't as though she was short of clothes. Her mother was good with a sewing needle, and Thelma more so. Brilliant in fact. Did she really need another outfit or pair of shoes? Plus, she was well fed, whereas this woman and her little boy...

'Here,' she said, taking the money out of her purse. 'I've been saving it up for a dress, but your need is greater than mine. Take it.'

'No, I can't do that.' Sybil was adamant.

Tilly was determined to help. Nobody should be so alone and so destitute.

'Tell you what,' she said brightly. 'I'll set a snare for a rabbit. Do you know how to skin a rabbit? If you don't, I can show you how.'

She said it proudly. It stemmed from the day Mr Forester had trapped and brought home three rabbits. Tilly could see them now, their glassy-eyed stare, their floppy bodies and her revulsion when Mrs Forester had shown her how to fold the skin from the body and take it off from the legs – like trousers. That's what she'd said. There was rabbit stew for dinner that night.

'I'd love to learn. Love to eat rabbit stew too.' Sybil called to her son, asking him if he too would like to eat some rabbit stew. 'What do you think, Jack?'

'You might make Jack a winter cap from the fur,' Tilly suggested.

Sybil laughed at the prospect and instantly looked ten years younger.

Tilly looked westward to where the sun in a burning glow would slip behind the hills before long. 'I'd better go. The cows are almost ready to be herded up and taken back for milking.'

She brushed the grass from her clothes whilst noting that Jack was curled up in a tump of long grass, sound asleep.

She couldn't go and just forget them. She wasn't made that way. Sybil needed someone to care for her, and Tilly was a natural born carer.

'I'll come back and see you tomorrow or the day after and we'll talk some more. Will that be all right with you?'

Expression wary, Sibyl took a few minutes to think about it before she replied, 'Yes. That would be nice.'

* * *

The cows went before her, hiding her presence in a tight packed herd as they hurried up the field, keen for the heaviness to be milked from their udders. Thus it was that John didn't look beyond her to the old cottage at the bottom of the field.

'You bin out here all day. Fall asleep, did you?'

'No need to be sarcastic.'

He smirked as he looked at her sidelong. 'I'm not being that. Sorry.'

'It was a nice day and, yes, I did fall asleep. The sunshine made me feel a bit faint, so I thought the best thing was to lie down in the grass and wait until I got better.'

She was unsure whether he believed her or not. It was difficult to read his expression, but something about it made her cheeks turn warm.

'Best 'ave some cod liver oil when you get back to the farm. Or some liquid paraffin,' he added with a wide grin. 'It's a cure-all for anything, if my old mother is to be believed.'

Tilly pulled a face and shivered. 'I think I'd prefer to stay ill.'

John's face brightened. 'I've got my own cure for feeling not too well. Half of cider at the Black Horse. What do you think?'

Him asking her came as something of a surprise.

'That would be lovely. Your treat?'

'My treat,' he said, looking pleased and just a little surprised that she'd willingly agreed.

Another attractive smile, a flouncing off behind the cows, a tap on their rears to get them moving more quickly.

'Then you're on,' she called over her shoulder.

8

Gloria Crawford, Jenny's younger daughter and Tilly's younger sister, often thought about the first time she'd met Damien Fox, the man she'd become quite obsessed with. From that moment of their first meeting, her world had changed, and the memory was still fresh in her mind, played repeatedly like a gramophone record she couldn't get enough of.

A friend of the owner, he'd come into the place where she worked, Thomas Cousens and Sons Limited, and been closeted in the office of Mr Thomas. They had discussed business; what kind of business she had no idea. The door had been tightly closed, so all she could hear was a rumble of conversation, not clear words.

Right from the first, she'd stared at this impressive man whose very presence hinted at money and power. Nobody wore such clothes in Knowle West or Bedminster, the world she'd grown up in: soft woollen suit, crisp white shirt, silk tie, leather shoes shined to the nth degree.

On that first occasion, she'd been bent over the filing cabinet when he'd come out and Mr Thomas had told her they were off out for bangers and mash at the Victory Café and would be late back.

They had indeed been late back, Mr Thomas a bit the worse for wear. She guessed that lunch at the Victory Café had been followed by a visit to the Barley Mow, for a few pints to wash down the bangers and mash. By the looks of him, he'd poured enough down him to drown the meal, not just wash it down.

Damien had instructed her. 'Just give me a hand getting him in his office.'

She'd complied with his request and with Mr Thomas flopping like a rag doll between them, they had half dragged, half carried him into his office.

Once Mr Thomas was safely seated in his chair, his head resting on his arms, which in turn were resting on his desk, Damien had closed the door on him, stating, 'Best leave him to sleep it off, love.'

Alone with this stranger, Gloria's legs had turned to jelly. Her eyes had seemed to take on a life of their own, fluttering as she tried to make up her mind whether to look at him or away at something nondescript: the wall, the files on the desk, the wire filing tray.

'What's your name?'

That was the first question he'd asked.

'Nice,' he'd said after she had told him. His dark brown eyes had looked her over as though she was one of the items he had come to buy. She'd been wearing a slim-fitting dress in navy blue; her hair held back from her face by a matching Alice band. 'Fancy coming out with me tonight?'

'For a drink?' She presumed a pub. All the boys and girls she knew met up at the pub or the pictures. If money was tight, it was just window shopping around the city centre.

'Now would I take a classy chick like you to a common pub?

No, I would not. I'm talking high-class nightclub. How would you like that?'

Although she blushed profusely, he'd instantly made her feel like a film star. And grown up.

Him asking for a cup of tea had broken her trance.

'We'll drink it here,' he'd said. 'That okay with you, love?'

She was reminded of her father. His voice was kindly and there was affection in his eyes – until he winked. But still she fancied there was a resemblance to the father who had loved her more than he had her sister.

'I promise I won't eat you, love. Now go on. Put the kettle on. Two sugars for me and don't worry about running out. There's plenty more where that came from.'

Another wink followed, suggesting to her there was no need to rely on rationed sugar. His sort had their own source of items in short supply.

Her hands had shook when she was making the tea, but somehow she had managed to get through it without a cup or saucer being smashed.

Whilst carrying out the task, she'd told herself to stop acting like a child. 'Don't be a goose,' she heard herself say. 'Shoulders back. Head up. Courage. Never let anyone get the better of you.'

The words were not entirely hers, but those of her father who she'd always looked up to. She recalled a long-ago day when they were still living in Blue Bowl Alley, a medieval area of Bristol that was no more. He'd been carting off a mattress infested with bugs. She'd followed behind him, even helped him light the bonfire he burned it on. Tilly had hung back along with her mother.

'Tilly was never as brave as you.' That's what her father had said to her. 'You're my best girl, Gloria, and don't you forget that.'

You can do anything if you've a mind to.

She couldn't recall for sure if the words had definitely been said by him, but they were certainly typical.

* * *

That first date had happened six weeks ago. Now here she was out with him again, picked up by car and treated very differently than on the dates she'd been on with younger men. He could afford to indulge her, buy her champagne – at least he told her it was champagne. She didn't know for sure because she'd never drank it before. All she did know was that it made her giggle. She also noticed that other girls eyed her enviously, at least she thought that was what she read in their eyes.

Whispers were rife that she was hardly the first young woman to saunter into a nightclub hanging on his arm and nobody questioned whether she was old enough to drink or not. Whatever Mr Fox willed, Mr Fox got.

A sharp-tongued older woman of at least twenty-five, cigarette poised like a stiletto knife, said, 'But you're certainly the youngest, you silly little girl. Got you straight from school, did he?'

'You're just jealous.' That was what she'd hissed loudly into that vicious expression. It was also what she told herself.

In the preceding six weeks, he'd taken her to nightclubs several times. He'd also taken her to the theatre to see a play, something she had never experienced. She'd watched the play spellbound, went for dinner afterwards, excitedly asking him about the plot and the lead actors.

'I've always wanted to be a film star, but I wouldn't mind being an actress.'

'You were that excited?'

Was that surprise in his eyes? Perhaps also a trace of pride.

She'd nodded avidly and spouted the first response that came into her head. 'I almost wet myself.'

She'd blushed when he'd laughed loud enough to attract the attention of people close by.

She'd felt a fool. 'That was the wrong thing to say, wasn't it,' she'd whispered.

He'd been incredibly reassuring. 'It was honest. That's all that matters. That's what I like about you, Gloria. You say the first thing that comes into your head. There's nothing wrong with that.'

And so here she was again. He'd told her that tonight was going to be special. He was going to give her a present as a mark of his esteem. 'Seeing as it was your birthday a while ago. I was busy so didn't have time to get out and buy you a present.' He grinned. 'But I've got you one now.'

Gloria had a way of dressing that made her look older. She liked to think of herself as a woman, not inclined to go out with boys close to her age. She gasped at the bracelet he brought out from a blue velvet box, soft and shiny. The way the stones sparkled almost blinded her. He slid it onto her very willing wrist, his thick fingers ably fastening the clasp whilst she gulped and tried to find her voice.

'Well,' he said taking a half-smoked cigarillo from his mouth. 'Do you like it or what?' The smoke curled up in front of his face.

Her sky-blue eyes met his black ones. Everything about Damien was dark, which to her mind made him even more intriguing. His hair and eyebrows were black, his skin swarthy. Never was there a hair out of place, never had she seen him wearing a creased shirt or an unpressed suit. Rarely did he wear the same suit. She'd teased that he was a bit of a dandy. In response, he'd smiled widely, exposing a gold tooth towards the back of his mouth.

'If you can afford it, flaunt it,' he said with his usual bravado, brushing his sleeve and making sure he didn't dip it in the spilt beer on the table. 'I can afford it.' He clicked his fingers at a waitress, motioning for her to clean it up. Dividing his smile and a salacious wink between waitress and Gloria, he said, 'This suit cost me twenty knicker. Wouldn't want it ruined.'

There was subdued lighting in the Green Silk Club. The naked flames of candles flickered in a way that animated the most stolid features. The candles were stuck in empty wine bottles, the wax left to run down the sides. Gloria thought them wonderful.

All around her, featureless figures moved in the foggy haze of smoke, men and women at tables crouched towards each other. The brightest point was the bar, where electric lighting and a mirrored back made bottles and glasses gleam.

The barman was a bald man named Norman; his hairless skull shiny beneath the lighting reflected from the back bar, just like the bottles and glassware.

She'd learned from the first that Damien wasn't just at the club for pleasure. It was also where he met men he called business colleagues. That's what he called them. Not friends. They came over to whisper in his ear. He'd nod. She never knew what was being said and she wasn't interested in business.

'What are you daydreaming about?'

Damien's eyes were fixed on her.

She jolted out from her daydreaming and smiled. 'The day we met. I never thought I'd ever own something like this.'

As she held up her hand, the light reflected from behind the bar caught the sparkling stones of the bracelet.

He shook his head and smiled. Forbearance, he thought to himself. She's only a kid. You've shown her a different world. Give her time to grow up.

He went back to discussing business with his cronies.

She went back to her daydreams and the first day he had appeared in the office where she worked. And the days after when she'd watch him drawing a hip flask from his pocket, undoing its silver top and adding a few drops of something into his cup.

'Will you join me?' he'd asked. Right from the first.

Officially she was too young to drink but would not admit it – not to this powerful, wealthy-looking man who reminded her of the Hollywood film star, Edward G. Robinson. And anyway, she had had the odd shandy – beer and lemonade mix – though was bright enough to know there was something much stronger in his hip flask.

'Young lady,' he'd said when she'd hesitated. 'I won't ask you again.'

She relished the memory. Calling her young lady instead of young girl clinched it.

'Yes,' she'd said with a smile and a confident toss of her head.

That was how it had started. A cup of tea. Strong drink added. Then him asking her out.

On that first date, he'd picked her up from outside the London Inn in a car. How he got the petrol for it, she couldn't even guess but didn't care.

Her assumption that he would take her to a pub had proved incorrect.

'I do go in pubs,' he'd told her, 'but it's a place for blokes not beautiful women. A beautiful woman like you deserves the best.'

With those words and his treatment of her, her childhood was instantly left behind. She melted at him saying that she was a beautiful woman. Suddenly, her world had changed. She was on the arm of a handsome man of the world who made her feel as if she was walking on air.

'You off in fairyland again?' His attention had turned away from the men he consorted with and back to her.

'I was just thinking about this bracelet. It sparkles,' she said in a hushed voice. 'I've never seen anything sparkle like this.'

He leaned forward until there were only a few inches between them. 'Just like your eyes.'

The blush on her cheeks spread like a rash all over her body. She tingled, she shivered, and her stomach tensed with excitement.

'Fancy going for a run the weekend?'

'Run?'

Her first thought was that she hadn't done any running since she'd left school. Young ladies in high-heeled shoes did not run. She was about to say so, but he got there first.

'I'm talking about a run out in the car. You didn't think we were going on a cross-country, did you?'

'Oh.' She felt a fool.

He went on. 'We can drive down to Brockley Combe. Get a bit of fresh air. Sunday would be best for me. I can pick you up at twelve outside the London Inn. Fingers crossed the weather will be good.'

'Yes,' she answered breathlessly, relieved she didn't have to pound the streets in shorts, navy blue knickers or daps – plimsolls to use their correct name. 'Yes. That would be lovely.'

In her mind, she was working out what she would tell her mother.

Right from the first, Damien had been most conscientious about getting her home before midnight.

'Don't want to upset your old lady,' he'd pronounced in a fatherly manner.

She'd turned quite defensive. 'My mum is not an old lady.'

'Just an older version of you, sweetheart?'

'I'll show you a photo.'

She'd done just that, taking out a snap of her mother. Thelma had taken the photo, chuffed to bits that her new man, Peter the pilot, had bought her a camera for her birthday.

Damien had narrowed his eyes as he studied the forty-something woman who was Gloria's mother. 'Nice-looking woman. Hope to meet her someday. Dare say I might.'

Gloria had taken back the snapshot and slipped it into the side pocket of her handbag.

'Not yet though,' she'd said, face looking down so he wouldn't see the confusion there. She'd avoided admitting that she was going out with a man old enough to be her father. Her mother rarely questioned where she was going at night. All she did say was to be careful and not to wander in dark places. She'd also said for her to enjoy herself and not to tie herself down until she was ready.

'Wartime can throw people together. Enjoy yourself and don't get too serious about any young man you might meet,' she'd said.

Gloria never let on that there was someone. Let her mother believe she was merely out with girlfriends, enjoying the here and now before another bomb fell on the city.

She rehearsed the excuse in her mind. 'I'll be going out with June.'

She'd mentioned her workmate before, so there would be no further questions.

Live for the moment. That's what she was thinking as Damien raised her hand and kissed the inside of her wrist. She held her breath. Nobody had ever told her that soft lips brushing that area could make her feel so helpless, so ready to surrender.

When his dark eyes focused on hers, she felt she was drowning.

'So that's a date. And that,' he said, indicating the sparkling bracelet, 'is a mark of my regard for you.'

She held her breath, unable to speak. How long, she wondered, before he said those three little words, 'I love you'? Dared she hope?

'Oh, Damien. I don't know what to say.'

'Nothing,' he said, and let her hand go. His smile vanished and a look of warning hardened his eyes. 'Just be there on Sunday. I'm counting on you.'

'I promise. I promise. I'll be there.'

* * *

As usual, she declined a lift all the way home. She didn't want anyone she knew to see her. 'Just to Queen Square. I can get a bus from there.'

His eyebrows rose as they always did when she insisted on this. 'Ashamed of me, are you? Is that it?'

She fancied he was teasing, but still proclaimed, 'No. No, of course not. I know you've got business to attend to.'

The stiffness left his face. A smile returned. 'You've got that right, babe. I'm a very busy man and getting even busier.'

His gold tooth glinted.

'I'll get Reece to walk with you to the bus stop.'

Reece was his right-hand man and driver.

Gloria sighed with relief. It was true that she didn't want anyone to see her with him, not out of shame. Going out with a man close to her mother's age would not win approval. For now, at least, Damien had to remain a secret. For the same reason, she would take the bracelet off before she got home. That way, there would be no need to explain and no condemnation of her having fallen in love with an older man. And she was in love and, for better or worse, she wanted him badly.

Reece Davies escorted her to the cloakroom where she'd left her coat. He manoeuvred her through the late-night crowd laughing and pushing their way into the red-carpeted foyer of the nightclub. A tidal wave of humanity, they parted as he barged his way through, respectful of his broad shoulders and above-average height. The vivid red scar on his right cheek added to his air of strength and menace.

Without looking from right to left, Gloria made it to the steps leading up to the main door. Because of that she did not see Margaret Routledge and her look of surprise.

Margaret herself had drowned two schooners of sherry, two gin and tonics and half a rough cider. The cider she'd bought herself. Obliging men had bought her the rest. Recognising her young neighbour through eyes blurred by excess drinking wasn't easy.

'I'm sure I know her,' she said to nobody in particular and therefore got no answer. Looking around with bleary eyes, she caught sight of a woman friend she'd come in with. 'I'm sure I know her that just went out.'

Her friend, Ivy, was in the same condition as she, her answer just as slurred as the question. 'You mean her with Reece Davies, him who works for Damien Fox?'

Margaret thought about it. 'Yes,' she said at last. 'I recognise her.' Her frown deepened as she searched her blurred brain for the identity of the young woman she'd seen being escorted out.

Ivy was an amiable sort who made friends easily and that included many members of the US army. 'You wouldn't know Damien and he wouldn't want to know you. You're not his type.'

Sensing she'd been insulted, Margaret bristled. Drunk she might be, but she couldn't let it pass without comment. A small irksome piece of her mind wanted to know more, wanted ammunition to fire at those who looked down at her. 'Are you sure about that?'

Ivy stuck a cigarette in her mouth after handing over her coat to the cloakroom attendant whose ample cleavage was on public view. 'Yes, darling. You're the wrong side of thirty. Come to that, you're the wrong side of twenty.'

Her aching head cleared. Slights both real and perceived grated in the aching space behind her forehead. The Crawford girl! Too young to be here. *Bet you don't know what she's up to, eh, Jenny stuck-up Crawford?*

A man in uniform offered her a drink.

Her red lips spread in a wide smile. 'How can I refuse, darling. How can I refuse?'

9

In the village close to Merryweather Farm in the heart of the Suffolk countryside, a big event was in the offing – big for a country village where the passing of the seasons dictated people's lives. There was a dance at the village hall tonight. Farmer Forester and his wife were going along and taking Tilly, Christine and their son John.

Mr Forester announced in his usual grumpy manner, 'Not enough fuel in the car for gadding about, so we're going in the dog cart.'

Mr Forester was wearing the suit he wore to church on Sundays plus his knee-high spats – a clean pair with shiny buckles, not the muddy ones he'd worn all that day.

Mrs Forester was wearing a flowery dress that looked pre-war vintage, a dull greyish green, a yellow cardigan thrown over her shoulders and a hat made of straw, a bunch of cherries jiggling on the brim.

The jangle of harness and clopping of hooves announced the arrival of the cart.

John looked directly at Tilly, who was still in working gear. 'Ain't you ready yet?'

'I caught my dress on the barbed wire on Tuesday. It needs mending before I go dancing in it.'

She took on the disappointment in his face. The plan had been for the two of them to go to the pub. That was before hearing about the dance.

'I'll mend it and come along later.'

Mr Forester tutted and shook his head. 'You girls. Why didn't you mend it sooner?'

He did not appear to notice the disappointment on his son's face.

Mrs Forester threw Tilly a smile and her husband a look of disapproval. 'You needed her to do other things, so she didn't have time.'

Mr Forester looked disbelieving that his wife thought him to blame.

Frustrated by the whole debacle, Mr Forester snatched the reins from his son and flicked them across the horse's back. 'Women!' he declared, clucked at the horse and moved off.

'I'll walk along later,' Tilly called after them.

Once they were out of sight, she bolted into the farmhouse. If anyone did look back, they would think she was off repairing the tear in her dress. The original tear had been small. Nobody would have noticed, and it looked perfectly acceptable.

The farmhouse stairs were narrow and winding. There was only one small window halfway up and, as evening came, the stained dark wood of stairs and panelling became darker.

On she climbed, past the first floor, all the way to the attic rooms at the top of the house.

Within minutes, she had mended her blue dress and put it on. On days she wasn't working on the land, she went barelegged. Thanks to that habit, there was no need to wear stockings; her legs were brown. A shine was added with the application of elderflower cream supplied by Mrs Forester. Even wearing boots, her legs did not look unattractive. The boots were for the interim. She'd change into her court shoes when she got back after doing what she intended to do.

Her footsteps echoed off the stone walls of the narrow staircase. At the bottom, she paused and listened. The sudden flare-up of coals in the kitchen range, the bellowing of a pregnant cow sequestered in the barn for the night, not happy being locked in away from the herd.

The coast was clear for her to carry out what she wanted to do. With that in mind, she headed for the larder with its stone shelves and dark space on the floor where vegetables were stored.

There were two large sacks of potatoes, far too many to carry. Tucked into the corner next to these, she found a sack with a few potatoes at the bottom. Onions were strung together and hung from a nail on the wall. Bountiful bundles of carrots dangled from another. There was curly kale, used mainly as cow fodder, but also a substitute for cabbage and nutritious when added to soups.

The sack bulged with the basic vegetables, but she couldn't leave it at that. Now for butter, cheese, eggs, bacon and perhaps a tin of beans and one of Spam. Everyone had Spam. Everyone had tins of beans too, the latter itemised as essential food and part of rationing. As for Spam, the US army must have brought over a ship full. The sack was filling up fast, but there was plenty of room for the plugs of tea, and sugar followed, each carefully portioned and wrapped up in newspaper. Mrs Forester was not just careful but knew how best to store things.

Once the weight of the sack was just about manageable, she

found a spare tin opener, a rusty one she'd rescued after Mrs Forester had thrown it to one side.

With the aid of the bread knife, she cut a chunk off the loaf left underneath a protective net on the bread board and finally, once she was sure she had everything she could get away with, she heaved a sigh of relief.

Her last task was to rearrange the vegetables and other food that was left. Once that was done, she scrutinised how it looked.

Hopefully nobody would notice that anything was missing. The farmhouse larder was well stocked, so she didn't think it likely. There were other labourers besides the two land girls and Mrs Forester knew things were sometimes pilfered by hungry folk who put in twelve hours of work, sometimes more. Being of a generous nature, she never made comment, though surely must have known what was missing.

Sack slung over her back, Tilly marched out of the farmyard and between the high banks where scarlet poppies, feathery white cow parsley and yellow ragwort nodded in the breeze. The sack was heavy, and back before she'd become a land girl, she might not have had the strength to carry it. Working on the land had changed that and it pleased her.

The sun was warm upon her bare arms as she made her way swiftly down the incline to the field. Swallows and swift, lately arrived from warmer climes, were diving high in the sky on an abundance of flying insects. Behind the ruined cottage, sunset peach and pinkness patterned the sky. It was a perfect evening, but she'd acquired the ability to smell the weather, to read why the birds were diving down to where insects were gathered. Rain was on the way.

The gnarled wood of the door was rough beneath her knuckles before gently pushing it open.

The room was warm, and a pleasant smell came from the

saucepan hanging from an iron hook above a log fire. The draught from the open door caused the logs to spit and spark. Logs only. Whatever coal there might have been in the outhouse left by those who used to reside here was long gone.

Sybil was lying down. Jack was playing with what looked like a wooden sword, which he was using to prod a ball made from what used to be a rabbit skin, tied tightly with string to prevent it falling apart.

He looked up and smiled his toothy smile on seeing her. Sybil struggled up onto her elbows and greeted her.

'Hello.'

'Hello to you,' returned Tilly.

She noted that the hollows beneath Sybil's cheeks were deeper than before and there were dark shadows under her eyes. She wondered if she'd been ill, but didn't like to ask. Sybil was a very private person, wary – scared perhaps?

Tilly lay the sack on the ramshackle table. Placing her hands on her knees and holding on to her smile, she leaned over the bed.

'Sybil. How are you today?'

The woman, looking so ill and forlorn, managed a weak smile. 'Just a bit tired.'

'Have you had anything to eat today?'

'I ate the last of the rabbit stew.' She smiled. 'Thank you for teaching me how to skin a rabbit, and for setting a snare. I wouldn't have known how to do it.'

'I'm glad it worked.'

She didn't add that it was John Forester who had taught her how to do it.

Back at the table, Tilly began to take her gifts from the sack. 'Here's some bread and cheese. And a slice of cake.' She smiled at Jack. 'I bet you'd like a piece of fruit cake, wouldn't you, Jack?'

She broke off a suitably sized piece for the little boy. Eyes shining with delight, he took it and began taking big bites until his cheeks were bulging.

Tilly grabbed some of it back, holding it above her head out of his reach. 'Careful. You'll choke.'

She turned her attention back to Sybil.

'Shall I make you a cup of tea?' She held up the pinch of tea, enough for four pots if used carefully. 'And I have sugar.'

Sybil nodded weakly. 'That would be nice.'

Tilly offered her a piece of the cake. 'Before Jack eats it all,' she added with a grin. 'I've also brought you some tinned things. Baked beans and Spam. And an opener. It would be downright annoying if you fancied a bit of Spam and didn't have an opener.'

Her eyes scrutinised the scruffy blanket under which Sybil's thin body was barely discernible.

'I'll see if I can find you some more bedding.'

She was no doctor but couldn't help thinking that something ailed Sybil, though she had no idea what was wrong with her.

'That's a pretty dress you're wearing.'

Sybil's comment took her off guard. She'd almost forgotten the dress or that she was going to a village dance.

'They don't go very well with my socks and boots,' Tilly said with a grin. 'I'm going to a dance. The rest of the family have gone on ahead of me. I'll have to walk.'

'You shouldn't have.' Sybil shook her head. 'It's very kind of you.'

'You can come if you like.'

'Oh no.' Sybil shook her head vehemently. 'I've got Jack to think about.'

'You can bring him with you. I'm sure nobody will mind.'

Tilly wasn't sure at all, but she had this need to make things better for Sybil, to make her smile, cheer up, enjoy life as she should.

Again, Sybil shook her head. 'I'm fine staying here.' She wound her arm around her little boy's shoulders, pulling him from standing into sitting beside her on the lumpy bed. 'Just you and me, isn't it, Jack?'

There was no point in pursuing the matter of the dance.

'Enjoy the food.'

'We will.'

That woman is an enigma, Tilly thought to herself as she closed the ramshackle door behind her. Even though her clothes were a bit scruffy, they looked of a good quality. Then there was her accent. She wasn't local, that much was true. Neither did she sound working class. And surely if her husband had been killed, she would still have had an army pension. If so, surely, she would be living somewhere more comfortable than a run-down cottage hidden at the end of a field.

Tilly hadn't even got to the broken garden gate when she saw him.

She stopped dead. Her jaw dropped.

John was standing directly in front of her, like a barrier between her and her escape route. 'What's going on?'

'I... um...' What could she say?

His expression unreadable, he jerked his chin towards the cottage. 'Is someone in there?'

She nodded.

'They've got no business here.' He made as if to push past her.

She grabbed his arm. 'John. Please. It's a widow and her little boy. She's homeless, ill and frightened.'

He stood still, looking down into her face.

She gulped back her guilt, unwilling for him to see the sack of food she had taken from his mother's larder. 'She's very frightened.'

Reading his face, she saw anger replaced by indecision and then an aura of calm.

'You won't turn her out, will you? She's got nowhere else to go. And no money.'

'You've brought her food?'

He surely read the imploring look in her eyes when she nodded.

'And you didn't think to trust me? Am I some kind of ogre?'

He grabbed hold of her arm and began to frogmarch her back up the field.

Long grass not yet clipped by grazing cattle whipped at her bare legs.

'I thought...' She shook her head. 'I don't know what I thought, only that they needed help. She didn't want anyone to know. She's frightened of anyone knowing that she's here.'

Halfway up the field, they stopped. He still grasped her arm. Their eyes locked. What would he do?

Looking at the ground, he shoved his hands into the pockets of his best corduroy trousers.

Keen to break into his thoughts, she touched his upper arm. 'I've a confession to make.' Her voice was small, not so much a squeak but like the sound her hairbrush made when she was forcing it through tangles.

Alarm came to his eyes and a grim set to his jaw. His muscles bulged when he folded his arms and said, 'I might have guessed... You women. You're all the bloody same.'

His comment surprised her. Surely her behaviour didn't deserve such a strong response.

'I was only trying to help. Stop them from starving.'

Now it was him who frowned. 'Explain yourself.' He said it slowly. It came to her that they were talking at cross purposes.

'I took food from the larder.' She hung her head. 'I know I should have asked first. That's what I'm ashamed about.'

His jaw dropped. 'You're confessing about taking food? That's it?'

Unsure about what she was hearing – and what she was seeing in his features – she nodded her head. 'Yes.' She frowned. 'What did you think I meant?'

Suddenly, the rigid expression relaxed, replaced by what she could only describe as relief. 'I thought...'

The penny dropped. 'You thought I was meeting with someone. Is that it?'

Was that a blush she saw on his face when he smiled? Very likely.

'It did cross my mind.' He let go her arm.

She stood in front of him, nervously rubbing her hands together, waiting for him to announce what his next action would be.

He shook his head when he looked at her. 'My parents aren't ogres either.'

Tilly blushed and looked suitably contrite. 'No. Of course not.'

Raising his head, he fixed his gaze on where peachy clouds were cloaking the setting sun. 'I was wrong. Bet you're going to think me a bit of a dunce now, not the sort of chap for going to the pub with.'

'I'd go to the pub with you. And to a dance. Shall we walk into the village?'

He seemed to think about it before looking her up and down. 'I'd walk into the village with you. But not with you wearing those boots.'

Arm in arm and laughing, they made their way to the gate from Brook Meadow.

He promised her that he would explain about the food being taken. 'I know how to put things,' he added.

Her heart filled with warm relief which carried over into her voice. 'I don't know how to thank you, John. I really don't.'

His hand resting on the gate, he smiled down at her. 'I do.'

His lips brushed hers before pressing harder.

Breathless, she suggested they make their way to the village hall if they were to squeeze in a dance that night.

He looked reluctant. 'I was thinking we could have a glass or two of the home-made cider which should be right mature by now.'

'Did you tell your parents you were coming back for me?'

He nodded. 'That I did, and they'll be wanting me back with the horse and trap to pick them up and get them home.'

'Another time then – for the cider.'

'Another time.'

10

It was Sunday morning, and Jenny was standing in front of the bedroom mirror, her fingers examining her left breast. At the same time, she prayed to God that it was no longer there, that its existence was imagined.

God wasn't listening, or he was setting the record straight, forcing her to face the truth.

I'll go see the doctor this week. Wednesday morning – or evening. She pursed her lips at her reflection and withdrew her hand. *Yes. I'll do it on Wednesday.*

Gloria came barging in. 'Lost something, Mother?'

Quickly doing up the top button of her blouse, her mother laughed it off. 'An earring Thelma gave me. Only a stud, but it popped off when I was brushing my hair.' She went back to examining her cleavage. 'It's down here somewhere. Never mind. It'll turn up.'

Jenny casually asked her daughter if she was going to church. 'Seeing as you're wearing your Sunday best.'

The question was delivered with humour. Asking her outright would be ill received.

Taking it as a joke as intended, Gloria laughed. 'No. I am not. Are you?' Her stance was cocky, her tone sarcastic.

'No. I was going to write to your sister. Might be nice if you got round to it too.'

Gloria peered over her mother's shoulder into the mirror and gently touched the smear of lipstick at the corner of her mouth. 'What would I write about?'

Jenny shrugged. 'Whatever you're up to. I'm sure she'd love to know.'

Gloria cringed. In her mind, she could visualise the words on the page if she wrote down the truth. And Tilly was such a little goody-two-shoes. She decided to compromise.

'I could write about work.'

'Not a boyfriend?'

'No.' Gloria's response was curt. 'She hasn't written to me and told me what she's up to, though I have heard there's a lot of American air bases roundabout where she is. And where there are American air bases, there must be Americans. She's bound to have met them.' She grinned mischievously. 'Maybe one of them might have taken her out of herself a bit.'

Jenny studied her pretty daughter. Both of her girls were good-looking, though in different ways. Gloria was pretty and bubbly. Tilly was handsome and serene. Chalk and cheese. What one enjoyed the other did not.

'Must go, Mum, or I'll be late.'

'Is he worth it?'

Jenny noticed a brief stillness to her daughter's face, a guardedness in her eyes.

'Who?'

Jenny wasn't fooled. Her daughter knew very well the manner of question. 'You know what I mean. You're off out with a boy.'

Gloria laughed. 'Sorry to disappoint you. I'm off with June and the girls from work. We're going on a picnic to Clevedon and then a half in the Salthouse – it's a pub, in case you don't know.'

Jenny was about to say that, yes, she did know the Salthouse, but Gloria had already gone to her room. Another attempt at perfecting her pretty looks, she thought. Her daughter's bedroom door closed with a determined click.

Sunshine spilt into the room as Jenny opened the bedroom window. A chorus of lawnmowers came with it. Across the road, Thelma would be preparing a high tea for daughter-in-law Maria and her grandchildren. It was hours before teatime and the family's arrival, but at least she would be occupied. As for herself, she would be spending the day alone, just her in an empty house.

Some of the neighbourhood kids were running riot on the green. Playing chase, by the looks of it. A group of girls were playing hopscotch, the age-old grid chalked out on the pavement outside next door.

Shrill laughter, chattering children and the continued rattle and buzz of lawnmowers.

Might as well join them, Jenny thought.

Gloria's bedroom door was still closed when she set off down the stairs.

Gardening. That was how she would spend an hour or so of a typical Sunday, an empty time when the shops were closed and those so inclined indulged in tennis or cricket at Redcatch Park.

It was hard work pushing a lawnmower through the carpet of daisies and dandelions on her front lawn, but necessary. The fluffy dandelion heads would breed even more. One year's seed would become seven years' weed. Shame about the daisies though, scattered like tiny stars against a blanket of green grass.

Jenny looked up when Gloria emerged from the house

looking as pretty as a picture in a pale lemon dress that went well with her tumbling dark curls.

'I'm off now, Mum.'

Her slender figure and impeccably made-up face made Jenny wish the years would fall away and Gloria was a child again. A child listened to a parent's advice, but her daughter – both daughters, if she was honest – were at an age when they thought for themselves. Her girls were growing up and there was nothing she could do about it.

Was it her imagination or was Gloria wearing more make-up than she used to? In the past, she had always been frugal with the application of powder and paint. Had it increased of late, or was she just a mother wanting to hold back time?

She stopped pushing the lawnmower, rested one foot on the blades and leaned on the handle. 'My. You do look a picture.'

Gloria preened like a bird of paradise showing off her plumage. She had always been something of an exhibitionist and, as if to prove the point, did a little twirl, her silky skirt billowing out just enough to make her look like a dancer.

'I've borrowed your white gloves. You don't mind, do you?' she asked pertly.

Jenny placed one hand on her hip and tutted as though she did mind. 'Not again.' A smile and a nod followed. 'Of course not. Now you go on and enjoy yourself. Tell June I said hello. And ask about her mother. She was ill last time I saw her.'

'Her mum's fine. Must go. I'll miss the bus.'

'Have a good time on the Downs.'

'Clevedon. We're going to Clevedon,' Gloria called over her shoulder.

'On the train?'

'Well, I'm not going to walk there, am I?'

Whilst Jenny watched her youngest daughter float off like a

flower in the breeze, Thelma came over to join her. She was wearing an apron spattered with flour.

'You look as though you've been busy,' Jenny remarked.

'Jam tarts. Cath made the jam. Her youngest kids went blackberrying last year, and she mixed them with apples and plums from the trees she's got out back.'

'Lovely. Your little ones will scoff them in no time.'

Thelma frowned. 'That's what I'm afraid of. Still,' she said brightening, 'if they eat the lot, it means my baking was not in vain.' She nodded to where Gloria had disappeared. 'She seemed in a hurry.'

'The weekend is short.'

'Oh well. Nothing to be done. Another year or so and she'll be bringing home some chap and you'll be getting out the best teacups.'

Jenny looked amused. 'He'd have to be an exceptional young fella to take on my Gloria.'

'Where's she off to?'

'Clevedon. On the train.'

'Really?' Thelma pulled in her chin, a signal of slight disbelief. 'I didn't think the trains were running to Clevedon on a Sunday. Something to do with troop movements.'

'Then she'll have to go somewhere else.'

Thelma shook her head. 'As long as she enjoys herself. I'm going to put the kettle on, give me a minute to check that I've turned the oven off.' Thelma tottered off across the road, the tapping of her heels disappearing as she negotiated the green, resuming once she was on the other side.

Only a narrow strip of dandelions and daisies remained. Jenny guessed that only a few minutes more and the job would be done.

'Yoohoo. Mrs Crawford.'

Mowing stopped. Jenny recognised the young woman standing at the gate. She frowned. 'June? Isn't it?'

She recalled that June was about a year older than Gloria, perhaps two. June had had the same vivacious personality as her own daughter. Her hair was golden, and her dancing eyes were blue. She too had been slender – but not now. Her belly bulged with the baby growing within.

Surprised, Jenny left the handle of the lawnmower resting on the hedge.

June responded to Jenny's enquiring look. 'Six months,' she said, running her hand over her swollen belly. 'I am married. See?'

She wiggled her ring finger. A narrow band of gold glinted. June looked mighty pleased with herself.

Jenny took a deep breath and tried not to look or sound surprised. 'Gloria didn't say anything.'

June looked at the house as though expecting to see Gloria hanging out of a window. 'I thought I might catch her in. Chance of a natter, for old times' sake and that.'

Her merry smile disappeared when Jenny shook her head.

'She's gone on a picnic to Clevedon.'

It suddenly occurred to Jenny that her daughter had not taken any food with her. How could she have been so stupid!

'Oh.' The corners of June's mouth turned down with disappointment. 'Oh well. It was only on the off chance...'

'How's your mother?' Jenny asked in the hope that changing the subject might make June feel better.

The brighter expression she hoped for did not occur.

'She passed over eight months ago.' Her hand gently smoothed over her stomach. 'Shame. She never got to know about the little one.'

And never went to the wedding either, thought Jenny. The proffered wedding ring had looked too thin, too brassy. Her heart went out to the poor girl.

'I'm so sorry. I didn't know.'

And Gloria didn't tell me. Why didn't she tell me? Because she didn't know.

Her suspicion was confirmed when June went on to say that she hadn't seen Gloria in months.

Yet you were supposed to be going with her to Clevedon! Gloria had told her an outright lie. So who was she with and where had she really gone?

June readied herself to leave. 'Tell her I said hello.'

'Of course I will. And best of luck to you, June. I hope all goes well.'

'Who was that?' asked Thelma, her head turning to watch the young woman who had just left Jenny's gate.

Jenny grimaced. 'The friend Gloria said she was going to Clevedon with.'

Thelma tossed her head and wryly commented, 'The only place that girl's going is the maternity hospital!'

* * *

'I think I need to have a word with your mother, just to let her know that my intentions are honourable.'

'No!'

Gloria was making herself as small as she could in the front seat of Damien's car.

'Are you ashamed of me or something?'

She wasn't sure whether he was being serious and, heavens above, she certainly wasn't ashamed of him. Head over heels in love was more like it.

'Just give me a bit more time so she can get used to the idea.'

The white patches painted on the back of the bus they were following seemed to blink at her as if in warning. Every bus in the city had white patches painted at the front and rear corners, a necessity in the blackout. Headlights were partially covered in a way that directed their beam downwards so the driver could see where he was going. The painted markers had been added to aid pedestrians crossing the road. Buses were big, but black and indistinguishable once night had fallen.

'Don't stop behind that bus,' Gloria hissed, sinking further into the seat. 'The people getting off might see me.'

'I'll let him go, then make my way into one of the side roads near where you live. I'll even turn the engine and lights off, so nobody hears or sees us. Will that suit you, Miss Crawford?' He sounded a bit annoyed, though not angry. She could cope with that.

'Yes.' Gloria breathed again.

He brought the car to a halt next to a patch of wilderness that had once been four houses destroyed the year before, though why enemy bombers had targeted Knowle West was a mystery. Rumours circulated that they'd thought they were over Filton and its aircraft factories. They couldn't have been more wrong.

Gloria straightened and breathed a sigh of relief. Damien couldn't have picked a better spot. The nearest houses, pitch-black without showing a single light, were far enough away not to notice anything happening outside their cosy homes.

'There, sweetheart. Satisfied?'

She said that she was and waited for his embrace. Instead, he lit up one of the cigarillos he was fond of. The smoke was pungent, almost sweet. He'd told her they were hard to get hold of but he had contacts. No surprise there. She'd cottoned on that Damien had contacts for most things, not that she pried into his affairs. Neither did she question how he made his living. Being with him was all that mattered. Anyone seeing them together would guess that she loved him.

He blew a cloud of smoke out of the window he'd wound open.

'Was that a nice day out or what?'

'Yes. It was. I didn't know you could drive.'

'Of course I can. Two's company, three's a crowd.'

'And Reece would have been a gooseberry.' She giggled.

Behind the smoky facade, Damien thought how girlish she sounded. She tried hard to appear sophisticated and older than her years. For his part, he'd tried hard to wean himself away from his attraction for her. *You're a cradle snatcher. She's less than half your age.* That was what he told himself. There had been other young women in his life, though not as young as Gloria. Okay, sixteen was the age of consent, but still...

He flicked the half-smoked cigarillo out of the window. A dot of redness, it landed on the edge of the derelict site, glowed for a while and then went out.

He reached across with one hand, his fingers threading through the glossy locks curling beneath her ear. 'Gloria, darling. It's been a grand day. Time for little girls like you to be in bed.'

He felt her go rigid. 'Don't call me that. I'm not a little girl.' She brushed his hand away, then instantly regretted it.

'You know people are talking.'

'I don't care.'

'I'm old enough to be your father.'

Tears stung Gloria's eyes. 'You're giving me the brush-off? Don't you want to see me any more?'

'Shh! Not so loud.' He wound up the window.

'I don't care.' When she swiped at her eyes, she knew her mascara would be smeared. So would her lipstick.

They'd rambled the clifftop behind the Salthouse in Clevedon and picnicked in a grassy area with a good view of the Bristol Channel. He'd brought champagne – Damien's favourite drink it seemed. The luxury food he'd brought had filled her eyes. She'd wondered what her mother would have thought. Tinned salmon. Chocolate. Slices of cured ham. Fresh bread and enough butter and cheese to last one person for a week.

She'd asked him why he favoured champagne. His face had clouded before he'd answered, because he could afford it.

'But it hasn't always been that way, sweetheart. It hasn't always.'

She'd tried nudging him to tell her more.

'My life's history!' He'd laughed. 'Not today. But one day perhaps.'

Damien looked out of the windscreen, though nothing could be seen. It didn't matter. He could see his thoughts. Funny that, seeing thoughts like pictures in the mind.

You have to let her go. It's for the best. A sad goodbye in his mind, her waving at him with a handkerchief soaked in tears. And him, resolved to let her go...

'Damien.'

He turned towards her indistinct features. The smell of her...

'I love you.'

It was, he thought, like being stung by a wasp or a bee. His resolve shattered and all his good intentions fell away.

She fell into his arms. He did not push her away, but held her tightly, rained kisses upon her face whilst breathing in the intoxicating scene that was her.

'My darling girl. My sweet, darling girl.'

He knew, just as she did, that there would be more tomorrows. She was obsessed with him, and he couldn't find the strength to put her aside.

* * *

Putting the key into the front door was easy enough. Closing it softly behind her would be harder, especially seeing as Gloria was carrying her shoes in one hand. Taking them off had been essential if she was to creep in without her mother hearing her.

Carefully extricating the key from the lock, she used both hands to close the door. The latch clicked, a small sound that seemed louder tonight than it usually did.

The hallway was dark and so was the staircase. She knew every tread of that staircase, well enough to find her way to the top without turning the light on.

Before she had chance to step onto the bottom stair, the living room door sprang open.

Her mother stood grim-faced, arms folded purposefully across her ribcage. 'How was Clevedon?'

Gloria swallowed her surprise. Feigned innocence. 'Lovely.'

'Train or bus?'

'Pardon?'

Her mother took a step into the very small hallway. Only one step and the way to the staircase was blocked.

'How was your old friend June?'

Gloria took a deep breath. 'Fine. We've promised to see more of each other.' *More opportunities for me to see Damien.* June was a useful excuse.

'Would that be before she gives birth or after?'

Gloria froze. A memory of winter from some years back came to her, a thick layer of snow sliding from the roof. Back then, she'd wondered what it would feel like if that sheet of snow had fallen onto her. Buried alive. Frozen to the bone. It was late May, but her blood had turned to ice. As if it fell on her now.

Her mouth opened, but she could find no words to voice into an equitable excuse.

'You've seen June?'

'Yes. She came round to see you. She's considerably fatter than the last time I saw her. Six months pregnant. Oh, and by the way, her mother passed away.'

'Oh.' Gloria bent her head. She'd so enjoyed herself today. It had felt as though the day would go on forever. But now this.

'You went to Clevedon.'

Gloria nodded. 'Yes.'

'But not with June.'

She shook her head. 'No. I went with a boy. He was on leave. I haven't known him for long. I thought you might disapprove, so I didn't tell you.' She paused. 'And before you tell me I'm too young, you weren't very old when you had Tilly and then me.'

There was silence before her mother asked his name.

Gloria thought swiftly, then said the first name that came into her head. 'Reece,' she said. 'His name is Reece.'

A look of relief came to her mother's face. She rubbed at her eyes with the fingers of her right hand.

It came to Gloria that she'd rarely seen her mother looking so tired. She only hoped that it wasn't her that had brought the worrying lines to her mother's face.

'Mum. Are you all right?'

She touched her mother's arm, the act of affection bringing a smile to her mother's face.

'You shouldn't have lied to me,' she said softly, the angry look gone from her eyes. 'Of course you can go out with boys. You can tell me about him, you know. I'd like to know.'

When they hugged, it was like being a child again. Her mother's body was soft and warm.

'I'm sorry I lied, Mum.'

'You can tell me anything, Gloria. I won't condemn you. Not ever.'

In bed, Gloria felt relieved that her mother had not asked her to promise that she would not lie again. It was a promise she could not keep, not if she wanted to carry on seeing Damien. And she did. She very much did, yet at the same time she wanted to share how she was feeling, to tell someone she was in love. That someone had to be trustworthy, capable of keeping a secret to themselves. There was only one person: her sister, Tilly. Tomorrow in work she would write her a letter telling her everything whilst swearing her to absolute secrecy.

Her heart soared at the prospect of sharing the ache she felt inside, one that would not go away.

11

Mr Bertram waylaid Thelma in the part of the shop where second-hand clothes hung on rails with big notices above them. EVENING WEAR, DAY WEAR, COATS, COSTUMES.

Shoes were layered on metal shelves donated by the store-room of a warehouse that had been damaged, the owner deciding to rebuild once the war was over. Women's shoes took up half of the shelves. Children's just shy of a half, and men's shoes the rest. Thelma put the paucity of men's shoes down to the fact that many of them had army boots either from this war or the last one.

Mr Bertram held the door to his office open. The way he was beaming at her gave Thelma hope that Bertrams was not for the chop just yet.

'Just a quick word,' he said somewhat apologetically.

He gestured for her to take a seat. She did so slowly, her eyes fixed on him, hoping for the best but expecting the worst.

His gnarled fingers were like the twisted twigs of an old oak, wrinkled and greyish as he folded them in front of him.

'Mrs Dawson, you are a valued employee. I am aware of

your love for Bertrams Modes. This shop was established by my great-grandfather as a general draper...' His voice petered out. His eyes raised wistfully to the ceiling. 'That was a long time ago, of course. I remember him well. He had huge whiskers and a thick moustache... very upright. Very Victorian...'

Thelma felt the need to interrupt his musing. She had work to do. 'You have told me that before. It was a long time ago.'

Her voice brought him back down to earth. 'Ah. Yes. Do excuse me. Now, where was I...? Ah, yes. A decision has been made. I will not be selling the shop, at least not until this war is over. That is the decision I have come to – with the assistance of my dear wife, of course.'

Thelma's heart seemed to be beating nineteen to the dozen.

'On the other hand, my dear wife and I ache to be in our little cottage beside the sea. Therefore...' He paused again, a faraway look in his eyes. Seeing a sparkling sea, thought Thelma.

Another nudge was needed. 'You were saying?'

'Ah yes!' It was as though he'd just woken up. 'Our plans for retirement will go ahead. Bertrams will remain open. The thrift department, for which you were responsible, will continue. So will that part of the shop specialising in new clothes, though, goodness me, I can't say the utility dresses are terribly impressive.' He shook his head. 'I can't see women putting up with so little material...'

'What's my part in this?'

He looked at her wide-eyed. If it were possible, the beam on his face had broadened. 'I want you to run Bertrams. I can't think of anyone who would do a better job. I would give you a little extra money – of course, that's if you're willing...'

Thelma leapt to her feet so swiftly, the chair she was sitting on fell over backwards behind her. 'Mr Bertram! I can't thank you enough. It's my dream. It's the best thing that's ever happened to me!'

Her outer exuberance reflected what she was feeling inside. In charge of her very own shop – well, not hers, but managing it was near enough.

She was still walking on air when she went back into the shop. The old mannequins were beginning to show their age. A nose chipped off. A finger missing. White plaster showing through where the flesh-coloured paint had chipped off.

A woman in a WVS uniform was flicking through the half-dozen new dresses on one of the rails in the 'posh' part of the shop. A younger woman hovered at her elbow, either her maid or a younger member of her family.

Eyes sparkling, Thelma nodded at Rosie, who waited to advise and serve should they decide to buy.

The other half of the shop was, as usual, more crowded. Women in silk bloomers, garters holding up their stockings, were squabbling over the few corsets with elastic suspenders intact.

Maisie and Gwen, two of her part-time sales assistants, waited by the till, ready to take cash.

Assured that things were under control, Thelma looked around to see who might need assistance. A woman was trying on a fur coat, far too warm for this weather, but it didn't hurt to think ahead.

The woman had her back to her. 'Getting ready for winter?' Thelma asked.

A hint of cheap perfume and moth balls wafted in the air when she turned round.

Margaret Routledge hugged the coat round her, clutching the collar at her throat. 'I might be.'

Her look was indignant. She always looked that way nowadays. Still, a customer was a customer.

'It suits you. A good price too. Only five shillings.'

The coat was a bit old-fashioned, the shoulders padded, which gave the wearer a bear-like look. All it needed was a set of claws.

Margaret spun away and proceeded to preen herself in a floor-length mirror with a crack in one corner.

They'd never spoken much to each other, certainly not since her son and husband had died.

'It looks smart enough to go out on the town,' Thelma continued.

Margaret threw her a caustic look. 'Any argument with that?'

Thelma shook her head. 'It's your life, Mrs Routledge.'

There was a flickering of heavily mascaraed eyelashes, as though Thelma's comment had taken her by surprise.

'I'll take it.'

She rather hastily flung the coat from her shoulders. Underneath, she was wearing a scarlet dress with a black cummerbund. It seemed odd for daytime, but who was she to criticise.

'I'll get you a bag. Come this way.'

Whilst one of the girls took Margaret's money, Thelma found a second-hand carrier bag with Harrods printed on the side. A long way from home, she thought.

'This should do.'

Margaret folded the coat up herself and put it in the bag.

'It's been a long time since you've been a widow. If you ever feel like having a chat, pop into my house and have a cup of tea. I'm a good listener. You can tell me anything you like.'

Thelma's invitation was coupled with a willing smile.

Margaret had little to do with anyone, including her sister-in-law, Cath Lockhart, who lived at the top end of Coronation Close.

'You must be missing your husband.'

She purposely didn't mention Albert Routledge, who had died roundabout the same time. Mention of the little boy might be too upsetting.

Despite the heavy make-up, Margaret's face drained of colour, and a haunted look came to her eyes.

Without saying another word, the Harrods bag swinging from her gloved hand, Margaret was out of the double doors of the exit, leaving them swinging behind her.

Thelma stared after her.

Rosie, who had seen everything, appeared at her side. 'She looked in a bit of a hurry, Mrs Dawson. Must have been something you said.'

Thelma responded, 'Yes. It must.'

She went over what she had said in her mind. Everything had seemed reasonable enough until she had suggested Margaret might be missing her husband. A scared look had come to her eyes, as though an old fear that should be buried had come back to haunt her.

12

Margaret Routledge knocked back two glasses of whisky before leaving the house. Cath Lockhart had given it her last Christmas – 'to steady yer nerves, what with all you've been through'.

Hah! If only you knew. Your precious brother was no saint, but then, you would not believe it if I told you.

Margaret had thanked her and put the bottle away in the dresser that took up one of the living-room walls.

Sometimes she imbibed of a glass, but only when she was stressed. Like now, with Thelma Dawson insinuating that she might be missing her late husband. If nobody mentioned him, she was fine. Someone voicing his name was an act of resurrection, his ghost bringing back his cruelty.

The whisky warmed her and helped drown the memory. So did the fur coat she'd bought. Five shillings and it made her feel like a queen.

She waited until both Howard and Judith had gone out before she left the house. They were old enough to look after themselves. Howard had gone out with his mates to the park where they kicked a ball about, sat on a park bench and smoked. Judith never told her where she was going, except to say, out with friends. Very upright friends. No worries there. If Albert her youngest had still been alive, she would have stayed at home. But he was dead, a grave she visited on a Sunday afternoon where she lay flowers. He was buried in the same plot as his father. The gravestone said so, though she'd smeared mud over Percy's name so that Albert's stood out.

The bus came on time just as a light drizzle began to fall.

She drew out a cigarette from a packet and smoked, a new habit she thought suited her – like drinking.

The Hatchet pub in Frogmore Street was a hive of noise, cigarette smoke, conversation and raucous laughter. Male sweat mingled with the smell of cheap perfume. Women accepted as being of loose reputation let their eyes wander over the male clientele. Men supped at pints or, if they could afford it, whisky, rum or gin.

Some of the women knew each other and although they nodded a welcome and had time for conversation, they mostly stood slightly apart from each other.

Deirdre edged sidelong to Margaret and mentioned that there weren't so many uniforms about tonight. 'Though enough to go round,' she added. 'Don't want to buy our own drinks all bloody night, do we?'

She laughed. Margaret joined her as she got enough from her purse for half a shandy. Her preference would swiftly change if a man offered to buy her a drink.

As Margaret sipped, Deirdre remarked on her coat.

'It's speckled with raindrops. You wanna watch you don't ruin it. Where did you get it from?'

'An aunt left it to me in her will,' returned Margaret. It was an outright lie, but she wasn't going to say that she'd bought it second-hand. She did add that her aunt had shopped in Bertrams before the war.

'There's posh,' said Deirdre. 'Keep you warm if you ever end up on Ladies Mile.'

'If that ever happens, I'll cut my wrists,' stated Margaret in no uncertain terms.

Ladies Mile was on Durdham Down, a known haunt of prostitutes down on their luck or not keen on hanging around in pubs. Conveniently, it boasted ladies' toilets half hidden beneath the trees but adjacent to the road. She'd heard it mentioned as a place where those selling their bodies could wash and freshen up after 'doing the business'. Margaret had no intention of ending up there. She wanted to taste the fun others had boasted of. It was her right. Wasn't it?

'Hope you never 'ave to, my lover,' said Deirdre in a strong Bristolian accent. 'It's a lovely coat. Give me first choice if you ever wants to get rid of it.' She gave the fur a gentle stroke.

Deirdre had a terrible complexion, her chin a mass of open pores that were only barely concealed by a thick layer of Vaseline and face powder.

Her gaze shifted to new clientele coming in through the bar door. 'Wouldn't mind a night out with 'im.' She jerked her greasy chin towards the man who was making his way to the bar. 'Looks like we've got business.'

Margaret resented Deirdre's terminology. So common. Tucking her fur coat more closely over her chest, she prepared herself to play the genteel lady fallen on hard times. A widow. Just here for a night out.

To some extent, it was true, and she certainly did look well-groomed and spoke in a very precise manner – just as Percy had insisted she should speak. She put on the voice now as she sipped the last quarter of her shandy.

'Yes, this coat belonged to my aunt, you know. She left me a few other bits and pieces in her will, including a lovely set of pearls...'

She took care to talk as though unaware of his presence. She purposely turned too quickly so that he couldn't help but barge into her. What was left of her shandy slopped over the rim of her glass and onto the floor. Some had dripped onto her hand, though, thankfully, nothing onto her coat – though she exclaimed otherwise.

'Now look what you've done. You should look where you're going.'

At first, his expression was unchanged, face as stiff as plaster of Paris. He half turned away from her before he seemed to have a rethink and turned back.

'Let me get you another drink. What are you having?' His voice was like a deep-seated grumble in his throat.

'It won't do my coat much good, but it might do me some.'

At her response, he raised a hand to summon the barman.

'Well, that might help,' she said in a tone that left him in no doubt that he'd upset her – when, on the contrary, he had not. In fact, he was just what she was looking for. 'A drink in exchange for you ruining my coat.' She brushed at the soft fur to add emphasis.

'Up to you.' He shrugged as though he couldn't care less whether she took up his offer or not. 'I'm offering. Take it or leave it.'

She decided it was now or never. 'Mine's a sherry.'

Holding up one finger, his eyes skewered the barman. 'A schooner of sherry for the lady.'

Margaret addressed the barman. 'Bristol Cream, mark you. None of that cheap stuff from Cyprus.'

Her new friend shrugged. Her eyes widened at the crisp

white fiver folded lengthways in his hand. He remarked that a sherry was a sherry as far as he was concerned.

Margaret's response was swift. 'I beg to disagree and assure you that there is a difference. And it's made in Bristol. Has been for two hundred years or more.'

When he looked at her as though impressed by her knowledge, something jolted inside. He was vaguely familiar, though she couldn't quite think where. Never mind. It would come to her.

She smiled pleasantly back and told him that her name was Margaret.

'Damien.'

She repeated his name, which rolled easily off the end of her tongue. 'Damien.'

Although the brim of his trilby hat shaded his face, she perceived angular features, high cheekbones and deep-set eyes the colour of cold steel. A little shiver ran down her spine. Those eyes were like ice and striking, but for all the wrong reasons.

Concern was pushed south with the shiver that had run down her back. She went back to surmising who and what he was. If he'd ever served in the armed forces, if his clothes were anything to go by, he certainly didn't now. He was at least five feet ten in height and his double-breasted dark grey suit was too sharply cut to be anything but expensive. The harp-shaped tiepin in his navy-blue tie had the glint of gold about it. He had money. She was certain of it.

Well, she thought, *this might be a man worth getting to know.* He had presence. He had money, that much was obvious.

'So, you've been left an inheritance. Lucky for you.'

'My aunt,' she said, continuing the lie.

'Not your husband?'

'My aunt, not my husband, though I am a widow. I got his pension though.'

Her smile was sad, as was expected of a grieving woman. She knew how to act the part even if she was far from grief-stricken.

She took a sip of the dark as blood sherry.

'Does it have your approval?' he asked.

Her face glowed as its warmth washed down. 'Definitely Harveys Bristol Cream.'

'Good.'

Not a good conversationalist and he kept glancing towards the door. It was down to her to make the running. Okay. She could do that.

'So, what's your line?'

He took a sip from the double rum he'd ordered. 'Businessman.'

'Really.'

She watched as he turned the tumbler and took another sip from the other side of the glass.

'Yes. Really.'

Definitely, a man of few words.

Keen to keep the conversation going and him close, she had to think hard of what to say next.

If the look of him was anything to go by, there was no point in asking him why he wasn't in the army. He was definitely over forty.

'Do you have a family?'

'No.'

'Never been married?'

'No.'

'Oh.'

Margaret racked her brains. Start with the mundane, outline details of her family. Everyone liked to talk about their family.

'I've got two children. Some women say it's difficult bringing them up alone, but I manage.'

No response, though he did jerk his chin as though he had heard. Drink barely touched; his eyes flitted around the smoky cloudiness of the public bar as though looking for someone. A woman perhaps? Had he arranged to meet someone here?

Back to glancing at the door.

Margaret clenched her jaw. It looked as though she might have her work cut out. This man, who she recalled was named Damien, could be quite a meal ticket. Well dressed, not afraid to spend a five-pound note and not pawing her and suggesting they go outside for a quick fondle – or more.

Hopefully if he was waiting for a woman, she might not turn up and she could step into the breach. If she could have a night out with all the drinks bought for her, it would leave her with money to spend on other things. Money ran like water through her fingers, what with new clothes, drink and cigarettes. Good clothes, of course. Good drink and fags too.

She was about to tell him more about her family, when he straightened, his gaze fixed on the lithe young woman who had come through the door.

The young woman wore a red jacket and a black and white dress. Her hair was dark and caught beneath a red bandeau she wore in lieu of a hat. She looked stunning, slender, young and prettily turned out. And recognisable. Gloria Crawford.

Damien left Margaret, caught hold of Gloria's arm and tugged her close.

Margaret heard him hiss, 'You're late.'

There was anger in the gravelly voice.

'Sorry, Damien. The bus was late.'

'You should let me collect you in the car.'

'You know why I don't want you to do that.'

The two of them seemed to glow, affection forming an invisible bond between them.

'Never mind,' he said, hugging her close. 'You're here now.'

Gloria showed no sign of being intimidated. It was in fact as if with one look, the ice-hard exterior of Damien Fox was in danger of cracking.

Well, she always had been a cocky little mare, thought Margaret, embittered that she'd missed her chance. *Well, little Miss Perfect, let's prick your bouncy little bubble!*

'Gloria. I didn't know you were old enough to be in a pub.'

The bouncy jubilance vanished from Gloria's face.

'Mrs Routledge.' She gave a perky little laugh. 'What are you doing here?'

'Does your mother know you come here? Does she know you're out and about with people she might not know?'

Gloria flushed bright red.

Damien's dark eyes flickered from the younger woman to the older one. 'You two know each other?'

It occurred to Margaret that he'd just uttered the most words she'd heard from him all night.

'We live in the same street,' exclaimed Gloria.

Tipsy she might be, but seeing Gloria in this place and with this man alarmed her. The old Margaret who had loved her children to distraction was still there, boxed deep in her soul. Gloria's presence had partially awakened the woman she had been. The lid of the box had been firmly closed except with regard for her own children. Gloria stood before her, the innocent child. Damien the predator, the man who would steal her youth and her innocence.

If the woman he was hitching up with had been a stranger, she would have considered it the luck of the draw. Even now, she half thought of retreating because it was none of her business.

The lid of that closed box eased open as she recalled Gloria's mother being kind to her on the night and days after she'd lost Albert. She owed it to Jenny to let her know that her daughter was consorting with older men. It didn't seem that long ago she'd left school.

Something sparkled on Gloria's wrist, catching Margaret's eye; a bracelet, far too glamorous an item to have been bought anywhere other than in an upmarket jeweller's. Unless it was stolen. She wouldn't put it past the likes of Damien Fox.

There was pleading in Gloria's eyes. No words were needed because that look was easily read. *Please don't tell my mother.*

Damien leaned away towards the barman and ordered a drink for the new arrival. She heard the words gin and tonic. 'Double,' he added.

Whilst his back was turned, Margaret looked at Gloria and shook her head disapprovingly – just as any mother would. 'Gloria,' she hissed, keeping her voice low. 'You shouldn't be in a place like this – and with the likes of him,' she added, her eyes pivoting to the man who was old enough to be her father.

Gloria glowered and hissed back, 'I'm not a tart. I love him.'

'You can't do! He's—'

'It's none of your bloody business.'

'I will tell your mother that I saw you here. She won't like it.'

Gloria's eyes glittered. 'And you think she'll believe you?' She laughed. 'Everyone in Coronation Close knows you're mad – that's besides being a slut.'

Margaret raised an open palm, ready to slap the cheeky look from Gloria's face.

Strong fingers wrapped around her wrist and held it high. 'No need for that. Drink your drink, darling,' he said to Gloria. 'And we'll be off.'

The glass was tipped back twice before it was empty.

'All done,' said Gloria, the liquid leaving a gloss on her lips.

Her attention was still fixed on Gloria. 'You're too young.'

The gloating look turned triumphant. 'We're not stopping. It's just a place for us to meet. Wouldn't want to be here by meself, would I, surrounded by all these old tarts?'

She looked around over the posing women, heard the ribald remarks of men out to pick up – and pay – for a woman.

Margaret felt the need to defend these women who had taken her under their wings with no questions asked. 'They're my friends.'

There was acid in Gloria's next remark. 'Tarts like floor covering – stretching from wall to wall.'

Margaret almost wrenched her arm in her efforts to escape Damien's iron grip.

He addressed Gloria. 'Ready?'

Gloria nodded.

Damien leaned in close and whispered in Margaret's ear, 'Behave yourself or it'll be my fist in your face.'

Margaret let her hand fall to her side. She looked around her as if only now seeing where she was. Deirdre and the other girls were here because they had no choice. But she did! As for Gloria...

'You shouldn't be here,' she persisted. 'You're a young girl. It's not right. Your mother would be mortified.'

Gloria smirked. 'And you're going to tell her?'

'Someone has to.'

'You're here. You're the talk of the street. Do you know that? Do you know what all the neighbours say? Fancy a policeman's widow out on the game, opening her legs for—'

Margaret didn't hold back but lashed out, landing a resounding slap on Gloria's cheek.

There was an intake of breath, surprise in her eyes. One hand covered the red mark on her cheek.

Damien's reaction was swift. A brazen finger stabbed forward within an inch or two of the tip of Margaret's nose. A hand followed, shoving at her shoulder with such force that she stumbled backwards. 'Get out.'

The force of the blow that landed on her face sent her sprawling. The blurred vision had returned, but not because of the drink. The dark, solid figure of Damien stood like the lid of a coffin about to fall over her and confine her to everlasting darkness.

'Be warned,' he growled down at her. 'Don't cross me or you'll be sorry. Ask anyone here, a tart who crosses me regrets it. Bear that in mind. 'He kicked at the sole of one of her feet before turning round to Gloria. 'Come on, babe. Let's be off.'

Drinkers fell back, dividing so he and Gloria could make their way to the exit.

Deirdre and another girl, Monica, helped Margaret get to her feet. Her nose was bleeding. Monica handed her a handkerchief.

'There was no call for that,' said Monica.

A man with a bulbous nose clutching a pint of cider in one hand suggested that she'd got what was coming. 'You're just a tart. Can't expect nothing else in your line of work.'

Deirdre, who was a tough old bird well known for standing up for herself, knocked the pint out of his hand. 'Shut your bloody mouth. What do you know about anything? All you do is drink.'

After Margaret had refused a drink and stated her preference to go home, Deirdre and Monica got her outside.

'We'll take you to the bus stop.'

Margaret's mind was in a whirl. It was as though somebody had shaken her awake from a deep and troubling sleep. She had not been aware of the best bits of the old Margaret being locked away inside, but she was now.

Blood from her nose was trickling into her mouth. 'I'm okay.'

'You're not okay.'

'Yes, I am! Honestly, I am.'

She sorely wanted to be home. She sorely wanted to be away from the Hatchet and everything connected with it.

'My children need me. That's where I need to be.'

'Sure you don't want one of us to walk with you to the bus stop?' Monica called after her.

'No,' Margaret shouted back. She did not turn round.

It was a damp night, the continuing drizzle cooling the air. Only a few people stood queueing at the bus stop, their heads bent against the rain or hidden behind open umbrellas which would not come down until the bus arrived.

Margaret ached to get home, to regain something of the woman she had been. Regardless of her husband's cruelty, she had always been a caring mother. Since then, she'd proved her point, lived a life that included all the things he'd disapproved of or disallowed her to do. She'd kicked over the traces, determined to be wicked – if embracing a wilder lifestyle was really that wicked. She'd been like a canary trapped in a cage and now she was free, but her life was about to change again. She wasn't sure quite how things would pan out, but one thing she did know was that she would never be returning to the Hatchet, and never pick up a man ever again purely for free drinks. At home, she would pour every alcoholic drink she owned down the sink. She would become the woman she should be, someone her children could be proud of.

The bus came to a halt at a bus stop before leaving the city centre. A woman got on and took the seat next to her. Margaret shuffled a bit closer to the window to give her room.

With a crunch of gears, the bus set off into the encroaching darkness. Men and women filled the lower deck on their way home from a night out or working a shift at a munitions factory.

The woman beside her wore an ugly headscarf and a coat that looked as though it had been converted from an old blanket. It was grey and held together just below the throat by a large safety pin.

The woman saw her looking. Her face tightened. Work-worn fingers played self-consciously with the oversized safety pin.

Margaret knew immediately that this home-made coat was all the woman had. Asking her personal circumstances would have been rude, but she could guess at her lowly existence. Perhaps she had lost her husband in the war, or perhaps she'd been a widow for some time – one without a pension. The job she did might be a necessity and not just triggered by war. Perhaps she had a horde of children at home, in which case clothing them came first.

Without another thought, she shrugged the fur coat from her shoulders and made ready to leave her seat – though this was not her stop.

'Excuse me.' The woman eased out of her seat.

Margaret got past and made her way to the platform at the rear of the bus.

'Excuse me, love, but you've left your coat behind.'

'You take it. I don't need it any more.'

I've done someone a good turn, she thought as the conductor rang the bell.

'Melvin Square. All ashore that's going ashore.'

She hopped lightly from the platform and didn't look back.

Leaving the coat was her good deed for the day, some kind of recompense, for so many things. For caring a little less for her children and more for herself?

The devil made me do it. That's what she would have been forced to admit if Percy was still around. Not the coat, but everything else.

The devil hadn't made her do it. Percy had made her do it, even the revenge that she'd been consumed with since his death. But no more. It was out of her system.

Raindrops speckled her hair, her face and her clothes. The skirt of her dress clung damply to her thighs and legs. She was getting wet but didn't care. The fur coat had been a heavy article of clothing – a bit like her life. Up until now, she hadn't realised just how heavy, weighing her down. *The skin of a dead bear*, she thought to herself, *weighing me down, like the past. And now I am truly free.*

The Hatchet. *Whatever did I see in that place?*

Thinking of its low ceilings and foggy atmosphere brought Gloria Crawford to mind. The girl was in danger. It was only right that Jenny Crawford should know that her daughter was involved with an older man. She had to be told.

13

Working as an usherette at the Broadway Picture House was only part-time, but the wage was enough to supplement Jenny's army widow's allowance.

Sometimes she was needed to cover for illness or other problems. Either way, it was a relaxing occupation. The customers were there to enjoy themselves so were usually good-humoured. There was also the added pleasure of watching the films, although by the end of the week she felt she knew the plots and dialogue off by heart.

That Hamilton Woman was the film being shown, a historical rendering starring a breathtakingly beautiful Vivien Leigh and a mesmerising Laurence Olivier. Set long ago, it offered romance, adventure and, more importantly, escape from the present war going on all around them.

'Excuse me.'

A couple had entered through the double doors at the head of the gangway. Jenny immediately dragged her gaze from the screen and gave them her full attention.

The couple were elderly and asked if she and her trusty torch

could see them down the sloping companionway and its inter-
mittent stairs for a place to sit.

Jenny accompanied them, making sure that the torchlight
followed their hesitant footfall. 'Go slowly. There's no rush.' She
directed the beam of her torch at two seats in the middle of D
row. 'In here all right for you?'

'That'll suit us fine,' said the woman.

'Don't want to miss anything,' whispered her husband.
'Nelson and the Battle of Trafalgar figure in it, so I 'ear.'

'It does indeed.'

'And that Vivian Leigh is such a pretty girl. As for Laurence
Olivier's voice, well it's enough to make you swoon.'

A loud hushing sounded from members of the audience
sitting close by.

'Be quiet.'

People sitting in the end seats in the same row got to their
feet to let them through, keen to do so as swiftly as possible so
they could sit back down again without missing what was
going on.

Everyone seemed fixated on the two film stars and the scan-
dalous affair of the historical characters they were playing.
Except for the young couples in the back seats, where the
goings-on were probably hotter than what was happening on the
screen.

Flashing the torch beam divided them for only a short space
of time. Once Jenny had moved on, they resumed what they
were doing.

A longing for times past hit her, not for that historic past but
back to when she was young and prone to the passion they were
feeling. She'd become a widow when Roy had died whilst he was
serving in the army, not because of fighting, but from a cocktail
of tropical diseases. His place in her life had been partially

replaced by Robin Herbert until his business had been destroyed thanks to his son and possibly his estranged wife, who likely had put him up to it. Devastated by his son's involvement in its demise, Robin had joined up with barely a backward glance, and certainly not much explanation.

It had been the end of an era. She'd not received a single letter from him, and it angered her.

On top of that, her two daughters were making their own way in the world. She hoped her youngest, Gloria, would be with her for a long while to come. Was it very selfish to think like that?

Standing at the back of the cinema meant she was looking down at the occupants of the back row. From this vantage point, she could also hear the heavy breathing and the whispered words of love. She suddenly heard a young girl sobbing.

'I love you, Colin.'

'Now, now. I ain't gone yet.'

'You're not well enough.'

'I was lucky. Truth to tell, I want to be there, Patsy. I want to do my bit.'

More shushing of course, though not sharply, certainly not from the other occupants of the back row.

Jenny surmised the story of these young people, a young man who'd been injured whilst serving his country but impatient to return as only the young could be.

Featureless forms, those of the audience who had already watched both the news and the film, were making their way for the exit.

Jenny made herself ready to focus her torch on the steep incline and steps leading to the exit.

The first wave was like a flood, people determined not to see the film yet again.

The stragglers came behind. Two people, a man and a woman, were next. Perhaps they would need the power of the torch beam or perhaps not. On noticing the man had a pronounced limp, she decided he would need her torch to proceed safely.

'Good evening, sir. Madam.'

Two pairs of feet were picked out by her torch: one a pair of men's brown brogues, the other a pair of tan court shoes.

The man and woman were at the darkest part of the upward sweep of the slope, over three-quarters of the way to the exit. The beam from the torch bobbed in front of them lighting their way.

Once they were through the exit and into the brightness of the foyer, she allowed her lips to smile and said, 'Goodnight, sir. Goodnight, madam.'

When the light from the foyer caught his features, the ground seemed to open beneath her. Charlie Talbot. The smile froze on her lips.

He was basically unchanged, although his hair was still the colour of ripe corn, his eyes blue as speedwell. He was leaning on a walking stick, so it seemed she was right about the limp.

His dark brows beetled, then rose as he accessed his thoughts and found his voice. 'Jenny? Jenny Crawford?'

She barely noticed the woman he was with and suddenly realised that she was holding her breath. Even after all this time, her heart fluttered like a trapped bird.

It hadn't mattered that he was of a different class to her, born into middle-class comfort. A man so different from her husband, she'd fallen in love.

She managed to say, 'Charlie. You haven't changed much.'

It was partially true, although there seemed to be more creases at the corners of his eyes and lips than there used to be.

Some men would have been aged by such lines. On him it merely enhanced. And there was the limp of course.

She managed to get her breath back. 'Long time, no see.'

'Indeed.'

Memories of their shared past came surging back, though not whole, as though the past was a smooth flat plain. It came back more as a patchwork of events, feelings, tender moments and those that had hurt deeply.

They'd met in the days when she'd lived in Blue Bowl Alley with her husband, Roy, and her two daughters. Although Charlie was from a wealthy background, he had a penchant for getting involved in the workers movement. He'd also spent a great deal of time in the company of older women, some married, some not. Later on, she'd found out that in exchange for escorting them, they'd showered him with gifts – both monetary and otherwise. If they were lonely, who could blame him? He was a charmer. That's what she'd told herself. He'd charmed the wealthy wives and lonely widows, and he'd charmed her.

'Charles. Aren't you going to introduce me?'

His female companion smiled, and although she must be wondering about this cinema usherette, there was no sign of animosity.

'Of course. I do apologise, darling.' He turned back to Jenny, one hand leaning on his stick, the other reaching for the woman's hand. 'This is my fiancée, Emily.' And to his companion, he said, 'This is Jenny Crawford. An old friend of mine.'

A hand coated in black suede was extended and Emily's smile looked genuine. 'How do you do.'

'Fine, I'm sure,' returned Jenny, who had never felt so taken off guard as she was now. Was it only to her ears, or did she sound a bit subservient? In awe of this beautifully dressed woman.

'Jenny knows me from way back before I ripped my leg open. I'm lately of the RAF,' he explained to her. He tapped his leg, which caused a ringing sound. 'Had a tussle with a Messerschmidt. Shot him down, but I was already on fire. Had to bail out.'

'I'm sorry to hear that.' She wanted to fling her arms around him and, like a doting mother, tell him that everything would be all right, that she was there for him.

She swallowed such sentimentality. This was the man who'd ran out on her. A man who was now engaged to another woman. *Look away. Walk away.* She did neither.

He grinned. 'I've adjusted. In fact, I like the acclaim on people's faces when I tell them.'

A fighter ace. Yes, she thought, he would like the resultant adoration.

'What are you doing back in Bristol?'

The way his face lifted when his mouth widened in a smile was still as captivating as she remembered.

'Working in the office at Bristol Airport. I'm involved in drawing up plans for a new airport south of the city. Goodness knows when it's likely to be built, but believe me, it will happen. Air travel will expand once the war is over. Flights will be about having fun, not about shooting down other planes. I foresee more people flying to go on holiday. Not at the present airport at Whitchurch, I'm afraid. There's not enough room. An airport hemmed in by a housing estate won't allow enough room for an increase in flights.'

His pronouncement seemed farcical and brought the *Tales of the Arabian Nights* to mind, especially the one featuring a flying carpet. And how many people would be able to afford to fly abroad? None of the ones she knew. But that was Charlie Talbot. He thought he had a grasp on working-class people, dismissing the fact that he came from the other side of the tracks.

She voiced her point of view. 'We're all hoping for a better world – although flying through the skies isn't likely to be cheap, is it.'

'Give it time.'

It both surprised and slightly annoyed her that his smile was still capable of making her go weak at the knees.

The next matinee was about to start, a good enough reason for taking her leave.

'Nice to see you again. I must go. It's dark in there and I don't want anyone falling over and breaking their leg.'

'No.' He tapped his leg with the stick. 'One is enough.'

'Nice to meet you,' said his fiancée, Emily.

'Yes. Will we see you again?'

'Possibly. We've got a house at Dundry, a village close enough to the airport but not on the doorstep. Who knows, we might indeed bump into each other again. I do like a good movie.' Tugging his arm closer to her side, Emily looked up at him adoringly. 'That's if he can drag himself away from the airport and take me out.'

Movie. She'd used the American word 'movie'. Not 'picture' as the locals did. Did she detect the hint of an American accent? Hard to tell. American colloquialisms and figures of speech had been easily absorbed into the King's English.

Charlie laughed. 'Mr Churchill insists he comes first in my life. At least for now.' He patted his fiancée's arm, an absent-minded action whilst his smile was fixed on Jenny's face.

There was a possessive look in Emily's eyes when she said, 'Take it from me that by hook or by crook we will be back to see another movie.'

'Goodbye then.'

Charlie took hold of his fiancée's arm and guided her through the blackout curtains that stopped the light from seeping out through the glass panels of the main exit from the foyer and outside.

Flustered and surprised, Jenny headed back through the double doors and into the darkness. Heart racing, she leaned one hand onto the wooden parapet at the back of the picture house, not trusting herself to stay upright without support.

She took a deep breath. People were beginning to come in. Charlie remained in her mind. He'd taken her completely by surprise. She was flustered, intrigued and left wondering when she was likely to see him again.

For a time, there seemed to have existed a conspiracy of hearts, the prospect of a relationship born of mutual need, hers perhaps more than his. She'd never quite worked out what his needs had been. Her marriage had stood in the way, and despite Roy not being the best of husbands, she had felt duty-bound to be faithful.

He wasn't that changed. She wanted to think otherwise, but his familiar image kept creeping back into her mind. Was it really possible that she'd loved him?

As her breathing normalised, she tucked her chin in and faced the harsh truth as she saw it. Regardless of what his fiancée had said, she doubted they would see each other again.

A sliver of amber light showed between the double doors at the top of the incline, which only happened if somebody was going in or out.

The silhouette of a man momentarily filled the gap before the door was closed behind him. Even before he came to her side, she knew he'd come back.

She smelled his masculinity, the cologne he wore, his form

and stance, and the memories came rushing back to heat her blood.

Why had he come back? For her? For another reason?

'I think I've dropped a cufflink,' he whispered.

A dropped cufflink? Such a mundane reason, though she hoped that it wasn't the truth.

She whispered the only response she could give him. 'There's no way I can find something so small until the lights are up again and that's likely to be a while.'

He offered a ready excuse that wasn't really an excuse. More a kind of appeal to be lenient with him. 'It's been a long while since I've seen you. Since that night, I think... when things changed.'

Jenny clenched her teeth. 'Yes. Since that night.' There had been a gas explosion in Coronation Close, and it was Jenny's house that had been damaged.

'You must believe me. I deeply regret that night.'

Three or four people turned round and suggested he keep quiet.

'Please. Go.'

He didn't go. Instead, he grabbed her arm, fingers tight, face still smiling as though there was no need to complain or worry about the fierceness of his grip. He'd held just such a tight grip on his fiancée's arm, affirmation of belonging. 'Jenny, I must talk to you...'

She wanted to tell him that he was gripping her too tightly. It also occurred to her to tell him to leave and never approach her ever again. But she didn't. She couldn't.

People began fidgeting, turning their heads, making shushing noises. The regular audience at the Broadway didn't have much patience when it came to people chattering and thus ruining their film.

Realising he wasn't going to give in easily and with him holding onto her arm, she guided him out of the doors and into the foyer.

There was no sign of Emily hanging around in the crimson and gold surroundings. Jenny had to presume she was waiting outside.

Shaking off his hand, she rounded on him, her eyes blazing like fire. 'I've got a job to do. In case you've forgotten, I work for a living. That's why the likes of me are called working class! If you want to search for your cufflink, you'll have to come back when the cleaners have done their job. They have work to do too.'

Her tone was vehement, delivered coldly, a reminder that he might think himself a champion of the working class, but it didn't wash. He would always be what he was, as would she.

She knew her barb had hit home when he flinched as though she'd smacked his face. Then he smiled, that old slow smile that she remembered so well.

He let arm go, then shrugged his shoulders. In doing so, the sleeves of his jacket rode up so that the cuffs of his shirt were exposed. A gold cufflink glinted from each cuff.

'You were lying,' she hissed angrily. 'Like to keep the workers on their toes, do you, looking for a bloody cufflink that you're still wearing?'

'I wanted to speak to you.'

Half turning away, she shook her head and raised the hand that held the torch, almost as though she might strike him with it. 'I have to go back.'

He grabbed her arm again. 'Jenny. I want to see you again.'

She glowered at the hand that grasped her arm, the manicured nails, the absence of callouses that usually evidenced hard manual labour. 'You're engaged to be married, and you want to see me? How can you say such a thing? It's dishonourable.'

His response was forthright. 'Easily. Jenny, you were always on my mind.' He raised her chin with one finger and looked into her eyes as though he would drown in their misted light. 'Come on, Jenny. Admit that you feel the same. That I'm always on your mind, just as you are always on mine. Tell me that your feelings have died, and I will walk away here and now. Tell me.'

Feelings she'd thought long dead simmered. Up until this moment, she had shut Charlie Talbot from her mind. Robin had filled the gap he had left. But here he was and suddenly the feelings had returned.

The main doors opened. The night air and the elegant Emily entered.

'Darling? Have you found your cufflink?'

On the surface, Emily sounded pleasant. Her smile was pleasant too, but Jenny couldn't help thinking there was a steely resolve beneath that amicable facade.

'In my pocket,' he said, turning round to her, smiling as he sported the erstwhile missing cufflink. 'There it is. I put my hand in my pocket for my lighter. It must have caught and slid off. No harm done.' Beaming, he leaned forward and kissed her on the cheek.

'I'm glad to hear it.' Her gloved hand brushed at imaginary specks on his shoulder. 'They cost me fifty guineas. I would never have forgiven you.'

There was a lilt to her voice. Definitely American. Jenny took in the details of her outfit. Nothing utility. A smart outfit that looked like cashmere. Impeccable make-up, glossy black hair caught in a chignon at the nape of neck, shoes of Spanish leather and, most telling of all, sheer stockings that could only be silk.

'Now come along. It's time we were going.'

I was right, thought Jenny. *Silky on the outside, steel on the inside*. Perhaps she was exactly what Charlie needed. Not her. Not a nobody wearing home-made or second-hand clothes.

'Thank you for your assistance,' Charlie shouted after her as she bolted for the dark safety of the auditorium. 'Nice to see you again.'

Her world seeming suddenly to have turned topsy-turvy, she said nothing but turned her back and rushed off. The sooner she entered the darkness of the auditorium, the better.

The main attraction had started on the silver screen. For her the main attraction had already occurred. The reappearance of Charlie Talbot. What was it his fiancée had said? They had a house in the village of Dundry? Were they living together even though they were not married? Or was there some other arrangement? A boarding house?

Under her breath, she whispered, 'Stop torturing yourself, Jenny. Get through this film then off home to bed.'

And that is what she would do, though she suspected she wouldn't sleep very well. Charlie Talbot was in her mind and, ultimately, might be back in her life.

Her heart was still racing after the last matinee when the familiar odour of nicotine, cheap perfume and stale sweat was more noticeable after the audience had left. Whoever had said that the cinema – or picture house, as it was called locally – was a place of wonder and dreams hadn't hung around when the lights went up.

Tonight, once the National Anthem had finished, the lights had come up and the customers had filed up the incline and out of the door, Jenny plucked with grim determination at the detritus remaining after three film showings. Cigarette packets, bits of paper, even more intimate items and used rubbers failed to obliterate the handsome Charlie Talbot, a vision of the past that she thought had disappeared forever.

He was back, but on the arm of another woman, one he intended marrying.

She could smell and feel him all the way home and was still doing so when she lay in bed, sleep elusive. Closing her eyes, she hugged the spare pillow in her arms and pretended it was him. The bulk of the feather-stuffed pillow was comforting but cold, not warm as she imagined his naked body to be. Just a pillow, but she leaned into it, all she had and all she was likely to have.

14

It was early morning, and Margaret watched as the contents of a bottle of port wine splashed into the sink and disappeared down the plughole.

She had expected to carry this task out before either Judith or Howard had risen. A loud yawn and dainty footsteps from behind proved her wrong.

Judith was quick in mind and movement, no questions asked, or acknowledgement given as she came to stand beside her. Like her father, it sometimes felt as though she was set on catching her mother out doing something she ought not do. She looked at the bottle and then at her mother.

'No more drinking? And about time too.'

The comment smarted, though Margaret pretended otherwise. 'Judith. What are you doing up so early?'

'I have some leaflets to distribute on the way to work. The new minister at the church asked me if I would. I promised and I don't break promises.'

Was it the chilly morning air or otherwise when, for one scary moment, her daughter's tone of voice reminded her of

Percy? It wasn't the first time she'd thought Judith turned after him. There were other signs that were hard to ignore. She still attended his preferred church, and her father would have approved of the way she dressed. No make-up. No frills or bows. Her clothes were steadfastly sombre and yet, perhaps because of her youth, she looked attractive in a fresh-faced way. Black especially suited her.

'Would you like me to get you some toast?' Margaret asked brightly, keen to deflect the conversation from where it was destined to travel.

Judith, too shrewd for her age by far, was not to be so easily put off.

'Thank you, God,' breathed Judith, raising her eyes towards the ceiling, as though by chance the crack around the lampshade had opened and heaven was easily viewed. 'Father would be appalled at how far you'd fallen. I'm praying also that you will no longer be out at night until the early hours.'

Margaret kept her eyes downcast as she sawed at the loaf of bread, two days old so only fit for toasting. Her face flushed at the fact that she was being chastised by her own daughter.

'I know my father's death came as a shock, coming as it did at the same time as Albert. You became a different person. I accepted you had to be given time to get through it and that, eventually, you would become the mother I knew, the one who sacrificed herself for family.'

Letting the knife fall from her hand, Margaret faced her daughter with a flaming red face and a fierce glare in her eyes. 'Judith, I loved my family, but that sacrifice you mention buried any vestige of the real me. Your father moulded me to suit what he wanted. He treated me like a slave, not a wife. There was no love, only an ongoing discipline that subjugated my soul, that made me feel worthless.'

Judith looked surprised, her deep-set eyes like chips of coal against a naturally creamy complexion that had become white as snow, rosebud lips slightly parted.

Margaret gave her no chance to make comment. It was all coming out now and her daughter – son too – might as well know the truth. 'He was a cruel man, Judith. He turned my mind. Abused my body. Said it was all for my own good. Women are naturally sinners. So...' She breathed a huge sigh. At last, she was talking about it. 'I became the sinner he accused me of being. I did everything that would have appalled him. I suppose some might say I had to get it off my chest, but as far as I'm concerned, I had to confront my deepest self to get back the person I'd once been. Do you understand that, Judith, because even if you don't, I won't be asking for any forgiveness. I did nothing wrong; I was just trying to correct the mindset imposed on me. Do you understand?' she asked again.

Judith stood stock-still.

Margaret saw flashes of reaction flicker in her daughter's eyes, her firstborn, the child she'd so wanted. Her heart ached for her to understand but feared she would not.

She turned away, placed the slice of bread onto the plate and began to butter it, completely forgetting she'd asked Judith if she would like a piece of toast.

The silence seemed to go on for ages, though it must only have been minutes.

'Is there any jam left?'

Judith's voice was small. If she felt any condemnation for her mother's behaviour, it didn't show.

'Yes. A little,' returned Margaret. The rigid way she'd been holding herself lessened. It was 'off her chest' and her mind.

She placed the jam on the table. Judith helped herself. Margaret poured a cup of tea for them both.

Halfway through eating her slice of bread, Judith looked up. A small frown set a narrow crease between her brows. 'Will you still be going out at night?'

Margaret sat down at the table and pulled the cup of tea towards her. 'Yes. I will.'

'But I thought—'

'During this...' She paused for the right word. 'This illness of mine, I made friends who did not judge me. Your father would have called them loose women. I think of them as the salt of the earth. They didn't care about my background, where I lived or how I behaved. They accepted me as I was, and I accepted them. So yes, I will pop in and see them from time to time.'

She steeled herself for the puzzlement in Judith's eyes, which seemed not quite so intense as expected.

What Judith said next was unexpected. 'Will you be coming back to church?'

Margaret shook her head. 'Not in the foreseeable future. Perhaps in time, but for now... no.'

'I fancy some toast. Is none made yet? Never mind. I'll make it myself. I know how to do it...' Howard's stomach ruled his life. He liked his food and didn't ask what they'd been discussing. Neither did he make comment about the empty bottle of port left on the draining board.

With a bustling busyness, he sliced the bread, spiked the toasting fork through it and held it over a gas ring.

'I'm off now,' said Judith, finishing her tea and her bread. 'I might be home late this evening. I need to take back any leaflets to the Reverend Andrews.'

Margaret cocked an eyebrow. 'The Reverend Andrews? What happened to the Reverend Grinder?' The latter had been the church minister at the time of Percy's death. She reminded herself that some time had since passed.

'He retired. The Reverend Andrews is new. He's very good. You really should come along and hear him. You too, Howard.'

Howard growled a hasty response that he hadn't time to go. 'I'm joining the army cadets. They need me.'

Judith batted her eyes at him, the look an older sister regularly bequeaths on a younger brother she finds irritating.

'Never mind about him. Think about coming, Mother. I'm sure you'll like him.'

Not as much as you, thought Margaret on detecting the sparkle in her daughter's eyes.

'Give me time and I might. But I won't promise... not yet at least.'

Judith nodded. Just a simple thing, but there was something in it that hinted at understanding.

After they'd both left the house, Margaret thought about the friends she'd made at the Hatchet, the wildness she'd descended into. Nobody had condemned her, and her eyes had been opened to a world she'd never known.

Thinking on what Judith had said and her reaction to the new church minister also struck a chord. Her daughter was impressed with this man. She wondered how old he was and whether something more intense was developing other than mutual respect. Wondering that also brought Gloria Crawford and her involvement with an older man to mind. A young girl was easily impressed by a charming man. Didn't Margaret know that herself.

The dishes from this morning only needed drying. Once that was done, she would trot along to number two, and inform Jenny Crawford what her daughter was up to.

Before doing that, she reached beneath the sink and brought out the second bottle of port she kept there – a present from a Portuguese sailor.

After taking out the cork, she sniffed at the sweet aroma that hinted at sunshine, vine-covered slopes and the warmth of a hushed breeze.

'Off you go!'

So swift and so determined was her action that some of the dark red liquid splashed onto her apron. And then it was gone, and she'd finally turned a new page. After that new page there would be many more. Margaret was sure of it.

15

Attacking the draining board with a stiff scrubbing brush took a lot of effort. Jenny was going at it as though she hadn't scrubbed it for years, though that wasn't the case at all. Twice a week was the norm. Oddly enough, scrubbing a draining board helped her get her rampant thoughts into a more cohesive order.

After all these years, Charlie Talbot had reappeared, although she was uncertain whether that was a good or bad thing.

Had he known she was working at the Broadway? She applied extra pressure to the brush. In her head, she answered her own question. It was possible that he might have asked around. The shops on both the Broadway and Melvin Square were a hotbed of local gossip. She blamed rationing and the queueing for food. Time spent hanging around was filled by more chinwagging than in the years preceding war. Gossip helped ease the strain of waiting around.

A sudden knocking at the front door, and her thoughts shattered.

Throwing the scrubbing brush into the sink, she dried her

hands and tucked a stray tress back beneath her turban. On second thoughts, she whipped the scarf from her head. No matter whether a turban was formed from silk, wool or calico, she refused to answer the front door wearing one. Just in case.

In case of what? More likely whom!

'Hold your horses,' she shouted. 'I'm coming.'

Determination echoed throughout the house with every heavy-handed bang of the door knocker.

'Wait a minute,' she shouted again, annoyed that someone could be so demanding at nine o'clock in the morning.

The door seemed to fall open of its own accord, thanks to one of Margaret Routledge's feet on the doorstep, the other lagging behind, heel caught on the corner of the lawn.

When Jenny took a deep breath, her nose was assaulted with the smell of stale, cheap scent and something more pungent and fruitier. Sherry or port. Judging by the stains on her dress, it appeared Margaret had spilt as much as she might have drunk. At this time of the morning?

Jenny hid her disgust. Might as well give her the benefit of the doubt.

'Margaret.' Crossing her arms in defensive fashion and glancing down at the offending foot, she adopted a nondescript expression. It had been a while since they'd passed the time of day and even then, only a stifled good morning or evening.

'Yes. It's me.'

It was difficult to guess the reason she was here. Her tone veered between confrontational and guilty. Jenny prepared herself but kept her voice even.

'Is something wrong?'

She cleared her throat. 'I'm not quite sure how to put it.'

Despite the spillage down her dress and the ongoing smell,

she seemed to be sober. Jenny considered inviting her in but thought better of it.

Margaret blinked, seemed to think before plunging in.

'It's about your daughter. Gloria.'

Jenny's eyebrows arched with surprise and changed her mind about inviting her in. 'You'd better come in.'

Jenny opened the door wide. Margaret hesitated before entering.

'Nice room,' she said, her gaze scrutinising Jenny's three-piece suite, the bamboo table on which the wireless sat, the fitted dresser that all the houses had. On the top shelf were family photographs. On the lower shelves crockery and the odd bit of silverware she'd inherited from her mother.

'Would you like a cup of tea?'

Margaret shook her head. 'I expect you've got things to do.' Her gaze flickered around the room as though looking for those things.

'It's no bother.'

'I'm fine.'

'Do you want to sit down?'

A bit of thought this time before she shook her head.

'No. It won't take long.'

A clearing of her throat, a tangling of fingers, a turning away of her face indicated to Jenny that whatever Margaret had to say, she was nervous about it.

'Tell you what, I'll go back to what I was doing in the kitchen before you came in. Will that give you enough time to get your act together?'

Perhaps it sounded a bit sarcastic, but she'd prefer if her neighbour would get to the point.

Back she went to the draining board, the hot water in the

sink cooling, the bristles of the scrubbing brush as stiff and hard as ever.

She became aware of Margaret standing in the doorway, quite tall, but slim enough not to block it.

The draining board was almost white with scrubbing. Her brisk application could not clean it any more than it had. She carried on, waiting for Margaret to get whatever it was off her chest.

'I don't like causing trouble for anyone, but as a mother myself...'

It seemed almost funny to Jenny that she should say that, yet, in all honesty, she had been a model mother before... the occurrence! She had strayed off the straight and narrow but had remained there for her children – even though they were far from being little children any longer.

The hand that wielded the scrubbing brush picked it up and returned it to the water. Back arching against the sink, Jenny turned round.

'Margaret, we've both had enough bother in the past few years to last a lifetime. So come on, out with it. I won't fall to pieces.'

'You might do once I've said what I've come to say.'

Jenny sighed. 'Will you please get to the point? I haven't got all day. You said it's about Gloria.'

'Yes.'

Jenny wondered what she was about to hear. Her youngest daughter had always been precocious. That said, she had never got into any trouble with any of the neighbours. She'd never known her to shout insults at Margaret when she was drunk as some kids in the Close were wont to do. Still, there was always a first time. She prepared herself for eating humble pie, modifying her tone just in case.

'Has she done something to upset you? I'll have a word with her if she has.'

'Ha,' Margaret exclaimed, the chipped red varnish of her right hand coursing up and down her left arm as though she was priming herself for whatever might come next. It was then that Jenny looked past the stained apron and took in the lack of make-up, the neat oval arrangement at the nape of her neck. She looked different. Still, best get to the point. 'What she's done is more likely to upset you.'

What had her daughter done? Jenny's mind went over the last few weeks, the flouncing out in frocks she didn't know she had. So far she had not pried in her daughter's room. What would be gained from that? Letters perhaps? Expensive gifts?

She felt her resistance to sneaking in drawers and wardrobe crumbling.

'Oh. What kind of trouble?' She couldn't help sounding brusquer than she had done and markedly scrutinised the dark stain down the front of Margaret's apron.

Margaret went red when she noticed her disparaging look. 'I spilt some drink.' The hand that had been nervously travelling up and down her arm brushed at the dark patch. 'Port. I'd had it since Christmas. Gone bad, so I poured it down the sink.'

'If you're after borrowing some, I don't keep drink in the house – not even the odd half-bottle from Christmas.'

Margaret winced before seeming to come to a decision.

'All right, then. It's like this... your daughter is too young to be drinking. That said, she's going to get more than just drunk in a pub like the Hatchet.'

Jenny felt a hammering of blood flow in her ears, a throbbing in her brain. She'd heard of the Hatchet pub in Frogmore Street. It was common knowledge that it was frequented by ladies of the night and local villains. Margaret too had been said to enter its less than hallowed rooms.

Unwilling to let Margaret gorge on the effect she'd had, Jenny shook her head in disbelief. 'I don't believe you.'

'No, I didn't expect you would. Your darling little girls, butter wouldn't melt in their mouth. If you believe that, you're stupid. Anyone can go off the rails. I should know,' she added softly. She paused and took a breath before delivering the crushing finale. 'A man – especially an older man – can wind a silly young girl around his little finger. Your Gloria is carrying on with a man old enough to be her father. And he has form, a finger in a lot of pies that aren't all legal.'

'I don't believe you.'

How could she believe the message being delivered by a woman who'd gained herself a reputation since she'd been widowed?

'It's the truth. She's not just going into a pub underage. She's got herself a sugar daddy, a man involved in goodness knows how many criminal activities. I've heard it said that once he gets his claws into someone – especially young girls – he does not let go.'

Jenny swallowed. 'I see.' It was all she could say and knew that the colour had drained from her cheeks.

Was that a sanctimonious and superior pleasure she saw on her neighbour's face? Or was it pity?

It was hard not to call her an outright liar, but too easy to lash out. After all, any mother worth her salt stuck up for her own chicks, believed the best of them and not the worst.

'Why do I get the impression that you couldn't wait to bring the news to my door. Makes you feel better, does it?'

Margaret shook her head. It was definitely pity Jenny was seeing in her eyes.

'Far from it. I thought you should know. I know that place. Some are down on their luck, no other life for them.'

'So I understand,' returned Jenny in a clipped manner.

'I make no excuses for myself. As I've already said, I've been a bit adrift of late. But I'm not now. Anyway, I'm old enough to look after myself. Your girl is not.'

A pink flush spread over Jenny's cheeks. 'I think you'd better go.'

'I'm going, don't you worry. You're a widow too. There's plenty who drown their sorrows in drink and dancing, so don't come over all superior with me. You think you're better than me, Jenny Crawford. As a widow...'

'Then you should understand a bit better. You're not a nun, are you? And neither am I.' Her eyes narrowed. 'I understand that the late Mr Crawford was no saint, but I'll tell you now, he would have seemed like one compared to Percy. I only hear rumours of what went on between the two of you, but you hear nothing about what went on between me and Percy. He portrayed himself as a respectable upholder of law and order. Ask yourself; do you know what goes on behind closed doors? You don't! And that's a fact.'

Jenny followed her out of the door and onto the doorstep, her face coloured with rage. The fact was that Margaret's words had hit home as a grim truth. Nobody really knew what went on between husband and wife. Each house was a small empire known only to its inhabitants.

Chest rising and falling with exasperation, Jenny searched for a parting comment but couldn't seem to grasp anything suitable. She was shocked to speechlessness by what she had learned. As if she didn't have enough to worry about.

Margaret began taking backward steps before turning her

back on Jenny and her shocked expression. As her hand landed on the gate latch, she turned and hurled one last parting shot.

'Like it or not, Jenny Crawford, you're no better than me under the skin. And as for your girl, well, even the saintliest child can be led astray. I came here to tell you so you could stop her sliding into a life she might regret.'

Jenny clenched her jaw. She was furious with Margaret Routledge, furious with Gloria and furious with herself.

Cool fingertips felt the heat in her cheeks. Ranting about Gloria had been bad enough but suggesting that her morals were comparable with Margaret's angered her the most. Without another word, she slammed the door but remained leaning against it, her heart racing.

Gritting her teeth, she confronted the reason for Margaret's visit, the fact that Gloria was frequenting a pub. It wasn't that unusual for girls of her age to lie about their age. But there was more to it than that. The Hatchet had a terrible reputation. That was bad enough, but the news that she was seeing an older man was far worse. Much as it grieved her, she had to accept that Margaret had been telling the truth.

As the kettle began to boil, Jenny hit her forehead with the palm of her hand. She hadn't asked Margaret the man's name. How stupid was that? On thinking about it, she decided it didn't matter. She'd get his name from her daughter and at the same time would lay down the law to her in no uncertain terms.

The wireless that had been so distant earlier now seemed to dominate the mid-morning sounds of the house she had fallen in love with back in 1936.

'It is reported that gains have been made by the Eighth Army in North Africa...'

She reached for the knob and turned it off. The light at the front of the wireless set faded to a grey blank. If Gloria hadn't already left for work, she'd be having a set-to right now. It would have to wait until she got home. This was war – of a sort – on the home front.

16

Dear Tilly,

I hope you are well. I am only kind of well. The fact is I've fallen in love. Mum knows nothing about it, and neither does anyone else for that matter. I need to share how I'm feeling. If I tell you all about him, do you promise not to tell anyone else? Mum will go mad.

I won't write to you with the details unless you promise to keep it a secret.

Write back as quickly as you can, then I'll write back and tell you everything.

Love, Gloria

Tilly was dumbfounded. The one and only letter she'd received from her sister and straight to the point. On reflection, she asked herself, why would she expect Gloria to be anything else?

Well, well. My sister Gloria taking the time to write, though only in her own interests, thought Tilly.

She wondered about this keeping it a secret. What could be so awful with this boyfriend that she wanted it kept a secret? A truly dreadful thought came to her that perhaps he might be married.

Oh, stupid, stupid Gloria! My daft little sister.

Tilly was making her way back from the post box which was outside the village shop. The shop also served as a post office and sold everything from cheese and bacon to candles and garden spades. She'd also picked up some tea and sugar, necessities that the self-sufficient Merryweather Farm could not supply for itself. The farm was better off than most for food, certainly better than in towns and cities. They produced milk, cheese, butter, eggs and vegetables, besides making their own bread from the home-grown wheat.

Mrs Forester hadn't said as much, but despite being a bit abrupt at times, she seemed fond of the two land girls allotted to her, especially Tilly.

Daisies, buttercups and poppies waved like small flags in the grassy banks at the side of the lane. Cows lowed in the meadows and the distant purr of a tractor sounded from some way off.

A city girl born and bred, but Tilly had settled into a county of wide landscapes, wider sky and thatched cottages and farmhouses dating from the early Middle Ages.

Perfect peace.

* * *

Milking began at dawn. It was relatively easy to immerse herself in the heavy work required on the farm. Maureen, the new land girl, was buzzing with excitement thanks to a poster she'd seen in the village about a dance at the RAF base just a few miles away.

'I've never been to a dance on an air base before. Can't wait. What is it like? Exciting, I bet.'

'It depends whether you like that sort of thing or not,' said Tilly, stepping back as she uploaded a bucketful of swill into the pig pen. 'I've been to a few. Some were good, some not so good.'

'I thought you had been to loads.' Maureen looked surprised and a bit envious.

'Not loads. Enough both at the base and at the village hall.'

Maureen was full of breathless envy. 'What are they like?'

The new land girl's palpable excitement was extraordinary. She had been brought up in the Welsh borders, an area too hilly for airfields, and army barracks too were a bit thin on the ground. US army, that was.

Tilly couldn't help quoting the common saying. 'Some of them are Polish or Canadian. Charmers every one of them. Give them an inch and they'll take a mile.'

Maureen was unfazed. 'Oow. Lovely. How do they speak? Do they speak English?'

'Of course they do, just with a different accent. Think of the cowboys you've heard at the pictures, or any other American film star for that matter. The Canadians sound a bit like that. The Polish have more of an accent, them and a few others from all over the place. Fliers from everywhere.'

Awestruck by Tilly's comment, Maureen was in a trance for the rest of the day. For her part, Tilly was thinking the letter she'd received from Gloria. Her sister had always been a rebel; she must be bursting to tell someone of her love affair. She grimaced at the thought of what her mother might think – when and if Gloria ever told her.

Sunset dripped its coat of many colours across the sky, splashing it with gold, red, lilac and purple. The smell of a rich stew drifted in a succulent haze out of the farmhouse kitchen, where Mrs Forester urged everyone to wash their hands before sitting down.

At table, Maureen did her best to catch Johnnie's eye, throwing him enticing looks from beneath her coal-black eyelashes.

The subject matter of her conversation was for his benefit. She was saying something about only strong men being able to work on a farm, 'men with muscles'.

Johnnie looked up at her before he turned his attention back to his food, shovelling it into his mouth more quickly than usual.

He looked up from his food and caught Tilly's eye. 'I suppose you're going to the dance at the airfield tomorrow.'

Tilly thought carefully before answering.

'I think I should. I think we owe it them. A form of thank you for putting their lives on the line.'

Johnnie's disagreeable expression said it all. His jealousy came as something of a surprise. It had always seemed that they were friends more so than sweethearts. He'd shown her how to harness up the big chestnut horses to the plough. He'd shown her also how to clean their hooves after coming back from a muddy field, how to break up the hay in the manger so they could chew it more easily. He'd even allowed her to join him when one of the cows was being covered by a prize bull owned by a neighbouring farmer. She'd felt his eyes on her, searching for any reaction to what she was witnessing. There was admiration on his face when she showed no sign of embarrassment but asked pertinent questions to which he gave knowledgeable answers. They were friends. *And that is all we are*, she said to herself.

Spotted dick – a heavy suet pudding riddled with currants and cinnamon – doused in custard, followed the stew. Everything served at the farmhouse was designed to fill stomachs to capacity after long days of physical labour.

Tilly patted her stomach. 'I'm full up,' she said after downing a cup of tea. 'I need to walk it off.'

There was no argument. It was Maureen's turn to help Mrs Forester with the washing up. Tilly was keen to be away.

'There's a sack of food behind the manger in the cow barn,' pronounced Mrs Forester.

Tilly tried not to blush when she thanked her.

Johnnie had told his mother all about the occupants of the cottage at the far end of the sloping meadow where bees buzzed and butterflies fluttered around the flowering nettles. Instead of being angry, Mrs Forester had put aside food and other items Sybil and her son might need. She'd also visited her.

'Poor woman. Makes you wonder why she's hiding – and hiding she is, in my opinion.' She leaned in close to Tilly's ear so that Mr Forester wouldn't hear and accuse her of being nosy. 'I made a few enquiries in the village, but discreetly, you understand. Nobody knows anything about a woman and a little boy being reported missing. Still, she must have her reasons.' A faraway look came to her eyes. 'Brook Meadow is our favourite meadow. Me and Fred used to go courting there. It's always held a place in our hearts. Every so often, mainly at sunset, either one or both of us go down there to reminisce about old times.'

Tilly gulped. 'Oh. I didn't know that.'

Mrs Forester drew in her chin until it looked as though she had no neck. 'Tell me, Miss Dawson. Have I not treated you well enough for you to realise by now that I am not a hard-hearted woman who would see anyone starve?'

Feeling acutely embarrassed, Tilly didn't know what to say, until finally, 'No. You're not,' she said softly.

'We guessed someone was down there. She wouldn't be the first to take shelter there. There was a German there a while back. He gave himself up. Last we heard, he was in a prisoner of war camp somewhere – one of those where they let them out to do a bit of farm labouring in the area. He seemed a nice sort, but there you are, 'tis them at the top who cause wars – that's my opinion.'

'I'm sorry.'

'Tell the poor woman to come up here whenever she needs anything. She won't be turned away.'

With those parting words, Mrs Forester turned to the bread oven at the side of the range to check on the two loaves and an apple pie. The smell was enough to make anyone's mouth water.

After taking the loaves from the oven, she wrapped one of them in a piece of muslin. She handed it to Tilly.

'Go and take it to the poor creatures. Tell the woman she can come here for a meal and milk for the child if she so wishes. We do not turn the needy away from Merryweather Farm. Is that clear?'

Tilly nodded. 'Her name's Sybil. The little boy is named Jack.'

'I know. I told you; I went to see her. Nervous as a doe she was. Likely to leap away at a moment's notice. There's something deep she's scared of, and someone's frightened her, if them bruises and cuts are anything to go by.'

'I think her husband's dead.'

Tilly tried not to think of the bruises she'd seen on Sybil's face, that her husband might not be dead but that she just wished he was.

Mrs Forester shook her head. 'I'll not judge. She needs our help, not our judgement.'

Harbouring a mixture of surprise and relief, there was a spring in Tilly's step as she headed across fields bathed in the warm glow of sunset. Swifts and swallows were darts of blackness against the last golden rays.

Her heart sang as she imagined Sybil's reaction to Mrs Forester's offer of a decent meal and milk. Growing children needed milk. Her mother had always said so.

She would tell her mother what had occurred when she next wrote to her.

When she got to the cottage, Sybil was sitting outside on the three-legged stool. Tilly waved. Sybil lifted her hand, three fingers waving before swiftly dropping back into her lap. Her cheeks were pink, perhaps because she was feeling better or the fresh air might well have had something to do with it.

'I've brought you some food.' She looked beyond Sybil to the cottage door. 'Where's Jack?'

'Asleep.'

Sybil barely nodded as she pushed the sack into the cool aperture beyond the threshold of the open door and inside the house.

Tilly pulled up a bucket, turned it upside down and sat on it. Excited by what she was about to convey, she rattled it off at high speed, how Mrs Forester didn't mind her living in the cottage, was willing to share food. 'And you're welcome to come up to the farmhouse for a meal – you and Jack – whenever you like.'

Her enthusiasm was not reciprocated.

Sybil shook her head. 'No. No. I can't go there.'

Tilly eyed her querulously. 'It's not charity; in fact, you might even be able to stay at the farmhouse in exchange for some housework. Wouldn't that be better than staying here?' Mrs Forester had said no such thing, but Tilly thought she would be quite amenable to having someone help her with the household chores. She had mentioned that her heart wasn't that good, that she was getting older and things were getting more difficult. Wasn't that as good as saying that she would accept extra help?

She looked around her at the green moss bordering the floor

where it met the walls, the broken windowpanes, the lopsided front door. That was beside the musty dampness, the view of the sky through the broken tiles.

Nobody in their right mind would want to stay here – not indefinitely. She felt a great urge to press the advantage of living up at the farmhouse compared with the semi-derelict cottage.

'It's fine in summer, but what about in the winter? It'll be very cold and damp. How would you manage? And your little boy...'

Sybil convulsed into a fit of coughing. Tilly imagined how much worse it might get once winter arrived.

The hacking cough lessened into a series of spluttering. Once that too had dispersed, Sybil shook her head emphatically, wisps of overly long hair escaping from the red scarf wound around it.

'I cannot live at the farmhouse. I don't want anyone to know I'm here. I must hide. I simply must hide.'

Tilly looked at her blankly before a frown pierced her brow. 'But we know you're here, and if we know, then other people will know.'

She wasn't quite sure whether that was true, but it was likely. Despite the wide-open spaces, news got around. Gossip flew like the birds in the sky.

Hair in need of washing and cutting was pushed behind one ear. Sybil's fingernails were dirty and chipped. Her eyes were downcast. Overall, this poor woman was a picture of despair and Tilly was determined to help her. She asked the question she had avoided up until now.

'Who are you hiding from? Will that someone hurt you if he finds you?'

She presumed it was a man, but Sybil had told her that her husband had died of battle wounds. Perhaps she was lying.

She looked for a ring on her wedding finger. There was something there, but if it was a wedding ring, it certainly wasn't made from gold. Brass perhaps – more like a curtain ring than one for wearing on a finger.

'Please. I can't help you if you don't tell me.'

Sybil swallowed and once again tucked some of the stray and dull-looking locks back from her face. A kind of watershed or dam seemed to breach. A decision had been reached. Sybil threw Tilly furtive looks as she attempted to explain. 'Someone who would take my boy away. Someone who would kill me if they could.'

Tilly was speechless that anyone would want to kill such an unprepossessing woman who looked as though she wouldn't say boo to a goose. 'Who? Who would want to do that?'

Sybil's large brown eyes looked out from beneath an over-grown fringe reminding Tilly of an Old English sheepdog. She shook her head. 'I can't tell you that.'

Tilly was confounded. She'd thought she was helping a woman who had merely fallen on hard times, certainly not one in danger of her life. 'Have you been to the police?'

A fluttery shiver ran across Sybil's shoulders. 'That would only make things worse.'

Although it was still light, stars were beginning to appear in a sky of metallic blue. Another hour and it would be a deep shade of indigo. For now, the heavens looked like a silk coverlet, vast and unending.

'How can I help you?' Tilly finally asked.

Sybil shook her head dolefully. 'You can only help by not telling a soul.'

Tilly promised. Not around here anyway. It was a different matter when she was home in Coronation Close. Her mother would know what to do. She always knew the right thing to do.

17

Earlier than usual, Gloria had stormed out of the house without saying goodbye. Even after she'd left, an icy atmosphere remained.

The evening before Jenny had barely given her time to get through the front door before asking about the man she'd been seeing.

'And don't lie. You've been seen. Was that who you were with last Sunday in Clevedon?'

Cold surprise had been replaced by hot response. 'He's nice to me.'

'I know that all right.' She'd brought out the velvet box she'd found in the top drawer of her daughter's dressing table, opened it to expose the glittering bracelet. 'He gave you this?'

Gloria's eyes had fixed on the sparkling piece of jewellery. There was no excuse but instant retaliation. 'You've been snooping. My things are private.'

'I'm your mother. I've every right to know what's going on in your life. You're not yet twenty-one, Gloria, and until you are, you're my responsibility. Now!' She'd snapped the box shut. 'I want you to give it back to this man and promise me that you will never see him again.'

For a moment, Gloria had looked as though she would fall in with Jenny's wishes. Her interpretation proved wrong.

'No. I won't give him up.' Gloria had been adamant, jaw set, determination fixed on her features.

'Gloria, you're in danger of ruining your life. Men like him entice young girls like you – girls barely more than children – ruin them and move on.'

'No.' A vehement shaking of her head that sent her hair bouncing around her shoulders. 'No. He's not like that.'

Jenny had thrust the boxed bracelet at her. 'You will give this back and do as I say.'

Expression full of anger, Gloria had snatched it. Her manner remained defiant and then, for no reason that Jenny could make out, had softened. 'You'd like him if you met him. His name's Damien.'

'I don't care,' Jenny had said, determined she would not like him. He wasn't suitable. Any mother would be as worried as she was. Grabbing her daughter's shoulders, she gave her a good shake. 'You will do as I say. Is that clear?'

There was no way of reading Gloria's thoughts or of laying down the law and saying she couldn't go out. On that particular night she'd already arranged to wash her hair.

Jenny had worked the late matinee at the Broadway, all the time seething at this man who had too great an interest in her daughter. If she ever got to meet him, he'd get a piece of her mind.

When the lights went up, her gaze had swept over the audience, the comings and goings – more especially the coming in of new arrivals. Each time the doors at the top of the companionway opened, she'd studied the cluster of men and women coming in.

Just checking, that's what she told herself. Making sure the seating capacity could cope.

Seating capacity, my foot! You're looking for him, aren't you? You're looking for Charlie Talbot.

* * *

The letterbox at number two Coronation Close was made of cast iron so lacked the more pleasant rattle of brass. Rarely did it rattle at midday simply because Jenny Crawford received most correspondence in the first post. Not that she received that much anyway, except for official notices referring to making the most of rationing, watching what you said in your day-to-day life. The probability of a spy being in the queue for potatoes or the back row of the Broadway Picture House was absurd.

On this occasion, she could tell the letter in the envelope sitting like a snowy island in a sea of coconut matting was not of the patronising kind, telling you what to do.

A tickly feeling, too subtle to call electricity, flooded over her. Tilly. It had to be from Tilly. Nobody else wrote letters on white lined Basildon Bond and used a matching envelope.

'Slowly,' she said to herself whilst relishing the thought of reading her eldest daughter's latest news from the far-off county of Suffolk. 'Take your time. You've got all day to read it.'

Holding off opening it until she was curled up in a comfortable armchair with a cup of tea, she began to run her fingernail along the sealed envelope, pretending she would be patient. Halfway along, she stopped pretending and ripped it open.

The goings on at Merryweather Farm leapt off the page and Tilly's vivid descriptions took her there. She could imagine the farmer and his wife, the ongoing troop of land girls that were there for a time, then gone again. Reading about the mother and child Tilly had discovered living in a tumbledown cottage stirred her emotions. Tilly had always been a caring soul. Taking these people under her wing was so typical of her.

'My sweet girl,' Jenny whispered, and began to read.

Mum,

It's me again. The top drawer of the dresser must be filling up with my letters. I hope that you and Gloria are well. Does my sister still have many friends? She always was the centre of attention at school – or out of it, for that matter – and liked going out and socialising far more than I ever did. Does she have a boyfriend? Have you met him?

I've been to the pub with John Forester, the farmer's son. He's very nice and about three years older than me.

I'm looking forward to coming home for a break. It's busy here now, so the date keeps being put back. I can't possibly leave the Foresters in the lurch.

I'm very much looking forward to seeing you both. We have a lot to catch up on. Tell Gloria we can have a good chat and catch up with what's been going on for both of us. Do take care of yourself.

Your loving daughter, Tilly

Tears filling her eyes, Jenny stroked the neat handwriting with one finger. Would she always miss her daughter as much as she did now? Yes, of course she would.

She stared at the letter, deep in thought, reread it for the second and the third time. References to Gloria seemed to figure quite a lot. Tilly had barely mentioned it before, not surprising really. They were chalk and cheese, one a little reserved, one far more outgoing than her sister. *I wonder what they'll be like if they ever get to be mothers*? she thought. *Would they get closer as they got older, or drift apart*? She hoped the former. Either way, she very much hoped to see it happening, to see their children and...

Suddenly, something snapped inside. It hit her so hard that the hand holding the letter dropped to her side. The other hand covered her throat.

Most mothers wanted to see their children thrive, didn't they?

She knew she did. She wanted to be around for them for many years yet. She couldn't do that if she was dead. Her health mattered if she was to see her daughters' grow up. Her darling daughter had inadvertently set it out in black and white.

Ensuring she lived to see that future, Jenny snatched the mantle clock with both hands. It had stopped. Surely it had read eleven o'clock when she'd last heard it ticking. It was now early afternoon. Evening surgery started at five and went on until seven. She had plenty of time.

Gloria would be home at around six. *More haste means less speed*, she thought as she scribbled a note on a scrap of paper, instructing her to make her own supper. Should she say where she was gone? *No. Let's see how things developed.*

Once the beds were made and she'd left bread and cheese beneath a muslin dome, she had a quick wash, changed her clothes and checked how she looked in the mirror.

Do I walk or catch a bus? That was the main question as she hurried out of Coronation Close and onto Leinster Avenue. Within yards of the bus stop, she capped her hand over her eyes and looked along the length of the avenue. No sign of a bus.

There were few other vehicles on the road, mostly delivering essential supplies. A black lorry owned by a man named Mr

Short, who was far from short and delivered coal. A vegetable cart, a few people on bicycles. A single black car coming her way.

Pulling back her sleeve ostensibly to check the time on her watch proved a wasted effort. Like the clock on the mantelpiece, it had stopped. Another casualty of her worrying about something she finally had to deal with, she'd failed to wind it up.

The solitary car she'd seen approaching pulled up beside her. 'Can I offer you a lift?' A man had wound down the passenger door window. He was about her age, smartly dressed and had the most incredibly dark eyes.

Since the beginning of the war and petrol being short, it was common for those who could to offer lifts to those without recourse to that luxury. Even so, Jenny was wary. She'd heard rumours of men pushing their luck, counting on a woman being impressed by what they were offering and hoping to get something in return.

She began to shake her head. 'I don't think so...'

He jerked a thumb to somewhere behind him. 'The bus won't be coming. The driver's back there dealing with a puncture. Where you going anyway?'

The need to get to the doctor's surgery was very powerful – surprising, really, seeing as she'd put it off for so long.

Doctor Adrian Stoddart's surgery was away from the estate on Wells Road. It was a long walk or a short bus journey.

'Thank you, but no thank you.' She began to walk on, turning nervous when she realised he had not gone away.

She clutched her handbag nervously as she debated whether to get in. Getting a diagnosis from the doctor was more pressing than it had ever been. She wanted to live for her daughters, but the fact was that she didn't know this man.

'Are you Gloria Crawford's mother?' he said before she'd gone three steps.

His question brought her up short.

He got out of the car, left the door open and invited her to climb into the back. It was then that she noticed another man was driving. He didn't look at her, just kept his eyes straight ahead, his hands, a tattoo on each finger, resting on the wheel.

'Mrs Crawford. I'm not going to abduct or eat you. Come on. Get in.' He shook his head and smiled. 'Honestly. I'm just being polite. Your daughter would expect me to be.'

Was it against her better judgement that she climbed in? The funny thing was that she didn't feel afraid. Getting to the doctor's surgery, something she'd put off for a long time, was all that mattered.

The car pulled away from the kerb.

He'd made himself comfortable in the front passenger seat. Sitting in the back seat gave her the opportunity to study the back of his head. On occasion, she glimpsed him looking at her via the rear-view mirror.

A possibility began to descend. She asked him where he knew her daughter from.

His arm rested on the back of his seat. He turned round enough for her to see his dark features and a glint of gold in one tooth as he answered her.

'Work. I call into the place where she works. Her boss is one of my customers.'

His answer went only some of the way to make her relax.

'I see.'

He was the right age and looked prosperous. He was also handsome – everything in fact that Margaret Routledge had insinuated. This had to be the man. He was also around her own age, perhaps older.

It was only a short journey to the Wells Road, a broad thoroughfare and the historic route out of Bristol to Wells.

Any concerns she might have had that the two men were not genuine vanished when the car stopped outside the bay-windowed Edwardian dwelling where Doctor Stoddart practised medicine on the ground floor. He lived with his family on the first floor.

'Thank you,' she said as he helped her out of the car.

'My pleasure.' His hand was warm on hers, his touch surprisingly gentle. He tipped his hat in a gentlemanly manner.

She didn't look back to see if he was watching her. It was just a lift, one that had been much appreciated. That was what she told herself.

Her heart was in her mouth from the moment she entered the vestibule on the outside of the house. She disliked the smell and look of the place, the bland decor of dull cream and an insipid green that made her think the walls had been painted with stewed cabbage water.

There were only three people to see the doctor before her: a woman wearing a feathered hat that looked as if it might fly from her head at any moment, a man in uniform who did not look up when she entered, nervously feeling for a chair. The third patient was a young woman who was hanging on with two hands to a cardigan with straining buttons over a waistline expanding with early pregnancy.

Absorbed in themselves and whatever was wrong with them, they kept their eyes averted. Jenny didn't want to talk anyway, neither to tell them her problems nor for them to tell her theirs.

I've got this bunion. That's the complaint she imagined for the woman with the flyaway hat. There were a few probabilities for the young man in uniform whose right foot tapped continuously on the floor. Nerves. A wound that wasn't clearing up as quickly as it should. Or he could have a rash that he was ashamed of. He wouldn't be the first one she'd heard of. Sailors, soldiers and airmen all got lonely and in need of female company. It was only natural.

As for the young woman hugging the cardigan around her...

Jenny looked for a wedding ring on the girl's right hand. There was one, but that didn't necessarily mean it was made of gold. Brass curtain rings had the same look.

She told herself she was being uncharitable. There'd been no harm meant by attaching labels to these people. Guessing their problems helped her get outside of herself and not dwell on her own.

But she was here.

The waiting room was warm but still she felt cold. Soon she would know.

She recognised her own voice in her mind advising her how best to cope. *Pretend you're not here. Imagine you're somewhere else. A ballroom, the sand dunes along the Somerset coast, a dark and glossy night of no blackout, only moon and stars.*

A woman came out of the nut-brown door dividing the doctor's inner sanctum from the waiting room. She charged out as though she had somewhere important to go.

The doctor appeared. 'Next.'

The woman with the feathery hat rose to her feet. She had an aloof air, not once looking to right or left, her expression held strictly in check.

The soldier followed, then the pregnant young girl, still clasping her shabby-looking cardigan around her growing shame.

Then it was her turn.

For the first time since arriving, she felt an overwhelming urge to turn tail and run all the way home. But she didn't. Whether the outcome was bad or good, she had to face it.

Her inner advisor was still there, telling her what to do,

reminding her that she wanted to see her two daughters grow up. *Pretend you're somewhere else.*

Finally, the question she'd dreaded was asked. 'When did you first notice it?'

She found her voice. 'I think it was about two months ago.'

It was one of those things that attracted a lie, the reluctance to accept that it had been there any longer – which it had.

'And how old are you?'

'Forty-four.'

'Married?'

'Widowed.'

'How many children do you have?'

'Two.'

A few more questions and she was invited to go behind the screen and strip to her waist.

The fingers that examined her breast were cold. She stared over his shoulder as he explored the soft flesh and the unforgiving hard lump that had refused to go away.

At last it was over. 'Get dressed.'

His instruction was brief and blunt as he turned his back on her and returned to sit behind his desk.

Feeling numb and an object rather than a human being, she slipped gratefully behind the modesty screen. After putting on her brassiere, she slid her arms into the pale green cardigan, the last item of clothing she had cast off so Doctor Stoddart could examine her left breast.

The screen around her was of the same colour as her cardigan and only a shade lighter than the waiting room walls.

The sound of Doctor Stoddart clearing his throat came from the other side of the screen and filled her with fear. Not that he was saying anything – not yet.

When fully dressed, she let her hands fall to her side and

took a deep breath, readying herself to face the doctor and hear what he had to say. Count to ten, she said to herself. Count to ten and prepare yourself.

'If you're ready, Mrs Crawford.'

'Just about,' she called back. She wasn't ready to hear this. Fear was like a tall hedge that she needed to jump over – like a horse in a race.

'No need to rush. Take your time.'

She gritted her teeth. If there was no need to rush, why ask if she was ready?

She came out from behind the screen like a prima donna about to take a bow, her footsteps light and carefully placed.

Doctor Stoddart was behind his desk, head bent. She eyed his shiny skull which was dotted with freckles. He was writing something down. When he'd finished, he raised his head a little, his horn-rimmed spectacles close against his eyes.

'Take a seat, please.' Without looking up, he nodded at the wooden chair immediately opposite his own before he went back to his writing.

She noticed one ink-stained finger and wondered if it had been there when he'd examined her and had left a fingerprint on her body. Her breast. She shuddered on recalling his cold fingers feeling the outline of the lump. He'd termed its position as being at six o'clock, in a direct line beneath her left nipple.

He'd already asked her how long since she'd first noticed it and she'd lied. She wondered if lying about it could lead to serious consequences. She'd told him she'd first noticed it two months ago. It was more like nine months, but she hadn't been able to tell him that because he would want to know the reason she'd left it so long. A stupid reason of course. Life had got in the way. She'd been busy. She had a job. A family. All had contributed to denial, not wanting to admit there was anything wrong.

Logical enough, though now, with hindsight, her excuses sounded trite.

There was one big reason above all others. Fear.

She sat stiffly, waiting for him to say that things were not looking good, but praying otherwise.

His eyes were unblinking behind the thick lenses. 'Well now...'

His slowness in getting to the point – whether she would live or die – pained her.

'The lump needs investigating by a specialist at the hospital.'

Her heart sank.

He picked up his pen, proceeding to scratch something more on the pad immediately in front of him.

'I'm going to phone the hospital and arrange an appointment at the special clinic they hold for such ailments as this. Can you make it there for ten thirty tomorrow morning?'

She'd been dipped in ice-cold water – that's how it felt. She nodded. 'Yes.' The word stuck in her throat.

'You may have to wait a while to be seen, but once you've been seen by Mr Palin, the specialist, we'll know what we're dealing with, and a course of treatment can be planned.'

She nodded again. Her mouth was dry, but she managed to ask what the treatment would entail.

'That I cannot say. Mr Palin is the expert in such matters and is in a better position to tell you that once he has examined you. He can then give an informed opinion.'

'Right.' She smoothed her skirt with both hands. Not that it needed flattening. It was newly pressed, but her hands were damp with nervous perspiration. 'Tomorrow at ten thirty. Mr Palin.'

'Yes. Mr Palin. The William Budd wing.'

William Budd. The name kept going round and around in her mind like a funfair merry-go-round. William Budd wing. Mr Palin.

She sat silently. Small details easily digested. She was vaguely aware of Doctor Stoddart taking off his spectacles, eyeing her intensely but considerately.

'Mrs Crawford, do you have anyone you can confide in? In my experience, it helps to talk things over with someone. Your children perhaps?'

'I don't want to burden them. They're only young, with their whole lives ahead of them. I only hope I'm there to see them grow up.' Her sigh was shallow and heartfelt.

'I understand.' He placed his spectacles back on his nose. 'A friend perhaps?'

She took a deep breath. 'Yes.' She gave a light laugh. 'Perhaps I should give it a name rather than say I have a lump or a serious medical problem.'

The doctor smiled. 'You wouldn't be the first, and besides, talking about it is the best way of coping. Giving it a name comes under that category and, to some extent, makes it seem less threatening.'

No more was said. The doctor showed her out.

Her mind was hazy, her footsteps quick as she headed for the bus stop. The traffic on the Wells Road was its usual bustling self, vehicles of all shapes and sizes heading away or to the Tramway Centre – although there were no longer any trams, thanks to enemy bombing back in April.

The bus was only minutes in coming and, just for once, seats were available. She would not have to stand, which was just as well. Her legs were like jelly.

A black car passed the bus, a handsome vehicle amongst the

lorries, vans, buses and horse-drawn vehicles. She wasn't sure it was the same car she'd arrived in but caught only a fleeting glimpse of the occupants. It was hard to tell if it was the man who had offered her the lift, the man who knew her youngest daughter from work. If circumstances had allowed, she would have asked him outright, starting with his name... Oh drat! What was his name? She hadn't thought to ask.

Craning her neck, she watched as the car threaded on through the worsening traffic filing down the Wells Road to the city centre.

Being so distracted not to have asked his name was bad enough but something just as intriguing came to her, a fact that hadn't hit her until now.

She was positive that they had never met before, so how did he know she was Gloria's mother?

18

How did he know that I'm your mother? How did he recognise me?
Those were the questions hovering in Jenny's mind, although
there was another more important question hovering at the fore-
front of her mind. What would the outcome be tomorrow when
she attended the hospital? She forced herself to push it to one
side and instead concentrated on Gloria.

Just look at her, she thought, watching as the little minx
sashayed up the garden path as though she owned the world.
And home from work a little later than usual. Where had she
been?

The instant she'd taken her coat off and come through the
door of the living room, Jenny was ready for her, arms folded
and thunder hovering over her eyebrows.

'I want a word with you, young lady.'

One beautifully shaped eyebrow lifted as Gloria casually
took off her cardigan and flung it onto the couch.

'Is something wrong?' Her expression was petulant, lips flickering between a smirk and a smile.

'Yes.'

'Are you ill?'

Jenny ignored the question. That was something she'd answer on another occasion. 'No. I am not ill, although from what I hear about you, it's enough to make me ill.'

Gloria was not a fool. Jenny saw the sudden realisation on her daughter's heart-shaped face. Placidity turned to rebuke.

'If you're going to lecture me, I'm off out.' She twirled on the spot, the meagre material of her skirt swinging with the speed of her turning.

Jenny got between her and the living-room door. 'Oh no you don't! Not until you've explained yourself.'

Rarely had Gloria seen her mother look so angry and knew she was in a scrape. She chose to hedge her bets, unsure of just how much more did her mother know? She knew a bit, but not everything.

'Mum.' Without a trace of shame, she placed one painted fingernail on her cheek, which riled her mother because it looked as though she was the adult and Jenny the one who was somehow in the wrong. 'I don't know what I could have done to bring this on. I go out, I enjoy myself – whilst I still can. You should do the same, Mum. Kick up your legs and live a little. After all, you don't look your age and there are plenty of men who might find you attractive. You might as well. Let's face it, Robin isn't going to reappear. No doubt gone on to pastures new, and believe me, there's a lot of pastures out there in need of ploughing...'

The blow from Jenny's right hand landed on her cheek. Gloria's jaw dropped. She laid the palm of her right hand onto her reddening cheek.

'This isn't about the war,' hissed her mother. 'We've already had this conversation. It's about you galivanting with a dangerous man. It's about you going into the fleshpots with him.'

Although her face smarted, Gloria maintained an openly defiant expression. 'Was that because I said you could still get yourself a bloke even though you're getting on in years.'

'You little minx...' Jenny raised her hand again.

Gloria flinched and crossed her arms in front of her face so no blow could land.

The look on her daughter's face chilled Jenny to the bone. Never had she seen such an angry and defiant look on her child's face. But that was it. The child that had been was no more. She'd grown up. The confident little girl had become a young woman, and her childish confidence had fed into a very adult independence.

'This man...'

'The one you think is dangerous. The one I won't give up,' said Gloria with a noticeable smirk.

'He gave me a lift this evening. I had no idea who he was but was surprised when he said he knew you. Even more so that he knew who I was, what I looked like. How did he know that?'

All semblance of arrogance left Gloria's face, replaced by disbelief. 'He gave you a lift?' Her daughter looked dumbfounded. 'He can't have done.'

'Why couldn't he?'

'Because I told him not to come around here...' The dumbfounded look remained fixed on her face.

'And he always does what you say?'

'For the most part. He loves me.'

Jenny shook her head soulfully. 'You stupid girl.'

Gloria hid her dismay behind a blank expression.

Jenny pressed the question to which she required an answer. 'How did he recognise me?'

The possibilities were chilling. Of course, she had no real reason to think that he'd been watching the house or following her. But what with everything else happening now, what might have been molehills were looking like mountains. She needed some kind of response that might ease her mind.

Gloria shrugged.

Jenny thought carefully about it and repeated what she'd already intimated. 'He knew who I was, yet I've never met him.'

Her daughter's blank look was replaced with one of guilt. A slight crease floated on her brow, then was gone again.

'I don't know.'

Gloria touched her red cheek, prodding at it as though she was torturing herself. Her gaze went to the rag rug in front of the fireplace and from there to the mantelpiece, a drawing of Jenny in a simple wooden frame.

'I showed him the photo I copied for that drawing.'

Both of her daughters were good at drawing. Tilly no longer drew, but to her great pleasure, Gloria had carried on. Only a few months ago, she'd sketched her mother lying full length on the sofa, one hand supporting her head. It had been a good representation. Both mother and daughter had been fond of it. And now it took pride of place on the mantelpiece, though slightly adrift from where it had been positioned.

'You were showing off.'

She nodded. 'Yes. He says I'm clever.'

'So that was how he recognised me, but then it still begs the question, what was he doing here?'

There was one obvious answer that made both mother and daughter feel uncomfortable.

'Looking for me, I suppose,' Gloria said softly.

'Has he done that before?'

'No.'

'No,' Jenny repeated. 'You meet regularly. He must know you

would be at work. There has to be another reason. What is it? Do you know?'

Gloria folded her arms and shrugged in such a way that squared her shoulders.

Margaret had said that he was a bad lot, a dangerous man to know. Jenny had seen herself that, although he'd been overly courteous, he had a lot of swagger about him. Clothes maketh the man – or might do. Just because he wore good clothes and travelled round in a car didn't mean his income was legally gained. Overall, his appearance and manner made her think 'spiv', black market.

Criminals involved in the black market secured stolen goods for resale. Their best sources were those stacked up in government facilities, tons of consumables, food, weapons and anything else that could be stolen and sold on. If she was right, the only place round here where large quantities of logistics were stored was the airport.

'Is he involved in the black market?'

'Of course not!' Gloria tossed her head as though the very idea of it was quite ridiculous. The blush that lit her face smothered any pretence of innocence.

It did no good to try to soothe the ache she felt in her head by rubbing it with one hand. Jenny shook her head despairingly. 'Gloria, my girl, you think you're a woman, but you really are still a child. Men and women who patronise the Hatchet are out of a certain mould and from what I've heard, they certainly don't work for a living. Not an honest living anyway.'

'He's a businessman.' Gloria looked at her mother as though she didn't know what she was talking about. 'He used to come into the office and chat with my boss. They did business together.'

'What sort of business?'

'Just... business!'

'The firm you work for makes gaskets, but that doesn't mean that him and your boss weren't involved in other business.'

'Don't be ridiculous!'

If tears could fall inside, then Jenny would be shedding them, and a whole variety of tears they would be. Tears of frustration, tears of disappointment, but also of anger.

It was only a passing change in Gloria's expression, but Jenny thought she'd seen misgiving creeping in.

Gloria's customary defiance returned. 'Oh, for goodness' sake! You think he's up here thieving, don't you. What do you think he was doing? Robbing the Co-op in Melvin Square, the Broadway Picture House? One of the shops or the pub?'

Taken aback at the ferocity of her daughter's outburst, Jenny shook her head. 'No. He didn't strike me as the type of man likely to go into a shop, not even to rob it.'

'I'm off out. A quick wash and I'm off.' She grabbed the handle of the living-room door and jerked it open, then stood there, her face leaning against it. 'Unless you've got anything else to say to me.'

There was the option to say yes, ask her to sit down and tell her about going to the doctor and the hospital appointment, the worry she'd been keeping deep inside. The occasion was fleeting, and besides, there had been enough upset for one night.

Tomorrow, she thought, her head bowed. *Tomorrow after I've seen the specialist.*

19

A cooling breeze was blowing through Coronation Close. Jenny leaned over the garden gate relishing the coolness diminishing the red flush of anger from her cheeks.

Of course, she knew that her anger was allied with fear. Yes, she feared for the consequences of her daughter's behaviour, but she also feared for herself and the appointment tomorrow morning. Despair weighed her down. She needed someone to confide in.

She looked across at number twelve Coronation Close, but it stared back at her empty and without her dear friend and neighbour, Thelma Dawson. Bertrams was almost like a second home to Thelma. Jenny could understand that. It gave her life purpose, something more than just family who, of course, were growing up fast.

A bus filled the gap at the end of Coronation Close, most likely the number four which ran between the end of Leinster Avenue and Brislington. It had stopped for someone to get off. Probably someone coming home from work. She waited to see who it was.

Once it was gone, Annie Davis, the ginger-haired woman who manned the ticket office up at the Broadway Picture House, came trotting into the end of the Close, three children of varying ages trotting along behind her. Like a mother duck with her ducklings, all in a row.

Annie waved.

Inwardly groaning, Jenny hardened her heart to what she was likely to say. The most likely was that someone had dropped out tonight and they needed an usherette to accompany people to their seats.

She primed herself to refuse even before the question was asked. 'Annie, I know what you're going to say, but I can't. I've got to...' She searched her mind for a suitable excuse but couldn't come up with one. Her attention was drawn to the ragbag trio of children. One of the kids was stuffing the last of a sugar sandwich into his mouth. Once his cheeks were bulging, he wiped his sticky hands down his mother's skirt.

'Don't do that, Arnold.' She clipped him around the ear before turning back to Jenny and filling her in on why she was there. 'It's nothing like that, me lover. We're covered for tonight. It's just that an old friend of yours came into the Broadway and asked if I could deliver you a message. Well, he said he was an old friend. I was out with my kids 'aving a picnic and thought I'd call in at the picture 'ouse and check the till were all in order ready for tonight. Plenty of sixpences and pennies and all that. Everyone seems to have half-crowns, and two-shilling pieces nowadays and then want change. Best to be prepared.' She looked pleased with herself, as though it was the wisest thing anyone had ever uttered. 'Anyway, whilst I was there, this bloke came in. Nicely dressed bloke. Good-looking – for 'is age. Looked as though 'e 'ad a gammy leg. Anyway, Gert was on the kiosk today. He asked her if you were around. Gert told 'im she didn't know, so seeing as I overheard, I stepped in and told 'im you wouldn't be on until tomorrow afternoon. Looked dead disappointed 'e did. Then he asked if I could give you a message. I told 'im to come in tomorrow, but he said 'e couldn't do that. Had important work to do. So I said I could deliver a message to you from me own mouth – if he'd like to cover the cost of me bus fare. Me and the kids that is. A nice little outing for them. That's what I said to 'im. So he did.'

Jenny felt a strong urge to give Annie a shake, anything that would get her to the point of her visit. 'So you've brought me the note?'

'That I did. Like I said to 'im, I weren't really going that way so I 'ad to 'ave money for the fare.' An impish look came to her face. 'As it turned out, me luck was in. My old man, Tom, was driving the number ten down and offered me and the kids a free ride. So dropped us off. I'll cadge a ride on the next one going back up. So bringing you this message didn't cost me nothing. And it gave the kids an hour out.' Annie beamed at her good fortune whilst her children poked and pushed each other in some kind of game.

'He wrote it on a bit of paper. There you are.'

Her ginger hair crimped around her head like a close-fitting cap, Annie handed her what looked like a page torn from the bottom of a letter where the words hadn't gone more than two-thirds of the way down. Perhaps the writer hadn't found enough words, thought Jenny. Whatever the reason, the edge was ragged as though it had been torn off in a hurry.

Jenny unfolded the note, her eyes skimming what was written.

Jenny. I'll wait for you outside the Broadway tomorrow at six o'clock. Charlie.

She sucked in her breath. Short and to the point. Guessing that Annie would read it, he had not included any terms of endearment. Yet Jenny fancied she could hear them in her head.

'He asked what time you're working tomorrow night. 'Ope I weren't speaking out of order, but I thought there was no 'arm in telling 'im.' She craned her neck to peer closer and see what was said. 'Anything important, is it? I mean, is he... you know...'

'No. Just an old friend who was injured when he was in the RAF. I think he wants to invite me to his wedding.'

'Oh.' Annie looked quite dejected that nothing salacious was divulged. Jenny would not have told her if there had been. Annie could spread gossip faster than the BBC could broadcast the news.

Jenny turned back towards her front door. 'Thank you for bringing it.'

Shepherding her brood with a few clouts and shoves, Annie called out, 'What do you think happened next?'

One foot on the concrete doorstep, Jenny paused. She couldn't think Annie would have anything else to say, anything she would be interested in. 'I couldn't imagine,' she replied. It crossed her mind that Annie was well suited to meeting, greeting and taking money at the box office up at the picture house. She knew everybody's name and their business.

'Then I saw Thelma. She's stood up there on Leinster Avenue looking as though she'd picked up a farthing and lost a five-pound note. I asked her what was wrong, and she said she was thinking of going up the Venture Inn for a drink. All by 'erself too.'

Jenny was instantly alert. It wasn't like Thelma to think of going into the Venture Inn – or any other pub – by herself.

'Are you sure it was her?'

'Of course I am. I spoke to her. Asked if she was looking for company – you know. A man. But she said her man was away fighting and she didn't mess around. I did ask 'er about that Dutch bloke she bin seeing...'

'And she told you to mind your own business.'

Annie looked affronted. 'I was only being friendly. It's nothing to me if she wants a bit of company. Not necessarily a bloke, just someone to talk to. Not that I know for sure, that is, but you can tell when somebody's dwelling on something.'

Jenny jerked upright, the suddenness of her movement making Annie stop short with her chattering. 'Are you sure about that?'

'Thelma going to the pub? That's what she told me.' Annie lingered. Perhaps she was expecting a cup of tea. Jenny dare not invite her in. Over tea Annie would fix her with those piggy little eyes and press her about the smart-looking man who spoke like a gentleman.

Turning her back on Annie and her scruffy children, Jenny closed the gaping front door. It might seem rude, but it had to be done. She had no intention of giving answers to Annie's prying questions.

The smell of supper drifted out to her and reminded her to turn off the oven. Once that was done, she brushed her hair, applied a little lipstick and headed out.

It was a short walk to Melvin Square and the pub, a large brick building, the handsomest in the square. On the way there, she found herself taking in her surroundings more thoroughly. Facing one's own mortality did that. She'd read it somewhere, although she couldn't think where. For a start, the sky seemed bluer, the red brick of the houses she passed brighter than usual. Flowers flooded front gardens with a riot of colour. Even her sense of smell seemed intensified: a mixture of garden scents of course, but also the smell of cooking. People were gossiping at their garden gates, children playing in the street.

A man wearing overalls passed her and wished her good evening. She returned the greeting and did not recoil at his smell of oil and sweat. Two children were turning a skipping rope for a little girl in a patched dress and worn Clarks sandals. There was a sweetness to the smell of children, likely because one of them – or perhaps all of them – had lately eaten something sweet and filling, like rhubarb and custard.

Her stomach rumbled, reminding her that she'd not eaten before coming out.

'Never mind. Never mind.'

Meeting up with Thelma was more important than her grumbling stomach. She imagined her friend standing at the bar with half a shandy, or something stronger. For her part, it would have to be something stronger. There were so many things she needed to talk over with her friend, her very dear friend.

From their very first meeting, she and Thelma had shared confidences, concerns and pots of tea – rather weak tea since the war had started. Tonight, she would share with Thelma the reason she was going to the hospital tomorrow. A problem shared is a problem halved, that's what they said, didn't they?

Then there was Gloria. Both had daughters so tended to share the same concerns.

And finally there was Charlie Talbot. Should she bother to tell her that she'd received a note from him, that he wanted to meet up with her? She'd already told Thelma that she'd seen him. No doubt a warning would be forthcoming. Thelma was nothing if not level-headed. A wise old owl who had lived and loved and risen above whatever people thought of her.

The Venture Inn dominated one end of Melvin Square, sitting on a corner dividing Leinster Avenue from Clonmel

Road. It was a huge brick-built place complete with dart boards and a skittle alley. There was even an area outside where kids could sip lemonade and eat crisps whilst waiting for their parents to come out. There were a few there already, dried snot between their nostrils and their mouths, knees caked in dirt and dried blood, one sock up, one down, clothes patched and worn.

'Penny for the guy, missus?'

'Guy Fawkes night isn't until November the fifth.' She was tempted to spit into the dirty palm held out to her but couldn't help but admire his cheek. 'Here's a farthing.'

The boy looked at it disdainfully. 'That ain't much. Next to nothing.'

'Your guy is next to nothing. In fact, you don't have one, unless he's the invisible man. But if you don't want it...' She held out her open palm.

The boy closed his fist over the lowly coin and pocketed it quickly.

Jenny pushed open one of the heavy double doors, dimpled glass patched over with sticky tape set in dark wooden frames. In peacetime, the colours of the glass had shed streaks of colour over the dark floorboards. In a wartime bombing raid, the sticky tape prevented injury from flying glass.

Thelma was at the bar and just about to raise a glass to her lips. Not half a shandy, Jenny noticed, but a clear liquid that she guessed was gin.

Oh dear, she thought. *Things must be bad.*

'Thelma?'

Dark eyes widened and, unusually for Thelma, there was no sign of a smile. A questioning look piqued the dark eyebrows as though resenting her sudden intrusion.

'I didn't expect to see you in here, Thelma.'

'Jenny Crawford, you're fibbing. You saw Annie Banks and she told you. Right?'

'She insisted on telling me.'

'I bet she did,' Thelma grumbled. 'That woman spreads gossip quicker than the *Daily Express*.' She took a swig of her drink.

'Gin?' asked Jenny.

'You bet it is.' She sounded grumpy.

How often had she known Thelma to be prickly? Not often and there was no point on dwelling on it. It was the reasons that mattered. Jenny prepared herself to ask what was wrong, why she was there, but Thelma got there first.

'I've got lots to think about. It's been a long day. I got off the bus and couldn't face going home to an empty house where all I would do was worry about the things that...' She took a sip of gin as she searched for what she wanted to say. 'Things that I can't help but worry about.'

The war, thought Jenny. Most of what they had to worry about was war driven. Personal relationships would have been different if it hadn't been for the war. Thelma might have married Bert Throgmorton, and Jenny might have married Robin, though, of course, his wife was an obstacle to that.

Jenny was about to ask the landlady for a glass of shandy, but if Thelma needed something stronger, so too did she.

'Gin isn't usually your tipple,' she remarked, raising a quizzical eyebrow.

'I need it,' Thelma said in the same grumpy manner.

Jenny ordered the same.

It was natural for two women in a pub to gravitate to a corner table away from the more crowded area where men hogged the bar to the extent that made women feel unwelcome.

The legs of the wooden chairs scraped the bare floorboards

as they pushed them back from a small round table stained from years of spilt beer.

'I'd say cheers, but you don't look as though you've got anything to be cheerful about,' remarked Jenny.

Thelma lowered her eyes and sucked in her ruby-red lips before taking a sip of clear London gin.

'I'm waiting to make a phone call.'

Her red fingernails were like blood spots against the glass.

'You're waiting to make a phone call?'

'Yes. I can't phone until seven o'clock, so I'm killing time.'

Jenny pointed out that there was a phone box on the other side of Melvin Square.

'I know. Did you notice how many people are waiting to use it?'

Jenny said that she did – and for obvious reasons. Husbands and sons were away serving, their families left behind to worry about them. Although it needed a constant supply of pennies, the heavy black telephone in the red telephone box was quicker than a letter. Not only that, but it could bring tears to the eyes of a loving wife or mother to hear a real voice. Hearing the real person wrenched the heartstrings because it was true confirmation that their beloved was still alive.

'His message was that I should ring at seven o'clock.'

Jenny knew without being told that she meant Peter. It could only be Peter.

'His number here, in England I mean, the place where he's stationed?'

Thelma nodded.

Peter van Luntzen had been stationed in a security capacity at the airport down the end of Leinster Avenue at Whitchurch. Just a few months ago, he had applied for a transfer to an active unit. 'There are more important things to do once the invasion happens.' That's what he'd told Thelma. Knowing what he'd meant had turned her blood cold. He wanted to be there, in his country, getting involved from the inside, doing everything possible to aggravate the occupying forces. Blowing up trains, bridges – even people.

She held the glass with both hands, her eyes flickering between the unfinished drink and Jenny. 'Much as I wanted him to stay local, he couldn't do that. He's not the sort. He has to feel that he's contributing to freeing his country from occupation.' She looked around her at the dark wood and flock wallpaper of an ordinary English pub. 'Sitting here it's hard to imagine the battles going on. All those young men living out their youth – or at least part of it – trying to kill other young men. Not that Peter is a young man.' She laughed lightly. 'Not that age matters much. Dead is what matters. And Peter is over there, and if I know him, he's right in the bloody thick of it.'

'Oh, Thelma.' Although Jenny was eaten up with her own fears and concerns, there was enough of her left to have empathy with her friend. She said, 'Peter can take care of himself. He's been through some pretty tough times. Remember this was the man who escaped from Holland with the enemy breathing down his neck. But he got out, him and the air force he served in. Didn't he bring the Queen of the Netherlands with him?'

Thelma smiled when reminded of the memory. 'There's a telegram on its way from wherever he is. He's sent it through official channels, so it will get to me more quickly. It *must* be at seven.'

Her emphasis on the time left Jenny in no doubt how imperative it was that she received that message. 'I see.'

'Because of what's happening, call times are allotted.'

Jenny brightened. 'Well, that's good, isn't it? Presuming he's all right.' She paused as the most dreadful thought clouded her mind. 'He is all right – isn't he?'

Thelma nodded. 'Yes. As far as I know. We devised a code. If he refers to coming home that means he's in Holland. He wants to confirm a few things we discussed before he went away.'

'Nice things?'

Thelma blushed. 'Yes.'

'That's wonderful. So why the long face?'

Thelma paused before taking another gulp of London gin. This time, her face was slightly pink. Jenny guessed it was nothing to do with the gin.

'In the last telegram, he asked me if I've got the dress.' Her eyes smiled, but only for a moment. There was also a hesitant wariness, as though she was fearful of looking foolish. 'He means a wedding dress.'

'That's wonderful!' Jenny's exuberant exclamation faded into concern. 'You're not having second thoughts are you? He has hinted in the past that marriage was on the cards.'

Thelma nodded. 'Yes. He has, but...' Thelma's hand reached out for Jenny's, not in a gentle pat, but an anxious grip that scrunched her fingers together. 'I've lied to him. I told him that I was a widow. That my first husband died back in the Great War and then my second husband died at sea.' Her eyelids fluttered nervously, and alarm tautened her face, unlined even at her age, a couple of years older than Jenny. 'He won't want to marry me if he finds out that I've never married, that my children are...' She bit her bottom lip to stop herself uttering the informal and more vulgar word for children born outside marriage. 'I love my kids,' she finally exclaimed. Now her eyes were blazing in that ferocious way that all mothers of all species blazed when their offspring were threatened.

Jenny nodded. 'I know you do.' She felt Thelma's anguish

and knew for sure that Thelma loved this man and that her heart would break if she lost him.

Coming here she'd resolved to tell Thelma about tomorrow's hospital appointment. Hearing Thelma voicing her concerns about Peter held her own fears back, slotted into another time when it might be more convenient. There she was worrying about what might be something totally innocent for which there was treatment. Thelma, on the other hand, was worrying about the man she loved – the man who might or might not get through the bloodiest war in history.

She sighed, resolved to keep her own problems to herself and instead impart advice to a friend in need.

'First,' she said as light-heartedly as she could manage, 'we'll have another gin. Drink up. A problem shared is a problem halved.'

Two more drinks were ordered, the fiery liquid helping give eloquence to Jenny's simple words.

'It's not the drink talking, but I truly believe that Peter is a good man and won't have any problems accepting your past. It's water under the bridge. I've seen the way he looks at you. I'm convinced it won't make any difference to him.'

A calmer expression replaced the anxiety that had paled Thelma's face to a waxy whiteness that showed despite a generous application of face powder. 'I hope you're right.'

'I mean it. His eyes follow you around all the time.'

It was something of a relief to see a bashful smile come to Thelma's face. Jenny had never known her be bashful.

Recognising signs of recovery – and hope – Jenny continued.

'I don't think you have a problem. He adores you, and besides, didn't he tell you that you reminded him of his wife?'

'He did.' Thelma ran her finger around the top of her glass. 'One time he said that we were like a pair of lifeboats lost at sea

– just waiting to collide in all those miles of ocean. And we have.'

Thelma's tension was still there but lighter when they came out of the pub half an hour later. A quick glance across the green confirmed there was still a queue at the telephone box on the other side of the square. Jenny suggested that she use the one at the end of Leinster Avenue.

'It's not so central, so might not be so busy.'

They walked briskly back, Thelma with her head held high, Jenny contemplating when she might at last share her own concerns with her friend.

Her assumption about the telephone box proved correct. Nobody was waiting.

She checked her watch. It was almost seven.

Sensing that Thelma wanted to be alone, Jenny said she would leave her to it. As a parting shot, she gave her arm a squeeze.

'See you later.'

Thelma smiled and brought out a handful of copper pennies from her handbag.

Jenny didn't look back, and Thelma would not have noticed if she had.

Heart beating thirteen to the dozen, she tugged open the heavy door of the phone box. Once it was shut tightly behind her, she fixed her eyes on her wristwatch and waited. Were those tiny hands moving or had her watch stopped?

'No matter what happens. Be there at nineteen hundred hours.' Those were the instructions in the telegram he'd sent direct to her.

Seven o'clock. Seven p.m. That's what he meant.

During the last few weeks, she'd ached for him to get in touch: phone, telegram, letter or, most wonderful of all, in person. There had been something distant about him before that, not exactly nervous but most certainly apprehensive. It had taken a lot of persuasion to get to the reason why. It had been hard to refrain from telling him that he might be too old to carry out acts of sabotage and suchlike. He had his pride and was hurt. His country had been invaded. How could she possibly feel what he was feeling.

Tonight, they'd stick to the basics.

So here she was, feeling like a girl again as she waited to hear his voice.

As the little hand ticked on, Thelma counted the seconds before the due time for her to ring.

Five, four, three, two...

She barely gave the watch chance to reach three but pounced on the phone, the pennies clanging into the box, the nervous waiting until the call was connected.

'Peter!'

Her joy made her feel as though she was floating above the floor in the tiny phone box where there was little room except for her and the phone sitting squatly on its metal table.

'Sorry. It is not Peter. This is Erik. He may have mentioned me?'

Her heart sank. It could mean only one thing.

'I take it he can't phone me.'

'I'm afraid not.'

'He's abroad?'

'I cannot possibly comment. He said to expect a telegram but also told me to speak with you if he could not.'

'He's abroad.' Her repeated comment was muted.

'I have a telegram from him. Through secure channels. He said it would be quicker than sending it direct to you, that I should read it out to you before sending it on.'

'Please don't keep me waiting any longer. What does it say?'
She immediately regretted her impatience, but her disappointment was hard to handle.

Erik was quick in responding. 'He says to tell you that he is
almost home.'

There was crackling on the line, a sure sign that even Erik
was phoning from a distance on a military phone connection,
though in this country.

'Say it again.'

'He says that he is alive and well and just a few miles from
home.'

She knew he didn't mean home with her in England. Home
meant Holland. He'd reached his own country, the one he'd lived
in before escaping to England bringing contingents of the Dutch
air force with him.

'There's another bit. Another question he asks.'

'Go on. Tell me what it is.'

'He's asked the question before. Have you got your dress yet?'

'Dress?'

Her heart missed a beat. She knew very well what kind of
dress he meant. A wedding dress.

'You know what he means?'

She breathed her response into the phone. 'Yes. I know what
he means. It's a subject he won't let drop. Thank you, Erik.
Thank you for letting me know.'

'I will send the telegram on to you.'

'Yes. Please do that.'

Once the telephone was returned to its cradle, the interior of
the phone box turned extremely cold. Marriage had been
suggested from early on in their relationship. Peter had lost his
family when the enemy had bombed and then invaded the Low
Countries. He'd escaped and landed on her doorstep. Never in

her wildest dreams had she expected to fall in love, especially at her age. The thought of finally becoming a married woman was thrilling, but she feared whether the dream would come true.

Letting the door of the phone box shut heavily behind her, she hardly noticed a woman waiting to use the phone not until she complained about the door trapping her foot.

Absorbed in private concerns, Thelma failed to apologise.

'You trapped my foot.'

Not really taking it on board, Thelma stared at her. 'What? Is there a problem?'

The woman's face folded into itself like a punctured football. 'Typical of the likes of the women of Coronation Close,' shouted the woman, determined to have some kind of retribution for her injury. 'Coronation Close is like a bloody great rowing boat – oars on both sides.'

Thelma knew she meant whores but would not be drawn. She had more important worries than this woman and her bloody foot!

* * *

Jenny heard the 'yoohoo' from the back door and knew it was Thelma.

It was hard to tell from her face if things had worked out, so she asked.

Hand on her chest and breathing a sigh of relief, Thelma nodded. 'Yes. It's exactly as I thought. He's in Holland.'

Jenny was about to say that it was good but stopped herself. Instead, she said, 'At least you know where he is.'

'I've got a spot of sherry left over at my place.'

Jenny shook her head. 'Not tonight, thanks. I've got a load of ironing to do.'

It wasn't true. She had a yearning to be alone, to prepare herself for the hospital appointment tomorrow morning.

'Just as well,' said Thelma, sounding less than triumphant.

Jenny lit the gas beneath one of two irons. Each in turn would be heated, one replacing the other once it had cooled.

Perhaps she was taking too seriously an interest in the ironing because Thelma lingered at the door and asked if anything was wrong.

She could have told her there and then but chickened out. Not yet. Not until after tomorrow.

To add authenticity, Jenny laughed. 'I was just thinking that it won't be long and you'll be Mrs Peter van Luntzen and I'll be dancing at your wedding.'

Thelma brushed off the idea with a dismissive wave of her hand.

Once she'd gone, Jenny leaned over the pile of bedding spread over the kitchen table. She was happy for Thelma and truly believed the wedding would go ahead. As for her dancing on that great day, *well, let's wait and see what tomorrow brings*, she said to herself.

She looked at the headlines in the newspaper. War, war everywhere.

Tobruk Hanging On

'Let's hope they do hang on,' she said out loud. 'Here's to the future.' *And that,* she thought, as the darkness closed around her, *includes tomorrow morning. If I get through that, I can get through anything.*

20

Gloria eyed her reflection in the dressing-table mirror. Her eyes, the colour and shape inherited from her father, sparkled with excitement. Not the excitement that they held when she was looking forward to a night out with Damien, but one that smacked of courage. That was what was called for. She'd had one run-in with her mother about the man who made her feel like a film star but knew it wouldn't end there.

Last night, he'd told her about giving her mother a lift before she had chance to ask him what he'd been doing in Leinster Avenue.

'I gave her a lift to the doctor's. All right is she? Only she seemed a bit nervy, though only natural, I suppose, seeing as she was going to the doctor's. Never know what they're going to tell you.'

'Yeah. She's fine.'

Her cheery smile hid her sudden alarm. All day in work, she thought about what he'd said and began to worry that it might be something serious.

But surely, her mother would have told her if it was serious.

It wouldn't hurt to ask.

Her mother's response was to sneeze noisily into a cotton handkerchief.

'I've had a rotten cold. Nothing seems to shift it.'

And that was that. Gloria, wrapped up in her own life, readily accepted her mother's excuse.

Damien had suggested she moved in with him and that, she'd decided, was exactly what she intended to do. Twenty-one was the age of majority when you could make up your own mind about getting married or leaving home. Practicalities went out of her head in favour of falling in with anything Damien wanted.

He hadn't mentioned marriage, but to her mind that was what he meant and, anyway, it was what she wanted.

'When?' she'd asked eagerly. 'Tomorrow? Next week?'

'One step at a time,' he'd said to her.

In her mind, she rehearsed telling her mother she was moving out that very week, only curtailed by Damien's insistence that she was patient. He'd rolled his huge shoulders and smiled in a way that made her feel that just by reading her face he knew her secrets. He couldn't of course, because quite frankly she didn't really have any secrets, but that was a fact she kept buried. Admitting to having no secrets gave the impression that she hadn't lived long enough to have secrets. She didn't want to admit that, even to herself.

The smell of fried bread came wafting up the stairs. She would have preferred just plain toast and butter. Butter was on ration, but thanks to Damien, she'd given her mother half a pound this week. Her mother's eyes had flickered with suspicion, and although she could make use of it, there'd been a hesitant stiffening of her features.

'Make the most of it, Mum. It was free.'

She checked the time on the pretty watch Damien had given

her. It was quite ornate, made of marcasite and studded with what looked like diamonds. They were probably only rhinestones, but it didn't matter. Nobody she knew had a watch like it.

She scurried down the stairs, the sound of her thudding footsteps in time with her heart.

It was something of a surprise to see two slices of buttered toast awaiting her on one plate and a slice of fried bread on the other.

Her mother was standing with folded arms looking out of the kitchen window, her back facing her.

'Oh. You decided the butter wasn't poisoned,' Gloria said jokingly, but her mother didn't respond. 'Is something wrong?'

'Wrong?' Her mother looked surprised at being asked the question. 'Why should anything be wrong?'

'Sorry I spoke.'

She'd expected a rebuke, but her mother gave every sign of being preoccupied with other thoughts.

Still wondering, Gloria kept her eyes on her mother's back and bit into the toast joyfully letting the butter run down her chin, even though it took a rivulet of lipstick with it.

One piece of toast finished, she prepared to assault the second piece. Lunchtime was a long way off and sandwiches were boring. More bread. Possibly fish paste.

She glimpsed the slice of fried bread. There was a fair chance she would eat that too. Such a feast gave her courage for what she intended to say next.

'Don't go shouting at me, but tonight I'm off out again with...'

Damien's name remained unsaid. Her mother's shoulders were shaking and faintly, ever so faintly, came the sound of restrained sobbing.

'Mum? What's wrong?'

Fried bread left to congeal, Gloria got up from the table and looked up into her mother's face.

Her mother shook her head.

Gloria frowned and wondering what her mother was looking at, let her gaze wander out of the kitchen window. 'Is it something in the garden?'

It was a stupid question, but she'd never known her mother to be tearful these days. Her eyes continued to search for something in the back garden that might have upset her. There was nothing except the old apple tree beneath which she and her sister had played as children. In that long-ago summer, they had spent all day out there, although she had always been the one to leave playing on hearing her father arrive home. My, but he'd been a handsome man. Tall and strong, especially in his black uniform. That was before he'd joined the army and wore a different uniform.

It had been a long time since she'd thought of her father. Perhaps it was the similarity between him and Damien: his physique, the smell of him standing ramrod straight in his black shirt and trousers, thick leather belt at his waist. She'd loved him so much and been truly proud of him.

Her mother had blanched when she'd once remarked what a wonderful man he'd been, and Gloria had preferred not to remember anything bad about him. Her attempts were not always successful. If she delved deep enough into the memories, she recalled her mother crying. The arguments. The sound of smashing dishes.

Gently, for fear of making her jump, she touched her mother's shoulder. 'Mum?'

Jenny half turned, wiping the end of the tea towel across eyelashes that held a sprinkling of tears.

Alarmed, Gloria frowned. 'What is it? What's wrong?' All

thoughts of telling her she would continue seeing Damien and would dare to move in with him flew from her mind. Determined as she was to declare her future, she could not ignore her mother's tears. In fact, she tried to recall the last time she'd seen her crying but couldn't quite bring it to mind. Unless she went back to living in the medieval slum that was Blue Bowl Alley. She'd seen her cry then. Seen the bruised face, the blacked eye and the way she'd cowered away from her father, the father Gloria had loved.

'Nothing. It's nothing.' Jenny sniffed and rubbed her nostrils on the back of her hand. She even attempted a wan smile. 'Just thinking of you two growing up and me getting older.'

Gloria couldn't help heaving a sigh of relief. 'Is that all? What's the point of that? You can't stop us growing up.'

She said it with the confidence of a young woman who couldn't wait to attain the age of twenty-one and everything that came with it.

'Oh, Mother,' said Gloria, not without exasperation. 'You are silly at times. We must all grow up. We must all move on. Anyway, just think of the future, you and Auntie Thelma cuddling grandchildren. That's something to look forward to, isn't it?'

Gloria fully accepted that she was awkward with her mother, that Tilly had always been the preferred daughter – at least as far as their mother was concerned. Tilly had been close to her mother, whereas Gloria had been the apple of her father's eye.

She did as she'd seen others do, rubbing her hands over her mother's shoulders, telling her everything was going to be all right.

Satisfied that her mother's tears had dried, Gloria declared that time was marching on, and she had to get to work.

'I'm off. Are you sure you're all right?'

Her mother smiled. 'Just feeling a bit run-down. I think it's the thought of waiting in queues for offal we would have fed to the cat before the war.'

Gloria grinned. 'Lucky we don't have a cat. We'd be starving!'

Her mother's cheek felt soft but damp beneath the kiss she gave her. Then she was gone, leaving her mother all alone.

Jenny touched that spot after she'd gone. Harbouring a need to share her secret had come to nothing. She'd been almost ready to share it with Thelma last night and Gloria this morning, but something had stopped her. Children became adults, and yes, the blood ties were still there, but adults became characters with their own hopes, dreams and plans. She had no right to blight the futures they envisaged for themselves.

Pull yourself together, she instructed herself.

She did just that. Washed, changed, put on make-up in readiness for her appointment at the hospital. After that, she might have some idea of what would come next.

Studying her appearance in the same mirror Gloria had been looking in was reassuring. There looked to be nothing the matter with her; in fact, she looked attractive and well turned out.

She forced herself to smile whilst telling herself that there was nothing to cry about yet. Hopefully that was the way things would stay. If the worst was revealed, then she would finally unburden herself and let her very best friend in on the secret. Thelma would be informed before she told Tilly and Gloria.

Thelma would understand. Thelma would give her the support she needed.

* * *

Gloria had learned how to type. She'd found a book on how to touch type, which meant not looking at the keys.

She was typing now, though not on Thomas Cousens headed paper. This was on a plain sheet, A4, double spacing and done when Mr Cousens was down on the shop floor dealing with a production problem.

The fact that she'd found her mother crying was worrying, a problem she could not bear alone. Tilly had to be told.

Dear Tilly,

I found Mother crying this morning. She didn't admit to anything being wrong, though I'm sure there was. Do you know why she was crying? If you do, please tell me. After all, I'm here and need to know if there is something wrong.

Love Gloria.

Ps. She's met Damien, my gentleman friend. It isn't anything to do with that, is it? You would tell me if it was?

21

Just an hour after arriving at work, Thelma was summoned to Mr Bertram's office. She'd presumed it was to tell her that a buyer had been found for Bertrams. As it turned out, she was glad she was sitting down when he told her the news.

'You may recall my offer that you become manageress of this shop for the foreseeable future, at least until the war ends.'

She nodded. 'Yes.' Was he going to change his mind? She hoped not.

He poked his spectacles which had travelled down to the lower part of his nose. 'There will come a time, I sincerely hope, when this war is over. I have decided that you managing the shop is basically a short-term arrangement. My wife and I still wish to retire and pass the shop – and the business on.'

Thelma held her breath. It didn't seem as though he was going back on his word, but something was in the pipeline. She waited, hardly daring to move.

Mr Bertram resumed his long-winded eulogy. 'After taking relevant advice and if you are willing, once hostilities are over and this country is back on an even footing, my wife and I will have nothing more to do with Bertrams Modes. The shop is made available to you at a nominal rent.'

That was when Thelma's jaw dropped.

He went on, 'I have assured the bank that I will continue owning the premises and the business until victory occurs. After that, and seeing as you have never owned a business or leased a property, I will function as guarantor for five years thence. I think that is a very generous term and gives you time enough to establish yourself in the post-war period that is coming our way.'

As was his habit, he held his head to one side, scrutinising her face for reaction.

He'd always thought Thelma had a strong face and the mind to go with it. He wouldn't let her know that it had taken some persuading for the bank manager to see that a woman could make the business more successful than a man ever could. After all, it was a fashion shop catering for women. Didn't it make sense that women knew what other women wanted better than a man?

Mr Bertram's news went some way to helping Thelma cope with her concerns for Peter. Her thoughts raced like the *Flying Scotsman* going at full speed towards Scotland. She already had the general running of the shop reorganised and under tight control. Now her mind soared like a skyrocket on Bonfire Night, soaring into the future.

There would be stock to buy, a good cleaning and modernising throughout – though that would likely have to be on a budget. And they could have functions again, perhaps afternoon tea where models could swan around in clothes signifying a return to feminine form. Gone would be the utility clothes made from the minimum of material. In would come fuller skirts, or at least that's what she hoped. It all depended on whether the manufacturers could source suitable materials.

Feeling quite giddy at this surprise news, she fanned a hand in front of her face. 'My word. This is the best news I could have had. My word. My word!' She burst into laughter.

Mr Bertram joined her and even once he'd stopped, a beaming smile lit up his moon-shaped face. In the past, she'd thought it a sunny face, but that was when it had more colour. He was older now and sunshine had turned to moonglow, a paler face overall with grey pouches beneath his eyes. There was also less hair, a few white strands combed over a speckled scalp.

'Are you amenable to looking so far into the future?'

'Yes,' breathed Thelma. Her head was still spinning. She got up from her chair. 'Absolutely.'

Before dashing out of the door, she held out her hand.

'I can't thank you enough, Mr Bertram. It's been a pleasure working for you.'

His fingers were birdlike and cold between her own. Nevertheless, she shook them as though she were trying to empty his hand of every single bone.

'And it has been a pleasure having you work for me in these troublesome times.' He wobbled a little and got to his feet. His fist, bony as it was, punched skywards. 'Onwards and upwards, Mrs Dawson. Onwards and upwards!'

22

A biopsy was taken at the hospital and was only slightly painful, a long needle, a withdrawing of a tiny piece of her.

'We'll write to you once we know the result.'

'How long before I hear?'

'Possibly two weeks.'

'And then?'

The nurse seemed a bit offhand, but the consultant had a warm smile and a kind voice. He also had patience. She was hardly the first worried woman he'd met. He took the time to explain what might happen next. 'It all depends on the outcome of the biopsy.' He'd told her the possibilities, the difference between benign and malignant. She'd left the hospital with her head spinning, unsure whether to be pleased she'd got it over with or nervous at what was yet to come.

One blessing was that the rest of the day would not give her time to muse on what might happen next. It was her shift that afternoon. At least she'd watch a film to take her mind off things. Unfortunately, bad news came first. Tobruk had fallen and many prisoners had been taken.

The mood in the cinema was sombre, but war was something people had learned to put up with. Forget about what you could do nothing about; gird your loins and face the future.

The film that followed harked back to a time when the Empire had been at its height. Set on the Northwest Frontier, *Four Feathers* was the story of a military man branded a coward who proves that he was not. Loud music accompanied the hero in the battle scenes when he was outnumbered by a dastardly foe. But he'd won through. The British Empire had won through. Hopefully, in modern times, it would do so again.

Jenny rested her elbows on the wooden rail at the back of the theatre, where she had a good view of the audience as well as the film. Sometimes it was more interesting to watch the young lovers in the back seats than it was the film, although that happened mainly in the evening matinee. Mostly older people and mothers with children attended the afternoon matinee, anyone not involved in war work, alone at home and in need of a bit of escapism.

The sound of crunching, sucking and loud chewing came from the stalls.

Tobacco smoke drifted upwards, meandering between her and the screen. At times, it seemed as though the smoke was part of the film, a bluish fog adding a little colour to the greyish images on screen.

There was no break between matinee and evening performances. When audiences were swapping over, going out or coming in, was when Jenny used her powerful torch to show people out through the darkness and into the well-lit foyer.

The change in audience would happen soon after this film ended and the next show began.

She wore no wristwatch and didn't need to, telling the time by the length of the films, the ten-minute break between the news and the main feature, the smaller break between the end of the main feature and the lights going up as the National Anthem played.

Public information films came up like clockwork, an encyclopaedia of advice, though some items Jenny thought ordinary common sense. The latest advice on charging up your wireless battery was useful. The most efficient use of in-season fruit and vegetables less so. It was something they'd all been doing for years.

The news usually followed on from the plummy voices advising – mostly women – on how best to use what little resources were available.

Back towards the beginning of the war, the films had been more worrying. Air-raid siren sounding off, take cover. Air-raid siren sounding the all-clear. Bombs were dropping back then, not so now, except in London, where flying bombs nicknamed doodlebugs were doing widespread damage.

The newsreels were more uplifting since the storming of the Normandy beaches. People cheered at soldiers of all nations smiling into the camera and waving – just in case their mothers or wives were watching.

Six o'clock. The end of this afternoon's matinee signalled the end of her shift.

Light flooded in from the foyer when Annie, whose shift it was, swept in.

'I've brought chocolate,' said Annie. Her tone was furtive. 'My Peggy's got a Yank boyfriend.'

That explained the chocolates.

'Lucky you.'

'She told me she's going to marry him.'

'Lovely.'

'I'm not so sure. He's the same colour as these chocolates.'

Someone in the back row hissed at them to shut up and close the door. The light was breaking into the darkness. People liked to have total darkness. It helped them concentrate on what was happening on the screen.

The door closed with a sound like a broom brushing over autumn leaves.

Relief intensified with each step, off home, supper, the wireless perhaps, a bit of mending, knitting. She'd taken care of the housework that morning. One less thing to impinge on a long evening with only herself for company.

Her fingertips touched the door handle when she spotted Charlie Talbot. Her breath became tight in her chest. His message had said that he would be there, but she'd chosen not to believe it, and anyway, he'd let her down.

He was standing to one side of the entrance, his gaze latching on her, one hand half raised in greeting. Where he stood gave him a clear view of where she was going.

Her hand clutched her trusty torch more tightly. What did he want? Whatever it was, she wasn't ready to face him. Panic set in. With determined swiftness, she made a dash for the door marked private, which seemed the best thing to do in order to avoid him. Once through that she could pick up her coat and handbag from her coat hook and sneak out the back way.

The door was ajar by about six inches. He used his walking stick to prevent it closing further.

'Jenny. Can we talk?'

She blinked, thought about it, and shook her head. 'No. I have to get home.'

'Surely, just a few minutes.'

'What is there to say?' She said it gruffly. Inside, her heart was beating like a drum.

Lines at the corners of his eyes deepened. A touchable tenderness appeared on his lips. 'Will you ever forgive me?'

'What is there to forgive? We were nothing to each other.'

His hand held the door. If she pulled it shut, his hand would be trapped – the fingers at least.

'You know that's not true.'

'You disappeared without a word.' Her words trembled. She trembled.

'I felt I was intruding. Your family. Your neighbours.'

The way he stated such a feeble excuse went some way to reducing emotions that had soared like a swallow. She was jerked back to that night when a gas leak had caused her house to explode. Of all the times she had needed support, that was it. But where was he. A new anger fermented itself inside at the memory of him taking off at high speed. Disappeared whilst she was left dealing with the damage done. She could still taste her disappointment.

She fixed him with a searing look. 'That wasn't quite true, was it. You saw Thelma and knew she'd seen you with other women. Women who paid for your companionship.' It was an ugly concept, women paying for his company – and whatever else they wanted.

His fingers tightened over his walking stick and a tremor of embarrassment crossed his face, then was gone.

'Let me explain...'

She waved her hand dismissively and turned away. 'I don't want to know.'

'Look, it wasn't quite what it seemed. There was a very good reason for what I did. I used that money in the struggle to help my fellow man. The working man.'

Her eyes blazed. 'It's not exactly what every man who gets caught out says, though still an excuse.'

'Whatever you may think, I want to make amends.'

'Does Emily know your history?'

He blanched. 'No.'

Her eyebrows arched and her expression was rigid. 'I could tell her.'

'You might let me explain.'

He might have done, but fate lent a hand.

Mr Croft, manager of the Broadway, made a habit of 'walking the floor', as he put it, making sure that everything was tickety-boo. The term 'walking the floor' stemmed from his time working in a big store in London. He still looked the part, shirt, tie, dark suit and oiled hair.

Pencil-thin eyebrows met above his aquiline nose. Mr Croft had lost an eye whilst on fire watch. His glass eye was unmoving whilst his good eye scrutinised the queue and the box office. Finally, he turned his head so that both glass and natural eye fell on the man in the doorway that led to the staff facilities.

Tall, unbending and stiff-legged as though marching, he strode with head high, lips pursed and addressed the man. 'Excuse me, sir. This door is marked private, just in case you didn't notice. Staff only. Might I ask what is your business here?'

Charlie met the querying look with the air of a man used to giving commands to the lower orders. 'I was speaking to Mrs Crawford. She's an old friend.'

Mr Croft maintained a stoical expression, unflinching in the face of someone who spoke well and no doubt thought them-selves his better. He had faced the worst artillery barrage of the Great War. Charlie Talbot's defiant jaw was nothing compared to that onslaught.

Whilst the two men faced off, Jenny took the opportunity to flee for the relative safety of the ladies' cloakroom. After discarding her torch and uniform, she grabbed her handbag and raced for the back door. The door was always in need of a bit of oil, but she managed to push the emergency bar open. In her rush, she tripped on the step and tottered across the concrete apron outside.

Skirting the side of the building, her breathing rushed, she hurried with her head down past the burned-out remains of Robin's shop. Robin had been her lifebelt following Charlie leaving her high and dry. Now he too was gone. Would there never be a man in her life who might stay? Would another man support her in the private battle she was facing? She doubted it.

Charlie Talbot had swept her off her feet at a time when she'd been in an unhappy marriage and living in a down-at-heel place. He'd come along and given her hope and made her think that he cared for her. How did she feel about him now? His image had stayed with her, that was for sure; deep blue eyes, corn-coloured hair that now sported wisps of grey on either side of his temple. Had his arms always been so muscular? She didn't recall. It was his voice and his eyes that had stayed with her, a focal point in her mind.

Robin had been married and now Charlie was walking the same road with the elegant Emily. *You do pick 'em*, she thought to herself.

The bustle of the Broadway passed in a blur as she ran for home. The tightness in her chest seemed to be forming a dam that helped hold back the emotions she was feeling. Today had been like the ending and beginning of something. She still held the secret close, but once the results of the biopsy were through, the options would be advised and considered. The consultant had intimated that one option – one very likely option – was surgery. Dependent on those results, two weeks and the surgery would be over, the lump removed. *Now when will you tell someone?*

Telling anyone was steeped with reluctance. The consultation at the doctor's had cost sixpence, another half a crown for the consultant. The surgery would cost at least two pounds, plus all the medicine she might be prescribed. It would most likely drain her savings, meagre as they were. But there, it might not come to that. Look on the bright side. And get it off your chest. All good advice to herself.

So why was she averse to sharing her grim news? A problem shared can be halved. That blasted saying again. But who to tell? Her daughters? Or Thelma?

The heavens opened as she turned into Coronation Close. The rain poured and then stopped. A beam of sunlight broke through a crack in the clouds. She wasn't one to believe in omens, but perhaps it was a sign and a good one. She was home, the place where she could lick her wounds and tell herself that all would be well. Home was the cosy place where it could seem as though problems were left outside the door.

23

It was late afternoon the following day when good news broke.

Jenny was putting a bundle of tied up newspapers outside on the pavement when she saw Thelma. She was waving frantically and looking as if she'd won the football pools – which she couldn't have because she didn't do them. Jenny concluded that something good had happened.

Thelma dashed across to her, surprisingly fast on a pair of black court shoes with three-inch heels. 'Jenny. I've got something to tell you. Wonderful news. Have you got a minute?'

'You look like the cat that got the cream.'

'I have. Double cream. Cornish clotted in fact.'

'Indeed?' Jenny raised her eyebrows quizzically and promised herself that if it was good news, then it was time to share her own – which wasn't so good – until otherwise informed.

Just as she was about to ask her in, Cath Lockhart called from the other end of the street. She was running towards them, her oversize slippers flapping like foot-driven wings.

'Thelma. Can I have a word – in private.' She added the 'in private' bit, along with a cautious glance at Jenny. Obviously, she was not included in what she needed to say.

Somewhat reluctantly, Thelma told Jenny that she would see her later. 'Give me a minute to see what the matter is. Won't be long.'

Jenny entered the cool emptiness of her house, took off her cotton topcoat, placed her bag beside it on a chair.

From the neat living room, she passed into equally neat kitchen, a sunny place in both decor and aspect, a place she had always loved like a friend, a place she always appreciated returning to at the end of the working day.

Today she needed to feel at one with it. To that end, she boiled a kettle of hot water. Once it had boiled, she tipped it into a bucket, added cold water and soda crystals, took hold of a scrubbing brush and got down on her knees.

Try as she might, the bucket of water remained clean. The floor was not dirty, but then she wasn't scrubbing it to make it clean. Doing something helped keep the dark thoughts at bay. *Am I going to die?* That was what she feared being told, not on her own account but for her daughters.

Suddenly it felt as though her hands were on fire. *What a chump you are*, she told herself as she frowned at their red rawness. Rubber gloves should be worn when using soda-infused water.

She sat back on her haunches, though not for long. Doing nothing brought back her fear. How would she tell her daughters? What did the future hold for them all?

Splash went the water as she let the scrubbing brush fall back into it. The yellow and brown linoleum was once again soaked.

'Jenny?'

Thelma was back, standing in the doorway, one arm outstretched across the door opening, one suede shoe on a stockinged foot held in a pose in front of the other.

'What the devil are you doing scrubbing a floor at this time of night?'

Jenny wiped her hands down the front of her apron and laughed.

Daughter Gloria came in, said hello to Thelma before asking if her supper was ready.

Jenny got to her feet, emptied the bucket down the sink and wiped her hands.

'It's in the oven.'

'Oh good. I'm off upstairs to get ready to go out.'

Thelma looked at Jenny, the clumping of feet going up the stairs was followed by one bump, then a second above their heads as Gloria threw off her work shoes.

Jenny shook her head in response to Thelma's look of disapproval.

'I take it you've laid down the law.'

'Of course.'

Thelma had been uncompromising with Gloria's behaviour. After all, she was too young to go into pubs, let alone in a relationship with an older man.

'Do you think she'll take any notice?'

She pointed out to Thelma that lots of underage girls hung around in pubs looking older than their actual age. She shrugged. 'It's an uphill battle. The war has changed us all, and besides, who knows where we'll be this time next year.'

'Ah, yes. Next year! That's what I've come to talk to you about. The future in fact.' Thelma's beaming expression returned.

Without being invited – because quite frankly she knew she didn't need an invite – she pulled out one of the pine kitchen chairs and sat herself down.

Jenny eyed her with an amused look. 'Has somebody given you a whole parachute? Enough to make three sets of underwear?'

Thelma shook her head, her eyes bright. 'Bertrams! It's mine. Mr Bertram's arranged everything.'

When Jenny didn't respond, she repeated herself, though with a bit more emphasis.

'The shop! You know I told you that I'm now manageress, well there's more. Once this war is over, he's arranged for me to have a lease on the shop. It's a thank you for my loyal service. Isn't that wonderful?'

She rambled on about buying stock, about getting the shopfront painted, reorganising the interior once the war was over and the second-hand clothes sector of the shop was no longer needed.

'I'll return it to what it used to be, a high-fashion shop catering for discerning – and dare I say it – wealthy women.' Her face scrunched up suddenly as her eyes rose as if scrutinising the ceiling. 'I'm not sure I'll keep the shop name as Bertrams. It's a bit old-fashioned. Hopefully it will attract a younger clientele, the young girls and newly married wives returned from the war and keen to leave uniforms and woollen stockings behind. And who can blame them? And once I'm the owner of the business, I'll need a manageress to help me.' Her eyes glittered. She leaned forward, hands clasped tightly in front of her. 'You will be my manageress, Jenny. We'll both be bosses. You and me!'

She laughed at this but stopped when she saw that Jenny had not joined in her laughter. Her joy was diminished somewhat. This was not the response she'd expected.

She frowned. 'What's wrong?'

'I've never worked in a shop like Bertrams, let alone managed one.'

'But that's just the point,' exclaimed Thelma, sounding as though running a business was the easiest thing in the world. She so wanted to do this, but she also wanted to aid her friend Jenny in this new world that would come when the war was over. 'You worked for Robin, ran the place whilst his wife Doreen ran rings around him. You've got the experience.'

Jenny looked down at her hands, her fingers tangling as she thought about how to put what she had to put. She raised her eyes from beneath a dark brown bang of glossy hair and lowered her voice.

'I have a confession to make.'

Thelma took on an enquiring look, head tilted to one side as she surmised her friend's expression. 'Is it anything juicy? A bit of gossip I might have missed?' she asked jokingly.

If she was expecting Jenny to say something to make her laugh, she was going to be very much mistaken.

Jenny was only just hanging on to being her normal self and even for the sake of their friendship couldn't bring a smile to her face and yet she didn't want to burden Thelma. What if the tests said that everything was fine? Why burden someone with a worry she might yet get through? She'd give herself a bit more time to think about it – talk about something else – something trivial.

'What did Cath want?'

Thelma grimaced. 'Her cat's just had kittens. Wanted me to drown them for her. Even had the bucket ready.'

'Did you?' Jenny looked at her in horror.

'No. I told her there was enough killing of innocents in this world without us adding to it. I said I'd put the word around that good homes were needed. It shouldn't be too much of a problem. There's only three of the poor little mites – unless another's arrived since I've been talking to you.' Thelma screwed up her face like a squashed peach as her brain worked overtime. 'Working at the Broadway is a dead-end job. You could do better.'

'There are advantages. I do get to see the films,' Jenny retorted somewhat defiantly.

Thelma snatched the kettle from the stove, pushed Jenny away from the sink and turned on the tap. 'Working for peanuts and taking orders. Working for yourself will be so different. You and me.' After lighting the gas, she smiled. 'No taking orders.'

'Not even from you?' Jenny responded with amusement.

'I'm not a hard taskmaster.'

'Working in the shop is one thing. Being in charge of it might change your behaviour. You might turn into a right posh type!'

Thelma responded with a snort of derision. 'I'll act the lady when I need to and so will you. Come on. The kettle's almost boiled. Let's have a chinwag about it.'

Tea made and poured, Jenny made a big thing of blowing on the hot tea.

Enthusiasm shone from Thelma in the same way as a halo on the head of a saint drawing in the onlookers, Jenny included.

Descriptions of how the shop would look, what clothes they would stock, 'smart uniforms for the staff, perhaps a home delivery service'. Describing her plans for the shop made her look girlish.

Listening to Thelma's plans helped normalise her feelings. The abject joy on her face raised Jenny's spirits in such a way she felt as though a door had opened, a sudden belief that life was for living – for ever and ever – and that there was nothing to fear. That was one point of view that seemed to occupy one part of her brain, the optimistic part that held life would go on as it had always done. The pessimistic side was there too, lecturing her in a dour manner that life was only temporary and she might as well get used to it.

Thelma said at last, 'You cannot believe how excited I am.'

Her sigh told Jenny exactly how excited she was. 'I'm really happy for you.'

'I'm determined that you're going to be working there too.'

No doubt she was, but Jenny was still unsure of whether she would be around at the end of the war – whenever that might be. Hopefully it would end more quickly now the Americans had joined the battle.

'So? How about it?'

'Damn it!'

Thelma looked taken aback. 'What does that mean?'

Jenny tossed her head so that her hair bounced in waves before settling on her shoulders. She had a forthright look to her classic features, a sudden steely fix in her eyes that had only just come to Thelma's notice. 'You mean it?'

'Of course I mean it. Let's push the boat out. Climb the highest mountain. Live life to the full until we can't live it any more.' Thelma's face shone like the sun but diminished when she saw that Jenny's demeanour had become downcast.

She was eyeing her tangled fingers, nervously intertwining. Jenny at last found the courage to speak.

'Thelma. Before we go any further, there's something I must tell you.'

'What?'

The moment had come. Jenny sighed, untangled her hands and sat back in her chair.

Although Thelma maintained her bright-eyed gaze, there

was a new stillness to her face. She was watchful, looking worried about what she was about to hear.

'I've had a problem for some time now.'

Thelma leaned forward. 'A problem? What kind of problem?'

For a moment, Jenny's tongue cleaved to the roof of her mouth, which was dry, so dry that if she said something now, she was liable to choke on her words.

Finally, on the breath of a deep sigh, she got it out.

'I've got a lump. In my breast.'

For a moment, the silence was so intense in that little kitchen that looked out on rows of vegetables growing in the back garden. Like the striking of a cuckoo clock announcing the hour, a single note from a blackbird finally penetrated.

Shock dented Thelma's joy. Hesitantly, she asked if she'd been to see the doctor, fearing what the answer might be.

It was something of a relief when Jenny nodded. 'And the hospital. I've been there too. Had all the tests. I'm now waiting for the results.'

'Oh.'

That one word was said with feeling. Having breast cancer was a woman's worst nightmare. It meant an operation and perhaps the loss of one, if not both breasts.

Jenny did not raise her eyes to meet Thelma's focused gaze.

'Right,' said Thelma in a forthright manner, having taken back control of her shattered emotions. 'So what's happening? What treatment will you be having? Have they told you yet?'

There was not the faintest quiver of weakness in Thelma's manner.

'It depends on the result of the biopsy. If it's malignant, then...' She took a deep breath and raised her eyes. 'The very worst that can happen is that the lump will be removed or depending on its size my whole breast.'

Once the words were out, Jenny's eyelids became half shut. She rested her jaw on her hand.

'And if it's not the very worst?'

Jenny took a deep breath, which helped when she delivered the next sentence. 'I might have to have radiotherapy.'

'And that is?'

A sigh, a capture of breath prior to explaining what she knew. 'It's like an X-ray. Not just one, a series of X-rays.'

'How many?'

'It depends on what's needed – on how bad things are. How malignant, which means how likely it is to spread.'

The silence returned, during which time Thelma dissected what she had heard, listing each item alongside its likely severity.

After sieving things through, she got them into order. She was no gambler, so used pure guesswork. 'But you'll still be alive. You're not going to die.'

Thelma said it with great conviction, so much so that Jenny suddenly believed that her fear was just that – fear of what she didn't know much about.

She blinked and met her friend's forthright gaze. 'I hope not, though I don't know for sure.'

'And this biopsy. You told me that's what they've already done. What's that about?'

'Taking a bit of the lump and putting it under a microscope.'

'And that will tell them whether it's serious.'

'I suppose so. It might not be malignant. Benign, I think he called it.'

To Jenny's great surprise, Thelma burst out laughing. 'How long have you had this?'

'A while.'

'And you've just as long believed that you're dead and buried?'

'It's not funny.'

The laughter faded. 'No. Of course it's not, but you see what you're doing? You're taking the negative view, not the positive. Good grief, Jenny, we need to fix on the positive in times like these. Now come on.' Thelma reached across and squeezed Jenny's hand. 'You've lived through a war and now you're going to live through this. I guarantee it. And guess what, you and I will have a bright future running Bertrams. No arguments,' she said, raising a warning finger when it looked as though Jenny was about to protest. 'We've got a few more years in us yet. Shall we drink to that?'

It had always been hard to resist Thelma's boundless confidence. Jenny reminded herself that her natural exuberance was not just veiling her concern for her, it was doing the same for her concern for Peter.

Her dear friend had put things in perspective. It didn't make her feel one hundred per cent better, but it did veer her thoughts towards the positive. What if she did end up with only one breast? Did it really matter?

Thelma slapped her hands palms down on the table. 'Well, this calls for more than a cup of tea.' With that, she tucked her hand into her pocket. 'This might look like vinegar, but it isn't vinegar. This is brandy. Peter brought a few bottles with him from Holland. It was for toasting my news about Bertrams and drinking to our future. We can still drink to our future and, believe me, I'm determined we'll have one – both of us.'

It was hard to be down when Thelma was around. Jenny's spirits were lifted. *Yes, why not have a drink.*

'These teacups okay or would you prefer a glass?'

'I wouldn't care if it was a tin can,' chortled Thelma.

After adding a good measure of brandy to the dregs at the bottom of the teacups, Thelma was first to raise a cup in a toast.

'Good luck and here's to Madeleine's Modes.'

'Madeleine? Where did that come from?'

Thelma shrugged. 'No idea. Just popped into my head.' She took a sniff of the teacup. 'Must be the tea. Cheers. Here's to us.'

Feeling lighter than she had in ages, Jenny joined her in the toast. 'To us. To whatever we do and for however long it lasts.'

24

By day, the city centre maintained the same grey, war-weary look, an ongoing blandness of soot-smeared buildings, sandbags piled around their base. All manner of entreaties on varying sizes of billboards went some way to relieving the mediocrity. Economic use of potatoes and carrots, saving of newspaper and the ubiquitous 'Careless Talk Costs Lives', and Gloria's favourite, an elegant-looking woman wearing a slinky dress, cigarette holder held aloft in fingers with painted nails. She very much identified with this femme fatale – except for the suggestion that declared that the woman was not to be trusted. The slogan for her was, 'Stay Mum. She Might Not Be So Dumb'.

Once a velvet darkness fell, the blackout instituted back in 1939 added a frisson of excitement. Night-time was like a cloak falling over and hiding the bombed-out buildings, the weeds growing in exposed cellars. Not a streetlight or a chink of light from a window disturbed the total blackness. But there was a smell in the air, that of people out to escape their drab lives and enjoy themselves.

Nightclubs and illegal drinking dens had been set up in

some of the bombed-out cellars. Labouring for the war effort for twelve hours a day was draining, not just physically, but mentally. Night was the time for pleasure, drinking, dancing and recharging very run-down batteries.

Even though she didn't work six days a week, Gloria was no exception. Her day job was boring but well paid, which went some way to explaining why she was so quick at her job.

The truth was that beavering away made the day pass more quickly. It was the night she wanted, the escape to a tinsel-strewn fairyland where the drinks flowed, the music blared and sweet-smelling men with money to spend treated her like a princess.

The lighting was low, couples and men in groups, drinking and smoking. Their features were indistinct on dark shadows leaning towards each other, smoke circling their heads like funeral wreaths. Muffled conversation provided a muted back-drop, obliterated when the band began to play.

The five musicians were all black and wearing American uniforms. Damien had told her they were earning a bit extra. 'And enjoying a night out.'

The screaming of a trumpet – a horn, she'd heard it referred to as – blared out into the smoky atmosphere. It was like a signal for everyone to pay attention, to stop talking, to think about dancing, or at least sparing a moment to listen.

Gloria began tapping her foot, her attention fixed on music she didn't understand but was drawn to.

Swept away with the beat, the urge to have her feet fly across the floor, she leaned into Damien and asked if he would dance with her.

He'd been talking to one of his colleagues, a pock-faced man with a bulbous nose and loose lips. His appearance had always worried her. When she'd mentioned it, Damien had told her not to worry.

'Not now, sweetheart. I've got business to discuss.'

He left her sitting there, the light from the small stage where the band was playing lit up her sulky expression.

Damien didn't like dancing. This table, in this nightclub, was where he did his business. He was in his element, and although he'd prefer her not to bother him, he liked indulging this slip of a girl who tried so hard to be a woman. A pretty one too. She was exactly what he wanted. But she wanted to dance, and he did not. Indulge her. That's what he would do.

He crooked his index finger over the lit cigar he was smoking to a fairly new recruit to his team. 'Jamie, isn't it?'

The kid was blond-haired, blue-eyed and had a clear complexion, almost as soft and peachy as that of a woman.

Jamie responded. 'Yes.'

'My girl wants to dance. It would oblige me if you would oblige her.'

A quick jerk of a hairless chin. 'Certainly, Mr Fox.'

Gloria reluctantly took the hand that was offered her. She would have preferred it if Damien had danced with her. She eyed young Jamie disdainfully. No more than a boy.

'Can you dance?' she asked him.

'You bet I can. Can you?'

She scowled. 'Of course I can.'

The dance bordered on a jitterbug but not quite. It was a pleasant surprise to find that, yes, Jamie could dance. He twirled her like a top, making her fly out around him.

He flung her out, then hauled her back in again, saying close to her ear, 'You like jazz?'

'Is that what this is?'

Out she flew again. Then back in again.

'Yep. It is. Genuine thing. Those guys certainly know how to blow a tune.'

The dance floor was small and crowded, which meant the jitterbug had to end. Her body slammed into his, a fact she found a little disconcerting. In an effort to hide her blushes, she turned her head to study the band better and saw their uniforms.

'They're American?' She already knew that, but it was something to say.

'You bet they are.'

'But not fighting? I mean, there's not many Americans left, are there?'

'Not many, but them left work in logistics, the stores and all that stuff, sending on the stuff the infantry needs.'

'They're lucky. Serving well away from the front line and playing here.'

She felt his right hand tighten on her left hand as he glanced at the band. One of them looked directly at him and when their looks held, the joy of the music maker left his face.

In need of a break, the band dispersed. Another drink was placed in front of her.

Damien patted her hand. 'All right, love? Enjoy your dance?'

She smiled and said that she had.

She had to wait for about fifteen minutes before the band returned, and the music started up again.

It had seemed to her as though Jamie was about to ask her if she wanted to dance again, but Damien stopped him.

'I need you here. We've got business to do.'

Gloria slumped back into her chair. Was that a blush she detected on Jamie's face? A quick glance, almost of apology. She judged him to be only a few years older than her – around twenty perhaps. Or twenty-one.

Whilst they were so occupied, her heavily made-up eyes searched the clientele. In response to a request for a slow number, the trumpet player left the tune to the more muted instruments in the band.

She saw the trumpet player's eyes searching the dance floor. His expression remained tight until he saw her and smiled.

'Wanna dance, honey?' he said, leaning over her from a great height.

Suddenly aware that Damien was assessing him, he met the older man's look head on.

'Hope you don't mind if I have this dance with your lady, sir? If I can have your permission to borrow her for a minute?'

Damien looked thoughtful, before giving a curt nod. 'Take good care of her.'

'I will, sir.'

'And make sure you bring her back,' he added as a delighted Gloria unfolded herself from the chair.

His hand was warm and spanned her back across her spine.

'My name's Brett,' he said without giving her chance to ask. 'And yours?'

'Gloria.'

'Pleased to meet you, Gloria.'

The dance floor was packed even tighter than before. Twirling and whirling around was not an option.

'Seems we need to kind of shuffle,' he said, smiling down at her.

'I don't mind that.'

She fancied she saw a question flickering in his eyes.

'Can I ask you a question?'

'If you like.'

He jerked his head to the table where Damien and the others were in earnest discussion. 'I don't want to be out of order, but is that guy...' He paused; his eyes still stuck on her. 'Is he a relative or what?'

She sensed there was a more direct question. It made her smile.

'You want to know if he's my father.'

His chortle was accompanied with a nod of his head. 'Forget it. I've no business asking.'

'You already have and by the sound of it you've made up your mind that he is not my father.'

'I have?'

She cocked her head in a saucy manner, with an equally saucy grin on her face. 'And you'd be right. He isn't my father. He's the man I'm going to marry, but he doesn't know that just yet.'

Brett was not the only uniformed man on the dance floor. There were others. Without these two noticing, three of them came together, heads together, exchanging cusses with each other and throwing hostile looks in their direction.

The other American servicemen were white and were dancing with white girls – which they considered their prerogative. Gradually, they moved in closer.

'Hey, nigger!'

Gloria had heard the word before but never uttered with such venomous intent.

The three uniformed men were close now, encircling the two of them.

Instinctively sensing that trouble was afoot, those outside their circle moved further away.

Brett gave no sign of turning the other cheek. A cast-iron tension stiffened his body. 'You got a problem, white boy?'

The band's rendering of an old jazz composition became fragmented as their attention fixed on Brett, Gloria and the three white soldiers.

A bullet-headed man, his head covered in the bristles of an

extra tight army haircut, hissed spittle into his face. 'Tonight is white night, but I got no problem as long as you stay with the rest of your kind and play the music. I ain't having you mixing with the rest of us on the dance floor.' He eyed Gloria with the utmost disdain. 'And dancing with a white woman.'

Brett wiped away the spittle with the back of his hand.

A bigger gap opened around them. Some of the space was taken up by more white American GIs. Behind them, the band had set down their instruments and stood in an opposing line. Black against white.

Someone close by suggested the MPs were called.

Gloria was frightened. Brett saw her fear and carefully eased her a foot or two away from him.

'Stay out of the way, honey,' he said to her.

Just when it seemed as though the battle lines would clash, a steady and commanding voice broke in.

'If you boys don't want to get hurt, I suggest you leave.'

Damien stood like a bulwark between black and white.

The white boys, full of drink and the bravado of young men who'd not so long ago, had been working in an office, a factory or driving a truck or plough, burst out laughing.

'And who's to do the hurting? You're the same age as my pop and I can sure whip him.'

'As hard as he whips you?' Damien threw back.

The band remained where they were, looking apprehensive as they tried to evaluate what their role would be in this.

A soft hand caught Gloria's wrist, pulling her back before sliding in front of her, between her and whatever was unfolding.

She found herself facing Jamie's back. He was joined by other men she knew to be allied to Damien in his business dealings.

Jamie's clenched fists were hanging at his side, looking unusually misshapen and large.

When the light caught his right fist, she saw the glint of metal threaded through his fingers. Hard metal, that of a knuckleduster.

Glances were exchanged between the clannish gathering hogging the centre of the dance floor.

Gloria shrank back against the rough wall. The main lighting was brought up.

Damien's voice boomed out. 'Now you can see what you're facing, will you go quietly or do I have to order you thrown out? I can assure you it wouldn't be the first time I've had to throw my weight around. But, as you can see, my weight isn't confined to me. And we're professionals. We've always handed out chastisement when it was needed. Chance your luck if you dare.'

There was a strange moment of no movement, no sound either.

The first thing to happen was that Brett eased his way back to the band before they all returned to the stage and picked up their abandoned instruments.

The white soldiers, taking the view that they'd won some kind of victory, began to head for the door, though a few fancied they could stay.

Damien's loyal followers retrieved them, prodding and pushing them towards the exit.

Feeling as though her knees were going to give out, Gloria sank back into her chair.

'You okay, sweetheart?'

She told Damien that she was.

'I'm glad that's over. They won't come back, will they?'

A wry smile lifted one side of his mouth as he shook his head. 'No. But their type is likely to be waiting outside.' He jerked his head at Jamie. 'Phone the MPs. Tell them there's a load of soldiers outside causing trouble. Do it now before the band leaves. I'm a businessman. I don't want any trouble.'

Gloria was awestruck. Damien exuded power and influence. The muscles of his arm felt hard as iron beneath the soft cashmere of his overcoat as he escorted her to the car. Tonight, he was taking her home. Her mother knew about him now. There was no point in pretending. No doubt it wouldn't be long before all of Coronation Close knew about her man, and she didn't care if they did.

His lips were on hers before she left the car to head indoors. His hand covered her breast, his fingers pinching her nipple. The long skirt of her dress was folded up above her knees as his hand travelled higher. This was the night when it would happen. That was what she decided. If he'd asked her the question, why now, he might have got the answer that he'd been such a force this evening against so many other men. He'd been like a giant amongst them, power being the aphrodisiac heating her desire.

'That's enough.' He covered her up suddenly.

'But you don't need to stop,' she said through her bruised lips, surprised and disappointed by his hesitation at a time when she was ready to give herself.

'I want to do it properly. I don't want your mother to think my intentions less than honourable.'

She got out of the car feeling hurt and confused. What was he actually saying? She wasn't sure.

Not wishing to disturb her mother, she crept silently into the quiet, dark house pulling the blackout door curtain behind her.

In the little living room of the comfortable council house, she sat trying to make sense of it all. She couldn't. Perhaps someone else could.

Fetching a notepad and pen, she wrote to Tilly. Just a few

lines. Not much at all. More words were needed to make the postage stamp worthwhile.

Perhaps she needed to sleep on it.

Upstairs in her bedroom, she placed the notepad and pencil – she couldn't be bothered with inkwell and pen at this time of night – on the chest of drawers.

A low, lone wail sounded in the all-encompassing silence of night. Holding her ear to the bedroom door, Gloria heard the unmistakeable sound of crying. Her mother was crying.

If she hadn't been so tired, she would have entered her mother's bedroom and enquired what was wrong. She made the decision to ask in the morning. That was also when she would finish her letter to Tilly.

She couldn't bring herself to either admit or tell anyone else she suspected that Damien's business interests were not always legitimate. Did she want to know more? Not really. As her mother was wont to say, ignorance is bliss.

25

Thelma called in on Jenny the following night to ask how she was. She called in on the night after that too. Every night in fact after coming home from work.

'Thelma, you don't have to call in every night. I'm too old to be wrapped in cotton wool.'

'You've heard nothing?'

'I've heard nothing,' Jenny responded with a sigh. 'Get on home, Thelma. You must be tired. You've been working all day.'

Jenny was right about that. Keeping busy helped her cope with more pressing worries – more fears. Luckily, she had the following afternoon off.

I've become a worrier, Thelma thought to herself. First there was worrying about Peter and now she had her dear friend and neighbour, Jenny to worry about.

Chitlings for lunch, served cold with pepper, vinegar and a slice of buttered bread. Custard and tinned peaches. Two cups of tea to wash it down.

Once she'd washed and dried the dishes, it was nearly three o'clock and she was sitting in a chair with her shoes off. Mary had written her a short letter. Mary's letters were always short and to the point.

Not long now and the new baby will be here. I'm knitting a lot and making clothes. Keeping busy. Will write again soon.

Alice sent typewritten letters, mostly composed when she was on night duty. They went into detail about the ward, the staff and the injured men in her care. Some sounded a delight and made Thelma wonder if her youngest daughter might end up making a life with one of her charges.

Daughter-in-law Maria had told her she would have a houseful of children, though was unsure where she would put them all.

'I will need a bigger house,' she'd said laughingly. Then, more demurely: 'But I do like children, and I don't mind how many I have.'

Her musings about Maria, her daughters and more grand-children were interrupted when someone knocked at the front door.

She stopped rubbing her tired toes together and placed the letter to one side. Whoever it was would have to see her without slippers or shoes. Her feet ached and she had a right to rest them.

'Coming,' she called out, hoping whoever it was would clear off and leave her with a peaceful afternoon.

Her neighbours, including Jenny, always came in at the back-door and through the kitchen.

Somebody collecting for charity or asking if she wanted knocked-off meat or nylons, perhaps? The black market was rife, the Venture Inn well known as a gathering place for goods that had 'fallen off the back of a lorry'.

Peter had promised her a whole box of nylons – black market or not – once he returned from his latest foray.

Such thoughts accompanied the smile that played around her mouth as she tugged the door open, aware of bright daylight in behind a familiar figure. Her jaw dropped when she saw who it was.

'Bert!'

He looked a bit more gaunt and gangly but still carried an overall greyness about him.

This was the man who had suggested they should get married once his aged mother had passed. When the time came and his dear old mother had her angel wings, he'd got cold feet and joined the army – not as a fighting man but in the wages department at Aldershot. He'd left a note – a piece of paper long ago shredded and thrown into the fire.

He looked acutely embarrassed to be there.

'Thelma.'

He whipped off his army-issue beret. The way he did it was more apologetic than gentlemanly.

Speechlessness led to even greater difficulty closing her mouth.

Thelma frowned. She'd got over him quicker than she'd thought possible. Hadn't heard a word from him.

'What do you want?'

Looking decidedly nervous, he wrung the army beret with both hands. He opened his mouth to speak, but nothing came out. His wringing of the beret continued.

'Are you hoping to strangle that?' said Thelma, glancing downwards at the beret.

Both hands met as though in prayer, divided only by the squashed beret.

He licked his lips. A few false starts before he found his voice.

'I hope you don't mind me turning up unannounced after me shooting off as I did.'

Thelma glared at him. He flinched when she folded her arms. 'Just in case you haven't noticed, there's a couple of years passed since you shot off. Why now, Bert? Why now?'

Bert shuffled his feet and looked close to strangling his beret, twisting it this way and that with both hands. 'Guilt, I think.' He did look guilty. 'And missing you.' It was hard to read in his face whether that was indeed the truth.

She crossed her arms across her ample chest. Her hands were best tucked away. Fetching him a right hook to his lantern jaw wasn't beyond the bounds of possibility. She was livid.

'You bloody well should feel guilty!'

He blanched. 'I'm sorry.'

Thelma wasn't finished yet. 'No word of farewell – at least not face to face. Just a letter and not much of one at that.'

He appeared to search for something else that might curry her favour. 'I'm sorry.'

'Repeating that you're sorry doesn't cut the mustard.'

'I heard you were getting married.'

Ah, thought Thelma. *Could it be that good old Bert was jealous?* The thought amused her.

'What's it to you?'

'I was surprised when I heard.'

Was it her imagination or was that jealous anger she read in his eyes?

'Who told you?'

He shrugged like someone does when they've been found out and have no wish to go any further.

'It came as a surprise. I'd come back and thought—'

'Well, you thought wrong.'

'There's no need to be so angry.'

'There's every need.'

'Getting engaged behind my back...'

'What?' Her face like thunder, Thelma could hardly believe what she was hearing. 'Are you telling me you came back because you heard I was getting married?'

'I am but a man.'

His churchy comment made Thelma see red. Those tucked-away hands were itching to escape and throttle him.

She shook her head. 'What made you think you were the only fish in the sea? Did you think that other men wouldn't find me attractive?' She stopped suddenly as the unpalatable truth struck her. 'No,' she said more quietly but equally strident. 'You know about my children. You know I never married.'

He looked about to deny that this was why he'd assumed she'd wait for him indefinitely – even though he had not been in touch.

'We were close. None of that mattered to me. You were my muse, the model for my sculptures and paintings.'

Art had been Bert's way of escaping his mother, his leisure time when he entered another world. Thelma had been flattered to be the subject of many of his pieces.

'I've had everything put in storage. I'll make a present of one of my paintings if you like. Not yet, but when the war is finally over.'

'Your generosity overwhelms me,' she said sarcastically.

'Are you going to invite me in? For old times' sake?'

She didn't know quite why she said yes, though it could have been testing herself that everything that had been between them was in the past. She was one hundred percent sure that it was.

'I can't be bothered making tea,' she declared once he was in her living room. 'I haven't got as much crockery as I used to have.' She indicated the dresser.

Bert glanced at it very quickly, then turned away, turned his back on it in fact, him who used to buy her pieces commemorating a royal wedding, a royal christening and, most of all, a coronation.

'I don't want a drink. I just want to ask if there's a chance you won't marry this Dutchman…'

'How do you know it's a Dutchman?'

He stuttered that he'd heard it on the grapevine.

'Stick your gossip!' Thelma flipped. 'I am marrying my Dutchman and don't give a damn what you or anyone else might think.'

He backed away from her ire until his back slammed against the dresser, knocking off one of the few coronation cups and saucers still in one piece. The cup rolled from the saucer over the edge and onto the floor.

'There's another one gone,' Thelma said grimly. 'As you can see, there's not many left.'

'No.' He sounded sheepish.

'Not that it matters.'

'It doesn't?' He looked taken aback.

She shook her head. 'No. It was just a load of old china, that was all. I've changed, Bert. The lives and happenings with the royals no longer matter to me. I've got my own life to live. War's bound to have changed you too, away from your mother and all that. But then, so's the world for that matter. Now you shove off.'

His lips were like soft India rubber, making movements and shapes searching for words he couldn't utter.

If he thought she was going to change her mind, he had another think coming.

'Out!'

Opening the living-room door was swiftly followed by opening the front door. Door held widely ajar, she jerked her chin, commanding that he leave.

'Please, Thelma.'

'Get out of here, Bert. Get out of here before I land my fist on your chin.'

He looked at her as though only just realising that she was not, and never had been, a woman to be pushed around. She'd had too tough a life to lie down and play dead.

Why did I ever bother with him in the first place? she thought as she watched him from the doorstep.

It was fifteen minutes past four o'clock and school was out. Bert was leaving just as the schoolchildren surged around the corner like a mountain torrent, eager to get home. Just days before leaving school for good, Howard Routledge was one of the older kids coming into the close. Bending to tie up his shoelace, he looked up at Bert Throgmorton going the other way. He wore a curious expression on his face as he watched Bert's stringy figure stride off on long legs around the corner. Once he'd gone, Howard came racing up to Thelma's gate looking puzzled.

'I seen that bloke before. Saw him coming from the back of your place.'

Intrigued, Thelma came down the garden path. She eyed him quizzically.

'You saw Bert Throgmorton in my garden? When was that?'

'The night we...' He hesitated to commit himself. 'The night that nightwatchman said he'd seen us breaking in. The night when your stuff got smashed. Police let us off though. Me mum went down and reminded them whose son I was.'

Thelma glared after the retreating figure of Bert Throgmorton.

Howard kept his eyes on her. 'It was 'im, wasn't it?'

'If he was the man you saw that night.'

'It was. Honest it was.'

'I believe you, Howard.'

Her acceptance of his statement made him beam from ear to ear.

She considered running after Bert and demanding he told the truth. But what would be the point? She didn't care about Bert. She didn't care about her commemorative china either. They belonged to the past. There were far more important things to think about both in the present and the future.

26

The harvest was in, the hard work done. There was still work to be done on the farm, but the heavy graft was over. Home tomorrow! At long last.

Despite the caked mud on her gumboots, Tilly almost skipped behind the cows she was herding into the milking shed. The little case that held all she needed for her trip home was already packed and waiting. Mrs Forester had also promised to provide some fresh produce to take with her. Everything was looking sunny – except for Johnnie Forester. His face looked like a bashed turnip.

He was standing outside the farmhouse door, a deep V between his eyebrows and his strong hands – maulers, his mother called them – tucked into the pockets of his green corduroy trousers.

It was hard to read the expression on his face, but there was no trace of a smile. Convinced she could change that, she waved and smiled. His lack of smile was unyielding.

Had she done something to upset him? Her own smile froze, and a feeling of unease took hold. Such a look boded ill news.

Her first thought was that something had happened to her mother. Surely not a bombing raid. Bristol hadn't had any heavy raids since last year.

Feeling the colour drain from her face, she ran to him, gumboots sucking at the muddy yard.

Looking up into his face, she spoke the fears that had taken hold. 'What is it? What's happened? Is it my mother? My family?'

Her outburst seemed to shake him out of his sobriety. A half-smile came to his lips. His strong fingers squeezed her shoulder, an act of reassurance. 'Don't panic. It's nothing like that. Your mother's fine.' He jerked his chin towards the interior of the house. 'We've got a visitor.'

Muddy boots were not allowed in the farmhouse. Impatient to get inside and see who was there, Tilly dipped one foot, then the other into the horse trough, muddying the clear water.

'Whoa.' Johnnie grabbed her when she was in danger of toppling over. 'And not so quick.'

He still held onto her even when the task was over.

She thanked him somewhat sheepishly. Johnnie always seemed to be around when she needed him. Last night at the pub, something they were doing on a regular basis together, they'd talked for ages about their lives, about how it was at present and how it might be after the war. Neither of them talked about marriage, but she sensed it was there, hovering in the background and Johnnie just waiting for the right moment to mention getting serious. He barely touched on the matrimonial line, citing his mother as the reason for being cautious.

'Dad needs me. Mum needs me. I will probably get hitched, but whoever I choose must understand that I will never leave the farm. Not only that, but whoever she is will have to give a hand to my mother. Her heart's not good. Rheumatic fever when she was a child.'

So, there it was, a statement of intent hanging in the air between them.

'No need to look so worried.' A strong arm wrapped around her shoulders gave her a bigger squeeze than his hand had done.

Apprehensive, but assured by his words and actions, Tilly entered the farmhouse.

The kitchen was warm and smelled of whatever was cooking for tonight's supper.

Mrs Forester was sitting at the head of the table, lovingly observing Jack, Sybil's little boy, as he spooned rhubarb and custard into his mouth.

On catching sight of her, his face lit up. 'I've got rhubarb and custard.' Once it was said, he went back to shovelling more into his mouth.

In answer to Tilly's puzzled expression, Mrs Forester explained. 'We had to call an ambulance. His mother's been taken into hospital.' She nodded at her son. 'Johnnie found her.'

Johnnie stepped in to explain. 'I was down in Brook Meadow. Heard the little lad calling for his mother to get up. I managed to carry her back to the top field where I'd left the horse and cart. Mum took care of them both whilst I got my motorbike out and drove to the post office.' There was determination and a whole lot of love in the look he gave to his mother. 'Once this war is over, we're getting a phone put in – no matter what Dad says. In case of emergencies,' he added.

His mother's eyelids fluttered an acknowledgement.

Tilly nodded dumbly before asking if Sybil was going to be all right.

'We don't know yet, but...' Johnnie paused and shook his head. 'One of the ambulancemen suggested to me that she might have TB, what with that cough and the overall state of her. She's likely to be in hospital for some time.'

'Poor woman.' Tilly looked at Jack. 'He'll miss his mother terribly.'

Johnnie took a deep breath whilst exchanging looks with his mother.

'Ma thinks we need to contact the Children's Department in Ipswich.'

'Children's home?'

'They've got homes for orphans.'

'But he's not an orphan!' Tilly couldn't help but protest. 'He's got a mother. She's not dead.'

She met the blank expression on Johnnie's face with a fierce anger on her own. Until what they were saying sank in. It was as if every breath was expelled from her body.

And what about Jack? Was he listening to this? Did he understand what was being said?

One look at him holding up his dish for more custard was enough to tell her that he did not.

Mrs Forester smiled down at him as she ladled more custard into his dish.

Johnnie put an arm around Tilly's shoulder. 'Let's talk about this outside.'

His voice was soft and the arm around her shoulder was firm but gentle.

Feeling weak at the knees, she let him guide her outside where the air was fresh and cool thanks to an earlier downpour. Beyond the farmyard entrance, a rainbow arched above the treetops.

Johnnie nodded at it. 'A promise from the man up there.' He pointed to the sky where heaven was supposed to be. 'No more rain today.'

She sensed he was prevaricating. Thanks to the volume of work on the farm, it wasn't often he went to church.

'If there's something you want to say, go ahead and say it.'

He sighed. Patted her shoulder, his gaze still fixed on the colourful bridge between earth and heaven.

'The lad has to go somewhere whilst his mother is in hospital.'

She was about to suggest that Jack stay at the farmhouse, but Johnnie got there first.

'He can't stay here with us. If he was older, I could take charge of him, but him being a youngster, that wouldn't work. My mum's got enough on her plate and, before you mention it, you're here to work the land and not play nursemaid. Besides, you're off to see your mum tomorrow.'

His mention of her going home reminded her that she might not see Jack when she came back – or his mother for that matter.

'Is there anyone in the village, someone who's already taken in evacuees?'

She knew there were a number of evacuees in the village, mostly kids from London whose parents had sent them to the safety of the countryside.

'I've no idea, but even then, it will take some time to ask around and get something sorted.'

To her mind, they seemed to be in something of a maze, but wasn't there always a path through? A way out?

She thought of Coronation Close, the comfy home her mother had provided for her and her sister. Three bedrooms. One for her mother, one for herself and one for Gloria. There was plenty of room for one more.

'I'll take him home with me. It'll take his mind off his mother not being around.'

Her suggestion was spontaneous. She couldn't know for sure how her mother would react. But the poor little boy...

She felt Johnnie's eyes on her and found she had no alternative but to look up at him.

'My mum won't mind.'

There was no time to let her mother know, but the die had been cast.

'I'll pay for his ticket,' she added, determined to make this work out.

'No, you will not. I'll deal with that. There's room on my motorbike to take both of you to the station. Eight o'clock sharp?'

Something special had passed between them. She could see it in his eyes. They'd talked the hind leg off a donkey in the pub, but this was the first time she'd felt there was something more between them.

'That's very kind of you.'

'It's very kind of you too. I'm grateful and I'm sure Jack will be grateful. He adores you. It's there in his eyes.'

She wanted to say that it was in his eyes too, but held it in. There would be a better time and place to voice warm endearments.

'There is just one thing,' he said as they turned back towards the door that led out into the yard.

'Which is?'

There was everything he'd hinted at in that look; a hesitant wistfulness that he feared saying yet just had to say.

To her surprise, he kissed her forehead. 'Just make sure you come back here. I'll be waiting for you.'

27

'Stop fussing around, Jenny Crawford, and get going or you'll miss the bus.'

Thelma tapped her hand playfully. It was hard not to keep rearranging the cups and saucers, pulling the cake to the centre of the table, transferring the fish paste sandwiches from one corner to another.

'Jenny, for pity's sake. No matter what corner those sandwiches are in, moving them won't magically turn them into tinned salmon. Fishpaste is what they are, and fishpaste they will stay!'

Thelma had taken charge, but Jenny still couldn't resist giving the dish of tinned peaches one more push. Nearer the jelly and the tinned cream seemed a better place.

'Jenny!'

Thelma took hold of her arm, handed her a black and white crocheted handbag and pushed her towards the door.

'Get going. Your Tilly will be waiting for you. Goodness, how grand is that going to be?'

'I'm going. I'm going right now.'

It didn't matter what she said, Thelma continued to propel her out of the front door, frogmarching her down the garden path until the gate clanged shut behind her.

Jenny had been looking forward to Tilly coming home for a long time. It wouldn't be permanent of course, just a week away from the farm. Once they'd caught up on everything, she'd be going back to continue doing her wartime duty.

Not a soul was waiting at the bus stop. She consoled herself that it was after midday and the bus was most crowded morning and evenings. Earlier in the morning was when the workers piled on, mid-morning was the time for women off to shop for the family, and evening around six and after was when the workers came home.

She knew the cheap little wristwatch she wore kept time as it saw fit, though not necessarily accurate.

No sign of the bus.

Having Tilly come home was incredibly uplifting. Worries about hospital results were pushed aside. Nothing was so wonderful as having both daughters at her side – at least for a little while.

Her strained gaze looked along Leinster Avenue to where the next bus should appear. There was no sign of it.

Biting her bottom lip, she thought of what might be best to do next. A taxi? Goodness no. That would cost a fortune and there was no Robin Herbert to ask for a lift. His van had been a bit of a bone-rattler, but at least it would have got her to the railway station.

There was a bit of a heat haze at the far end of the road, at the point where it dipped down towards Whitchurch Lane. Beyond that were fields and the airfield.

Something squarish and black suddenly came into being, like a pupa punctuating the shimmering haze.

The shape solidified as it came closer and then it became larger, eventually recognisable. It became a car.

It was impossible not to watch as it became bigger simply because there was nothing else on the road – certainly no bus.

To her surprise, it slowed before stopping altogether.

The window on the passenger side was rolled down, the driver leaning full length across the front seat.

'Jenny. Do you need to get somewhere urgently?'

Her jaw went slack. Charlie Talbot filled the gap in the open window.

'I prefer to wait for the bus,' she replied hotly.

He shook his head. 'There's an unexploded bomb in the city centre. Buses and everything else are running late.'

Instant panic had her asking about the trains. 'Are they running late?'

'I couldn't say. I haven't heard of any unexploded bombs around the station. The one that's causing traffic hold-ups fell deep into the ground at the bottom of Park Street. It's only just been discovered. Can I help at all? Can I give you a lift?'

She hesitated.

He looked away, then back again.

'If you could just tell me where you're going, I can tell you if I'm going your way.'

Getting there was priority. She swallowed her reservations and told him she was meeting her daughter at Temple Meads station.

The door swung open. 'Get in. I'll take you there.'

The open door beckoned. So did the upholstered front seat. She slid in beside him. The car moved away from the kerb.

'Your daughter must be a young woman now.'

'Yes. She is.'

Keeping her eyes fixed on the road ahead helped her cope. If she didn't look at him, didn't see that brandy brown hair and merry blue eyes, she could persuade herself that it was not him, that it was just a taxi driver.

The subterfuge was gossamer thin.

'Is this the eldest one? Your daughter, I mean.'

'Yes.'

'On leave, is she?'

'She's a land girl.'

'And your youngest daughter. What does she do?'

'She works in an office.'

Throughout the exchange, she kept her eyes on the road, not daring to look at him.

He fell silent. She fancied him glancing at her but did not meet his look.

The silence lasted a few miles, all the way through Bedminster, past the tobacco factory, over Bedminster Bridge and up Redcliffe Hill. Until the spire of St Mary Redcliffe threw its shadow across their path.

Charlie said, 'I've been told that St Mary Redcliffe was the favourite church of Queen Elizabeth the First.'

'Yes.'

The silence fell again until, as the Gothic towers of Temple Mead Station at the top of the incline in front of the station, he said, 'Jenny. I know I hurt you. I think you should know that I bitterly regret many things in my past.'

'Like the women who paid you for their services?'

There was a bitter, accusing tone to her voice. What kind of man allowed a woman to pay for his company – and more?

'Ouch. I deserved that.'

'Does your fiancée know about your past?'

He sighed. A lorry pulled across in front of him temporarily preventing the car from proceeding. 'She does now.'

His response surprised her.

'Indeed?'

'I told her. The truth is that I saw you and made an instant decision to tell her all about my past – warts and all.'

'I see.'

Charlie Talbot had always had a glib tongue, knew how to get what he wanted – even if it meant lying. The fact that she wasn't sure he was telling the truth must have shown on her face.

'She gave me my ring back.'

How did she feel? Was she glad? She wasn't quite sure. Her face felt warm, but perhaps that was due to the sun shining through the car windscreen, blinding her almost.

The car pulled up in front of the main entrance to the grand facade of the station, where people were milling about, some going in, some coming out.

Jenny grabbed the gleaming door handle, turned it and flung her feet out of the door, followed by the rest of her.

'Do you still live in Coronation Close?'

His shout followed her loud and clear, but she didn't answer, didn't even look back. The coolness of the station interior beckoned. Flinging her arms around her daughter mattered more than flinging them around him. Let him stew.

She didn't check to see if he was still there and expected him to drive away, to go wherever it was he was going.

Thanks to him giving her a lift she'd arrived early. Tilly's train was not in yet.

A cup of tea in the buffet was welcome. Waiting gave her time to calm down and to think.

Her thoughts were jumbled. A few years had passed since she'd seen him last, and now here he was, large as life and as confident as ever.

Emily, the woman he'd been engaged to, was perfect in every way.

Whereas I'm just ordinary, not elegant and certainly not perfect. Yet she wanted him.

Her gaze travelled to the scene outside the buffet window. Women were embracing men in uniform lately stepped down from trains, their affection a joy to see. When they got home, were reunited in the matrimonial bed or whatever, they would make love.

Jealousy took hold of her as she imagined passion and naked bodies. Oh how she would like that with Charlie. But it couldn't happen. If the worst came to the worst and she had surgery, then she would not measure up – certainly not to Emily. She would be less than perfect. Charlie could have his pick of the perfect, so why would he bother with her?

* * *

A harassed-looking Tilly climbed down from the train, suitcase and carrier bag in one hand, her other hand holding the hand of a little boy.

There were hugs and kisses before Jenny had a chance to be introduced and she listened quietly whilst her daughter explained.

'I'm sorry. I just didn't have the time to tell you. It all happened so quickly.'

Over another cup of tea, squash and a currant bun for Jack, Tilly told her who he was and the fact that his mother was in hospital.

'I'll tell you the rest of it when we get home,' she whispered, her gaze sliding sidelong in Jack's direction.

Jenny's heart did a flip when she saw Charlie's black Hillman cooped up amongst the taxis, cars and buses. There were crowds behind her, crowds in front of her and no way to escape coming level with him. He got out of the car and went round to the passenger door, held it open and smiled.

'I'm free to take you home. All three of you.'

He'd waited for her. Pure chance that he'd come along when she'd been waiting at the bus stop? No. She didn't think so. He'd been on his way to Coronation Close, honeyed words on his tongue, ready to enchant her all over again.

His smile swept from her to Tilly and finally to little Jack.

'Fancy a ride in the car, little fella?'

Tilly saw the concern on her mother's face.

'Haven't I seen him somewhere before?' she said in a hushed aside.

We'll get the bus, a defiant response. She readied to deliver it.

'Car,' cried Jack and pointed.

The little lad's eyes had been closing, not surprising after the long journey from Suffolk. The car had aroused his interest. Both he and Tilly were tired. *Don't look a gift horse in the mouth, Jenny Crawford!*

Her mind was made up. The sooner she got them home, the better.

Young Jack scrambled through the narrow rear door and into the backseat, his face bright with excitement. Tilly followed, cramming the one piece of luggage she'd brought on her lap between them.

The back of the car was more cramped than the front. Even so, Jenny would have been more comfortable to sit there rather than next to Charlie.

Telling herself the trip was only short helped a bit.

The car on the move, she kept her gaze fixed forward and her mouth closed.

Eyes on the road ahead and sensing her mood, he directed his conversation at Tilly, who batted back answers with alarming confidence.

Yes, she was a land girl. Yes, she did know the difference between a cow and a bull. Yes, she could drive a tractor.

When Charlie's questions ran out, Tilly told Jack what to expect at Coronation Close. Jenny joined in, choosing a subject the little boy could engage with.

'Cath's cat has had kittens. Perhaps Jack would like to see them? Would you like that, Jack?'

Yes. Of course he would. Kids and kittens were a good mix.

Half an hour and they turned into Coronation Close. Jenny didn't wait for Charlie to come round to the passenger side but opened the door and almost flung herself out.

Tilly and Jack piled out of the car behind her, her daughter thanking Charlie for the lift.

His statement that he would see her around followed Jenny up the garden path. 'You've got a nerve,' she whispered. His past behaviour was not that easily dismissed.

The ample figure of Thelma Dawson stood waiting at the front door. Her gaze flickered between Jenny and Charlie standing in front of the car bonnet watching Jenny every step of the way.

Jenny didn't meet her gaze as she hurried with head down up the garden path.

Thelma's eyes slid sidelong at Jenny as she murmured, 'Charlie Talbot. Well, there's a thing.'

'The bus didn't turn up,' said Jenny as she swept past. She'd tell her the rest later.

'And Charlie did,' Thelma murmured. 'Welcome home, sweet girl.' She gave Tilly a hug before looking down at the snowy-haired boy and asking, 'Now who have we here? What's your name, little lad?'

Looking totally unfazed that a cuckoo had been brought home to the nest, Thelma smiled down at him. Jack looked up at her. His smile revealed babyish teeth, 'Jack,' he lisped.

'Hello, Jack. You can call me auntie if you like. I'm auntie to everyone around here.'

'Including me,' chuckled Jenny.

Thelma took hold of his hand. 'You must be starving. Do you like jelly and custard?'

Jack nodded.

'And apple pie?'

Tilly answered for him. 'And so do I. Come on, Jack. Let's get to that apple pie before someone else gets to it.'

Thelma held on to the door. 'I'm right behind you.'

Charlie Talbot's reappearance worried her and it must have shown on her face. It couldn't have come at a worse time. Jenny was at her most vulnerable.

Charlie returned her puzzled look with one that hinted at challenge as though he was daring her to pass judgement. Not that she cared what he thought. She wasn't going to let him take advantage of Jenny. The look she returned to him was just as challenging.

The moment held, neither of them speaking nor altering their expression.

He lifted his hat to her before getting into the car, starting the engine and travelling the full circle of the green at the heart of Coronation Close before disappearing. Only then did she close the front door.

'Good riddance,' she muttered; then, pasting on a smile, joined the others.

28

The handles of two heavily laden shopping bags dug into Margaret's hands. It was the potatoes that did it and what with waiting in the queue to be served. Her mood showed on her face. The corners of her mouth were downturned. Her jaw jutted forward like a bulldog about to take a bite out of someone.

Late afternoon, and Coronation Close was not yet bursting with the noise of children just let out of school. Some of her neighbours were out gassing on the doorstep. She sensed their eyes following her as she made her way to her front gate.

Usually, she would have thrown them a filthy look, but not today. Today her thoughts were fixed on her daughter, Judith. Why hadn't she noticed before how much she resembled her father?

Judith had openly admitted that she was attending the church where they'd once gone as a family. Percy had been a staunch disciple of Maurice Grinder, the minister there. It now seemed that their daughter had fallen under the spell of the new minister – younger so she'd heard, but no less a firebrand.

'I'm old enough to make my own choices as to whether I go

to church, or indeed which church I go to,' Judith had loftily exclaimed. 'You've chosen the sinful path, Mother. I've chosen a righteous one.'

Margaret had been stunned. No matter how much she shouted or threatened to beat some sense into her, Judith had stood staunchly by her principles. For someone so young, she certainly held her ground, not giving an inch despite her mother's threats.

Her stance and her words, so much like her father, caused Margaret to recoil. Why couldn't she be more like other girls of her age, like Gloria Crawford for instance?

Confronting Jenny Crawford about her wayward daughter shouldn't have happened. She'd grow out of her waywardness. Most people did as they got older. Waywardness, wildness was somehow normal.

But what to do about Judith? Daughter being so like father was unpalatable.

Staggering along with heavy shopping slowed her footsteps and gave her time to think and face what she had been and what she had become. Percy was to blame for her wild behaviour. That's what she told herself. Judith resembled her father, was taking a similar path, but was he to blame for that, or was she?

Her thoughts were confused. Her eyes fluttered like butterflies unsure of a safe place to land.

A thought came to her. How about she phoned the minister and gave him a piece of her mind?

The thought took root. She stopped close to the phone box on the corner before Coronation Close.

She might well have done that, but somebody was already in the phone box, a lifeline much used since the advent of war. Thelma Dawson. Probably talking to that Dutch bloke.

Thelma's back was to her. She was about to tap on the glass

when Thelma Dawson turned round, glowered and went back to her phone.

By then, Margaret had changed her mind.

The smack of a ball against a cricket bat sounded from the green.

'Mum!'

Howard came running over, the one and only cricket bat in the street tucked beneath his arm.

'You're out,' one of his mates shouted.

'I've retired,' Howard shouted back.

'Here. Carry one of these.'

He grimaced but did as he was told.

'Did you get the job?'

He'd been for a job at a cooperage in Coronation Road. Percy wouldn't have approved of his son making beer barrels, but Margaret had been told the apprenticeship would lead to a well-paid job. Everyone wanted beer and beer was stored in barrels made by the same method for centuries. A skilled job.

'Yeah,' Howard replied. 'I start next Monday.'

'Work hard and no messing about.'

Howard placed the heavy bag on the draining board in the kitchen. Unbeknown to his mother, he was assessing his chances of lying about his age and joining the army. Being tall for his age, he reckoned he'd get away with it. And anyway, his mother wouldn't be alone in the house. Judith would still be here, not the best of company, her sullen countenance rarely cracking with a smile.

'Auntie Cath said I could look at her kittens. Our Judith wanted to see them too. Oh, and Auntie Cath asked if you could drop in with a cup of sugar.'

'Why? Doesn't she have her own?'

Howard looked sheepish. 'She made apple pie last week and gave a load of it to me and Judith.'

His sister, who was getting ready to attend an evening sermon, made comment. 'Food doesn't appear by magic.'

'I don't think the Reverend Grinder would consider it a miracle,' Margaret replied acidly.

Judith was unfazed. 'You may mock, Mother, but he believes, and so do I, that miracles do happen.'

She eyed her mother calmly, her dark eyelashes brushing her cheeks.

Margaret's jaw tightened. 'Not in Coronation Close.' Her tone was bitter. What did her daughter know about what her father was really like? What did she know of the extreme grief when Albert died, her blaming her husband for his death?

Judith had never commented on her behaviour, never called her a tart, never questioned why she'd become what she was. But that look in her eyes, such a deep look, direct yet full of hidden meaning. It was as though she knew without being told.

Margaret owed Cath something, seeing as she was generous towards her brother's children. She filled the cup with sugar and handed it to Howard.

'Here you are.'

'Mum! I can't. I'm playing cricket.'

Bat beneath arm, the door slammed behind him before she could stop him.

Judith held up a hand, palm facing her. 'I think you should go. Go on. You haven't seen Auntie Cath for a long time. Pop in.' The way she said it was more than a suggestion. More like an order.

She sighed, rolled her eyes, then looked down at the sugar. Cath was not to blame for anything that had gone wrong in her life.

'I'll pop in.'

29

Brushing Jack's curly white tresses made Tilly laugh. 'Look at these curls. They've got a life of their own.'

Jenny laughed too. The little boy was chuckling, gleeful that his wild locks were making them laugh.

'I think that will have to do. We're only visiting Cath. And the pussycats,' she declared, bending down so that her face was level with the little boy.

They held his hands as they made their way along Corona-tion Close, one either side of him.

'He's such a lovely little boy,' said Jenny, smiling down at him. 'If I ever have children, I'd like one just like him.'

Tilly was easy to love, thought Jenny. She gave so much to everyone around her. Even Gloria had managed to stay in one whole night in honour of her sister's visit. The other nights were spent with Damien. She felt helpless to do anything about it. Traditional attitudes still existed beneath the surface of a world in turmoil but seemed to have been shelved.

Jenny had told Tilly as much as she knew, though avoided mentioning him giving her a lift to the doctor's surgery. If she'd told her that, Tilly would want to know why she'd needed to go to the doctor and Jenny didn't want to tell her.

A brown envelope that had arrived yesterday morning lurked behind the clock on the mantelpiece. Opening it could wait until Tilly had gone back to the farm. No news was good news, though she had taken it from behind the clock several times. Flicking it between her fingers, tempting her curiosity. So far, she hadn't succumbed. No news was good news.

The kittens were pretty, and Jack wanted one. Tilly had the task of explaining to him that it was a long train journey back to the farm. 'Kitty would be tired out!'

Jack settled for cuddling each kitten in turn.

A loud yoohoo sounded from the back door.

'Cath. I've brought your sugar back.' And there was Margaret Routledge.

Cath had been on her knees next to Jack, holding back the curtain hanging from the draining board. The curtain hid a vegetable basket and a potato sack. In winter the space beneath the draining board was occupied by a chicken coop, just enough for one or two in time for Christmas. At present, the space was taken up by an orange box occupied by the cat and kittens.

Cath knocked her head on the draining board as she got up. Sight of the cup of sugar seemed to take her by surprise.

Margaret explained. 'I borrowed it from you.'

'Did you?'

Intrigued by the arrival of yet another new face, Jack held up the black kitten he'd tucked beneath his chin. 'Look,' he said gleefully.

Cath grabbed the cup of sugar before it crashed to the floor.

Margaret's face, devoid of make-up, turned a ghostly white.

Jenny pressed a fingertip against her lips. If she hadn't, she would have blurted out that, yes, Jack resembled Albert. Not the same age, but same in looks.

'His name's Jack?' Margaret waited for confirmation. Jenny was inclined to think that if nobody said otherwise, Margaret might claim him as her own.

'His mother's in hospital,' she said, low enough so Jack couldn't hear.

'Are you sure?'

Yes, of course she was sure. More explaining.

'The farmer's wife is not in the best of health and unable to look after him with nobody else around, so Tilly brought him with her.'

Her voice was clear enough, but it was hard to tell whether the explanation sank in. The look of shocked surprise remained on Margaret's face.

Tilly added, 'He looks like your little boy.'

Jenny shot her a warning look. Referring to Margaret's loss might not be a good idea.

'This one's my favourite,' said Jack, unaware of the tense atmosphere that had descended following Margaret's arrival.

Jack's jaw, white as alabaster, snuggled against the fluffy bundle.

For some inexplicable reason, he fixed his blue eyes onto Margaret. 'Do you like this one?'

'Yes.'

The response was carried on a sob.

Cath suggested she sit down.

Gaze fixed on the boy, Margaret sank onto a chair.

Jenny offered to make a cup of tea.

Cath jerked her head. 'Good idea, Jenny. You know where everything is.'

Hot tears accompanied Margaret's sobs. 'His mother...'

Tilly repeated that his mother was in hospital. She didn't outline the circumstances of how she'd met Jack and his mother. Neither did she elaborate on Sybil's bruises and her suspicion that they might have been the result of blows from a violent husband.

A look passed between mother and daughter. Tilly had relayed her suspicions to her mother, but that was all. Nothing was proved.

'Does he need a home?' Margaret asked, a hopeful expression appearing as she lowered the pale hands that had covered her face.

'I don't think so. It all depends on if his mother is better. I won't know that until I get back to Merryweather Farm.'

'Are you staying for that cup of tea?' Cath asked Margaret. She glanced at the mantel clock.

Margaret's eyes were dreamy and fixed on the boy. 'He looks like an angel.'

There was an awkward silence. Was Margaret going to grab him and say he was Albert reincarnated?

'Your Albert was older.' Jenny's voice was firm.

Misty-eyed, Margaret asked Cath if she'd made a cake. Cath was well known as a brilliant cake-maker. Food, especially baking, was her way of showing love to everyone.

'Apple cake. That old apple tree keeps on giving. I'm still using up loads that I dried from last year. John reckons he'll end up looking like an apple if he eats much more of it.'

Amusement spread from one to another. Perhaps the worst was past.

* * *

Back at number five Coronation Close, Judith was preparing to attend the evening sermon. She checked the time and smiled to herself. Her mother had been at her aunt's house for over an hour, more than long enough to return a cup of sugar.

She'd seen the little boy playing with the kittens and his resemblance to Albert. That was when she'd planned the miracle. Her mother wouldn't have recalled whether she had borrowed sugar or not. Thanks to the drink, her mind had turned to mush. Judith understood how things had been between her parents. Her father's behaviour had partly contributed to her mother's behaviour in these latter years. But so had the death of her younger brother.

It was a long shot, but having her see Jack, a child that resembled Albert, might just shock her out of the lifestyle she'd fallen into. Improvement might not happen overnight, but there was a chance that the first building blocks would be laid. That was her miracle. She was now off to listen to the Reverend Andrews. Afterwards, she would tell him what she had done. He would approve. He approved of her very much.

30

Jenny's heart ached on the night before Tilly was due to leave for Suffolk.

Did Charlie Talbot have sixth sense? It seemed that way, when he drew up at teatime, parked the car and came knocking at her front door.

'I wasn't sure you'd be working or not, but called in at the Broadway anyway. They told me you weren't expected back until tomorrow afternoon once your daughter had left. Good Samaritan that I am, I came to offer my services by way of a lift to the station.'

They say that looks can kill, but hers didn't. 'You're no good Samaritan.'

His gushing enthusiasm lifted one side of his mouth – something between a smile and a grin. 'Father Christmas then. Only it's a Hillman motor car, not a sleigh. A lift to the station. How can you say no to that?'

Finding the fortitude to prevent her heart from melting was difficult.

Tilly was going. She was staying. As for Gloria, the writing was on the wall. Nothing was going to persuade her to give up Damien Fox. Love for a man or loyalty to her mother? She knew she would be the loser.

'Are you going to invite me in?'

'Yes.'

It seemed her abrupt response was unexpected.

'Can we begin again?' he asked, once he was standing in the middle of her living room.

'What do you have in mind?'

When that deep V showed between his eyebrows, she was tempted to smooth it out with the tips of her fingers. Yes, she wanted to resume their relationship. She'd known that from the first moment she'd seen him at the Broadway.

'You've always been on my mind.'

She shook her head and laughed. 'That's not any kind of commitment.'

'Mind if I sit down? This leg of mine...' He tapped his damaged leg.

She nodded.

There was a puzzled look on his face. 'I hope I've got this right. Your question. I won't run away this time. I'll stand by you, no matter what.'

He looked at her as if she'd gone mad when she burst out laughing.

'Through thick and thin,' she flustered through continued laughter. 'Can I hold you to that?'

Charlie played with the brim of his hat, looking down at it as though it was something he'd never worn before. A new hat. A new man?

He stopped twirling the hat. 'Yes.' Just like that, not knowing what he was letting himself in for.

She reached for the brown envelope from behind the mantel clock and gritted her teeth. *Let's see how you react to this!*

The puzzled look came back. 'What's that?'

The courage to open the letter from the hospital had taken a long time coming, but eventually, late last night, she'd done it. Nobody else around. No Thelma enquiring whether she'd heard. Tilly and Jack in bed. Gloria out and about with Damien Fox. Just her and whatever was in store.

Now somebody else who might share the burden – or might not.

She passed him the envelope which she'd rudely ripped open, just waited whilst he read it.

On first read, his eyes skipped over the words. He looked confused. Men tended to look confused when faced with illness – whether their own or someone else's.

He read it again.

Arms folded defensively against whatever was coming, whatever he might say, she said nothing. Just waited for him to digest what it said before committing himself.

'Cancer.'

One word. He'd voiced that one word.

'Yes.'

'It says you're going to have surgery.'

'Yes. My breast removed.' She said it softly but bravely. 'It's the only way to get rid of the lump.'

Thoughts that would usually be whirling in her mind seemed totally absent. This moment was like standing on a clifftop whilst contemplating the decision whether to jump off or go home and put the kettle on.

Whatever Charlie Talbot said next would sway her decision. He was the cliff, though he might not know that.

'Why are you telling me this?'

She sat down opposite him. 'Because if we do start again, you need to know of impairments. I have mountains to climb – or one mountain at least.'

She sat back in the chair, her fingers interlaced as she awaited his response.

He seemed to read it for a third time. 'Does anyone else know – I mean, your family, your friends?'

She shook her head. 'No. To be honest, the opportunity to tell you has made me stronger. I'm not going to tell my family.'

'Don't you think you should?'

She laid her hands down on the chair arms, smoothing them as she gathered her reasons.

'I don't want them worrying about me. My doctor informs me I have a good chance once the tumour – tumours – are removed. That's good enough for me. My burden, not theirs.' Her eyes met his. 'Yours too if you're sincere about rekindling our relationship.'

Tilly and Jack dashed through the back door, laughing and shouting, Tilly telling him one more dish of apple pie and custard and it was off to bed.

'We have a train to catch in the morning.'

She stopped and stared when she saw Charlie and her mother.

'Hello.'

'I've come to offer you a lift to the station in the morning.'

There was no trace of anything except bonhomie in his voice, no residue of the conversation he'd had with her mother.

The letter had been handed back, Jenny tucking it into her pocket.

'In the car again,' Tilly said to Jack.

The little boy was rubbing his eyes.

'Bed for you, young man,' said Jenny, getting to her feet.

'Right,' said Charlie. 'Then I'll see you all in the morning. Eight o'clock early enough?'

Tilly said that it was.

He left without ceremony, waving one last time from the garden gate before getting into his car.

Jenny was unsure whether he really would turn up. Or perhaps it was just an act of kindness for an old friend. Perhaps that was all she was to him. Well, it was up to him! He'd read the letter. What happened after that – between them... She pushed the thought from her mind. Nobody knew what the future might hold. She certainly didn't.

* * *

Twilight patterned the road with alternate bands of light and shade. They reminded him of mid-1940, limping back to base, flaming buildings and potholes in the runway.

So much owed by so many to so few.

And what did he owe? What did Jenny owe?

He was lacking a leg. Not just a damaged leg, but half of one. What woman would want half a man? He dared hope it would be Jenny, the married woman he'd taken under his wing in years gone by. A bond remained. Jenny wouldn't know just how strong that bond was, how fate and this war was like a chessboard, the two of them pieces in similar circumstances finally thrown together.

Take it easy. That woman is proud. She would not accept pity. But then, neither would you, Charles Talbot, old man. Neither would you.

31

A short visit. Now it was back to Suffolk.

Jack's face was pink, and his eyes were closed, his head cushioned beneath her arm. A picture of untroubled sleep.

He'd been a bag of excitement when they'd climbed into the railway carriage. Acres of fields and grazing cattle held his attention for a while but eventually the long journey caught up with him.

Suburbs and the counties in between them and London had passed slowly. People got on and off at each station, some in uniform. Everyone seemed to be going somewhere, and she wasn't the only person accompanied by a child.

People remarked on the length of Jack's hair, longer than normal on a little boy.

'It's how his mother likes it,' she'd explained.

Their expressions changed at mention of his mother. Up until that point some assumed that she was his mother, which made her smile.

She'd sent a telegram to Merryweather Farm detailing estimated arrival at Hadley Halt, the closest station to the farm and some miles before Ipswich. She had not expected or received a reply from the farm but trusted that someone would be there to pick them up.

Paddington Station was full of steam, smoke and people. This was where they had to change trains to connect with Bury St Edmunds, where they'd have another train before Ipswich.

It was a bit of a bother changing trains. In one hand she carried their suitcase, holding onto Jack with the other.

Jack was fascinated by everything going on around him but was just as excited when they got on the next train as he had been on the first, doubly so when Tilly got out the sandwiches. Her mother had packed them sardine sandwiches and apples. A lot of people hated sardines, but Jack gobbled them back without grimace or comment. But there, she thought. The little boy had known war and deprivation for the whole of his young life.

Shunting yards with their grime-streaked goods trucks and coal heaps were left behind. The sky above the yards became less grey as they passed through the suburbs, where a gap in between houses betrayed where a bomb had fallen.

The countryside beyond the cities and towns formed a wide expanse of green. Church steeples pierced through the heart of villages; slate, clay and thatched roofs grouped around like chickens seeking a mother hen.

Jack's interest in the passing scenery waned more quickly than on the first leg of their journey. The sandwiches, an apple and a drink of barley water all gone, he closed his eyes. His sleepy head fell onto her lap.

The fields became ever larger and ever flatter, proof enough that they were passing through Suffolk, Constable country, the painter who had captured its flat fields and vast expanse of sky.

Some way off were what looked like a whole cemetery of

black crosses travelling across the sky; aeroplanes going off to war. God bless them all.

There was enough time for her too to doze before they reached their destination.

Jack had not yet asked about his mother, though on several occasions he had awoke during the night back in Coronation Close, crying and asking where she was.

Speaking in a calm voice, Tilly had assured him that the first thing they would do when they got back was to visit his mother. Had he forgotten her promise? She hoped he had. The first thing she wanted to do was to have a bath. Never mind that there would be barely enough water to float a goldfish, it had been a long journey.

She didn't know how long she'd slept, but she woke with a jerk. Sunset was streaking the sky with strips of fluorescent pink and violet. Lengthy shadows patterned the fields. Cows were either gathered at a far gate or had vanished entirely.

Station names were only shouted out in cities and towns. Few villages and hamlets bothered. What made things more difficult was that the name plates that had once adorned lamp posts and station canopies had been removed earlier in the war.

Pressing her face against the window, she tried to surmise how far she was from her destination. One field looked much like another. Platforms on small stations gave little away as to location.

Panic set in, though only for a short while. Geraniums and aubretia, colourful displays hung at regular intervals. She'd noticed them on the way out, and here they were again, a cheerful welcome home.

She gave Jack's shoulder a shake. 'Jack. Wakeup. We're home.'

Cheeks rosy and rubbing the sleep from his eyes, Jack asked if he was going home to Mummy.

'Yes,' said Tilly with warm enthusiasm.

Johnnie waved from where he stood beside the car.

'Luxury,' Tilly said laughingly. 'Not the horse and cart?'

'And this.' Looking a bit sheepish, he handed her a bunch of roses. 'I bought them from the old chap who looks after the flowers here.'

Fingertips brushed fingertips as she took the bouquet, her cheeks as pink as some of the roses. 'They're lovely.'

'How's your mum and the family?'

'They're very well.'

'So a good visit?'

She sighed and briefly buried her face into the sweet-smelling flowers. 'It was lovely, but...' She hesitated then smiled. 'But it's good to be home.'

'Yeah. Always good to be home.' Johnnie too seemed to sigh in relief.

She wondered at what she'd just said, declaring that Merry-weather Farm was home. Did she mean it? Yes. She did.

Johnnie tousled Jack's hair. 'And how are you, soldier? Ready to see your mum?' He added an aside to Tilly. 'She's still in hospital. I've managed to get permission for Jack to see her. They don't usually allow in children under twelve, but I persuaded the ward sister.'

'That was quite an achievement.'

He grinned. 'I used my natural charm.'

Tilly laughed before pointing out that Jack had eaten all the food on the train. Johnnie responded by dipping into his jacket pocket and bringing out a bar of chocolate.

'For you,' he said to Jack. 'Half in the car on the way to see your mother and half on the way back.'

The car was ready and waiting for them to get in. Time seemed to stand still as they stood there silently looking at each other.

'Welcome home.'

That word again.

They kissed in the cool dusk of the summer's evening. Theirs had not been a passionate awakening, more of a leisurely walk. On each step of the way they had got to know each other better.

The moment was ended by Jack pulling at her skirt. 'Can we go now?'

* * *

Some things, thought Tilly, seemed only natural. On their return from the hospital, after she'd put Jack to bed, she walked with Johnnie to the orchard. Beneath a sky full of stars, he asked her how she felt about marrying a farmer. About being a farmer's wife.

Although his question was not entirely unexpected, her brows furrowed as she hunched her shoulders, as though the question took a lot of thinking about. Johnnie wasn't a romantic. But that, she surmised, was the way he was. A typical farmer. Practical in the extreme.

'I'm not twenty-one yet, so I'll have to ask my mother.'

'Only right,' he said in that matter-of-fact way of his. 'I can ask her if you like,' he added, somewhat eagerly for him.

'I'll write to her tonight.'

'I can phone her.'

'You don't have a phone and neither does she. Let me write. I want to tell her how things went today.'

Even though his face was only lit by starlight, she could see the understanding in his eyes.

Later that night, an ancient oil lamp throwing its meagre light over her writing pad, she composed a letter that would explain a lot. Johnnie's proposal of course, but also about Sybil and Jack.

Dear Mum,

Thanks for everything. Jack thoroughly enjoyed himself and has been promised a kitten when one of the farm cats produces some.

Give my love to family, friends and neighbours. I do hope everything goes well for Thelma and her shop, you too if you decide to join her.

My best wishes also to Mrs Routledge. She looked well when I saw her. You were right about her marriage not being a happy one.

I'd thought the same about Sybil and assumed her bruised face was down to her husband. It turned out not to be true.

Sybil fell in love with a German who she'd met before the war. Jack was the result. Her parents turned her out when they found out she was pregnant and would not have the child adopted. Back where she lived, there were threats against both her and Jack. Hence the bruises I saw.

They met up again when Gerhard, Jack's father, was captured and became a prisoner of war. They intend to marry when the law allows.

Thank Charlie for giving us a lift to the station. I do remember him. He seems a nice man.

Much love, Tilly.

PS. Johnnie Forester has asked me to marry him. x

32

No matter how many pennies Thelma fed into the slot, out they came. A third attempt and still they came out.

She swore under her breath. 'Blasted things.'

A tapping at the glass of the phone box drew her attention.

'Having trouble?' asked a familiar voice.

Jenny's youngest, Gloria, was holding up a cupped handful of pennies. New pennies, or at least not as worn as the ones Thelma was using.

Her shout was audible despite the thick glass. 'These should work better. I'm a dab hand at phoning from telephone boxes. If the coppers are a bit worn, they won't work.'

Thelma pushed open the heavy door and took a few. 'If you don't mind. I'll pay you with some of these.'

'Don't bother. There's plenty more where they came from.'

Thelma didn't let her gaze linger on the smart black and white checked jacket and white skirt Gloria was wearing. They looked top quality and expensive, but then they would be if Damien Fox was paying the bills.

Inserting the new pennies worked. Thelma got through on

the same number she'd used before. She asked for Peter's friend, Erik, but was told there was nobody of that name.

'But there must be.'

The woman on the other end asked what detachment they were with. She replied that they were Dutch.

'Sorry. They've moved on. It's ATS here now.'

Thelma couldn't believe what she was hearing. 'Where have they gone?'

'Sorry. I can't help you. Back to Holland?'

The answer was given in a sneering manner causing Thelma to bite her tongue.

Distracted by worry, she didn't thank Gloria for the coins.

'You look as though you could do with a drink,' remarked Gloria. 'You and my mum. Worrying about stuff that might never happen. Is that it?'

Without thinking what she was saying, Thelma snapped right back. 'I've got every right to be worried and so has your mother. More so in fact.'

The fierceness of her response pulled Gloria up short. Nothing shocked that girl, or so it seemed, until now. 'What do you mean?'

Thelma realised she had gone too far and backtracked. 'Well. What with you. What with Robin not getting in touch.'

Gloria fixed her with a look of sheer disbelief. 'I know when someone's lying, and you're lying.'

Nervously licking her bottom lip, Thelma took just two steps before Gloria grabbed her arm.

'You are lying, aren't you.'

It was a statement, not a question.

It wasn't often that Thelma was lost for words, but she was now.

'Ask your mother.'

* * *

It had surprised Damien when Gloria had called off meeting him. 'Not tonight.'

Thelma Dawson had everything to do with it. Though her mother's old friend wouldn't know it, she'd cut through Gloria's selfish disposition as easily as a knife through butter.

Gloria made a habit of appearing selfish, but there was softness beneath the brittle bravado, mainly for her family.

Her mother was a presence on the periphery of the world she inhabited, someone only deferred to in time of trouble. Or when she'd been a child. She'd figured more prominently back then.

The back door of number two Coronation Close was usually open so she didn't need to use her front door key, but this evening she decided was an exception. Thelma's manner had been unnerving.

A little time was needed to think how she would approach this. Ask her mother outright what was worrying her? *Probably about me*, she thought and smiled to herself. *She's told me enough times that I've always been a worry to her.*

The living room was empty. So was the kitchen. The sound of shears clipping at a hedge sounded from the back garden.

July. The evening air was warm. Insects were buzzing around like small aeroplanes darting in and out of sunbeams.

'Cutting the hedge again?'

'Because it needs it. A drop of rain and it grows quickly.'

A simple explanation. Gloria eyed her mother speculatively. Cutting the hedge was normal. Everything in the kitchen looked normal. Ditto the living room.

Sighing, she went inside and took off her hat.

Whilst in the process of tidying her hair, she had cause to eye her reflection in the mirror. The corner of an envelope peeped out from behind the mantel clock. It wouldn't be for her, but it wouldn't hurt to read the address.

Mrs J. S. Crawford. There was an official stamp over the right-hand corner which was hard to read. Just one word stood out. Hospital.

The envelope had been torn open and although everyone was encouraged to reuse envelopes, this one never would be. It was too badly damaged.

Without thinking of the consequences, she slipped her fingers in and brought out the letter, unfolded it and began to read.

Her blood ran cold. Each word was like a nail being hammered into her skull.

Dear Mrs Crawford,

I'm afraid the results of your biopsy are positive. I feel the only option is for an operation to be carried out. To that end, I have arranged for you to be admitted on July 29th...

'What are you doing?'

Gloria held onto the letter as she turned to face her mother, her face full of alarm. 'Mum. Are you going to die?'

She knew she sounded like a small child and that her eyes were filling up with tears. It couldn't be helped. She was yet again the little girl who had craved attention, firstly from her father and then from her mother. Deep inside was like an empty well in desperate need of feeling the cool comfort of water lapping against its sides.

Jenny's face was immobile and very pale. In a sudden effort to take control, her jaw tensed, lips clamped tightly before she said angrily, 'That letter was not addressed to you.'

'Why didn't you tell me?' Gloria held on to that childlike pleading, her eyes stinging with tears.

'It was private. You had no business...'

'Have you told Tilly?' The prospect of her mother having told her elder sister without telling her was galling.

Jenny stared at her before shaking her head. 'No.'

'So nobody knows.'

Jenny gulped. She hadn't wanted to tell either of her daughters until it was all over – one way or another. 'The only person who knows is Thelma.' Mentioning Charlie Talbot was an option that would only make her daughter angrier. Best left unsaid.

Gloria nodded tersely as the first tear ran down her cheek. She shook her head. 'Oh, Mother. Why did you block us out?'

Sinking into a chair, Jenny buried her face in her hands and asked herself the same question. Why hadn't she told them? They would have supported her through this very tough time.

The answer was instant. 'Because I didn't want to burden you. We've got through dangerous times. I wanted you to enjoy your lives – even if a bomb fell on us tomorrow. I want to feel that you've lived.'

A single tear turned into a flood. 'Mum. I'm so sorry for giving you trouble.'

Jenny peered through the fingers spread fanlike across her face. Her hand dropped. A look of unconditional love came to her face. 'If he makes you happy, that's all that matters.'

Gloria buried her face against her mother's neck, her arms encircling her shoulders. 'I love you, Mum.' The words were carried on a flood of tears.

'Hush.' Jenny lifted her daughter's head, her hands cupping Gloria's face. 'It was because of love that I didn't tell you, and just for the record, no, I don't think I'm going to die. If you had read on you would know that.'

* * *

By the time Thelma came knocking at the door, Gloria had dried her tears and walked to the phone box. Her mother was going to live so she had changed her mind about going out with Damien tonight.

The two women sat opposite each other, the kitchen table between them each nursing a problem.

Jenny asked first. 'Did you manage to find out where he is?'

Thelma shook her head. 'No. The unit's moved.' She shrugged. 'I don't know where to. It's an ATS unit now.'

'Didn't they know where the Dutch unit had gone?'

Thelma grimaced. 'The girl who answered said they'd probably gone back to Holland. Daft cow. I think she meant it as a joke. It's not funny.'

'Of course it's not.' Jenny paused before saying, 'Gloria read the letter from the hospital.'

Thelma's eyes blinked wide open. 'I'm sorry.'

Jenny shook her head. 'No need to be. She had to know some time. Tilly too for that matter, and no, I haven't told her.'

'But Gloria read the letter.'

'Yes. Actually, it doesn't read that bad. They're talking about an operation. But...'

Thelma reached across the table and covered Jenny's clenched fingers with both hands. She shivered on finding that Jenny's were cold as ice.

'The doctors don't know everything.' Thelma's voice shook as she said it and her eyes welled up with tears.

'You've told Gloria that everything will be fine?'

Jenny nodded. She touched her left breast. 'I keep wondering how it will feel, having only one breast.'

Thelma's sad smile was fleeting. 'You'll still be the same woman you've always been. There's still a future, Jenny. For both of us.'

'Looking on the bright side, I assume your good luck with Bertrams is going ahead.'

'Yep! I'm managing it, and more than that once this blasted war is over.'

'I'll work for you if you want me to.'

'Of course I do.'

As long as we're all still above the ground, thought Thelma. She made a mental note to herself to ask daughter-in-law Maria if she could go to church with her. The Catholic Church did a lot of praying to saints who might lend a hand to a sinner like her.

'Does Peter know about you starting up a business?'

'No, but I know he'd be delighted.'

Her countenance fell as the old question came into play. How would he feel about her children being fathered by three different men.

Reading her mind, Jenny clasped her fingers as though they might scurry off if she didn't grip them tightly. She reminded Thelma that Peter's family had been killed during the early months of the German invasion.

'He will have gained a family by marrying you, one to replace those he lost.'

Bang, bang, bang! Somebody was banging on the front door knocker hard enough to smash the door in.

'Who the devil's that?'

Jenny got to her feet.

Thelma stayed her with a firm press on her shoulder. 'You rest. I'll get it.'

Margaret Routledge was there, her face devoid of make-up yet looking more attractive for all that.

'I thought you'd be here. I was buying some butter from Frank Turner's barrow when the phone box rang. It's for you.'

The meaning in the look she gave Thelma was easy to read.

'I think it's your Dutch fellah.'

Thelma threw her hands over her face. 'Oh my God. Is he all right? What did he say?'

'He said could I get you. He'd hang on until I did. My Howard's guarding the call, but you better run before he rings off.'

Thelma didn't need telling twice and Jenny almost pushed her out of the door.

When she got there, puffing and panting, she grabbed the phone as a drowning man might a life raft. 'Peter. Peter. Is that you?'

'It is me.'

'Where are you?'

'Paddington Station. The trains are crowded, and it will be close to midnight when I leave. Will you stay up for me?'

She could hardly breathe, and her legs seemed to have turned to jelly. She managed to say that, yes, of course she would wait up for him.

Speaking to him added wings to her heels, or at least it felt that way as she raced all the way back to Coronation Close. Jenny was looking out of the front window but headed for the front door on seeing an out-of-puff Thelma leaning on the post at the entrance to the street.

'Is there news?' she shouted as she headed to join her.

Thelma fanned her pink complexion with her hand. 'He's coming home. Peter's on his way home.'

A feeling of warmth seemed to encircle them both.

'You're home,' said Jenny with a smile. 'That's what home means to him.'

She leaned against the privet hedge. A flake of withered paint floated down from the fading paintwork declaring that this was Coronation Close. It was the council's job to maintain paintwork, but the war had put a stop to that. There weren't enough painters and decorators to do the job.

Jenny looked up at the sign and felt instant affection. 'Do you know what, Thelma, I know that name was only given to this street in honour of King Edward the Sixth, the king who never got crowned. But to my mind it will always be down to your collection of coronation china. You were here before then.'

Hand on chest as she caught her breath, Thelma shook her head. 'Well, I'm a bit like him. He didn't take the throne for the love of an unsuitable woman. I'm not collecting any more coronation china.'

'Not because Peter is unsuitable. He's hardly that,' Jenny said laughingly.

Thelma laughed with her. 'He's the most suitable man I've ever met.'

Arms interlaced, the two of them strolled round the back of Jenny's house and into the kitchen. With the touch of a match, the gas jet on the stove burst into life. Once filled the kettle was placed on the circle of flame.

Two friends of the same mind and destined to be so for as long as they lived.

* * *

Lying in bed that night, Jenny felt the full impact of that small word: home, and home was where the heart is. Whether it was Tilly with her farmer's son, Thelma with Peter or even Gloria with Damien Fox. That was what home really meant. Being with those you loved regardless of what the rest of the world might think.

For her it meant her daughters and ensuring their place in the world. She hoped she'd done a good job of bringing them up. Whatever the future might hold, she knew they would cope with everything that came their way.

* * *

MORE FROM LIZZIE LANE

The next instalment of the gritty and gripping Coronation Close series is available to order now here:

https://mybook.to/CoronationClose6BackAd

ABOUT THE AUTHOR

Lizzie Lane is the author of over 50 books, including the bestselling Tobacco Girls series. She was born and bred in Bristol where many of her family worked in the cigarette and cigar factories.

Download your exclusive bonus content from Lizzie Lane here:

Follow Lizzie on social media here:

f facebook.com/jean.goodhind

X x.com/baywriterallat1

© instagram.com/baywriterallatsea

BB bookbub.com/authors/lizzie-lane

g goodreads.com/lizzielane

ALSO BY LIZZIE LANE

The Tobacco Girls
The Tobacco Girls

Dark Days for the Tobacco Girls

Fire and Fury for the Tobacco Girls

Heaven and Hell for the Tobacco Girls

Marriage and Mayhem for the Tobacco Girls

A Fond Farewell for the Tobacco Girls

Coronation Close
New Neighbours for Coronation Close

Shameful Secrets on Coronation Close

Dark Shadows Over Coronation Close

Tough Times on Coronation Close

Bad Company on Coronation Close

The Strong Trilogy
The Sugar Merchant's Wife

Secrets of the Past

Daughter of Destiny

The Sweet Sisters Trilogy
Wartime Sweethearts

War Baby

Home Sweet Home

Wives and Lovers

Wartime Brides

Coronation Wives

Mary Anne Randall

A Wartime Wife

A Wartime Family

Orchard Cottage Hospital

A New Doctor at Orchard Cottage Hospital

Family Affairs at Orchard Cottage Hospital

Bleak Times at Orchard Cottage Hospital

Echoes of War at Orchard Cottage Hospital

The Kowloon Series

Doctor of Kowloon

Escape from Kowloon

Standalone Novels

War Orphans

A Wartime Friend

Secrets and Sins

A Christmas Wish

Women in War

Her Father's Daughter

Trouble for the Boat Girl

Sixpence Stories

Introducing Sixpence Stories!

Discover page-turning historical novels from your favourite authors, meet new friends and be transported back in time.

Join our book club Facebook group

https://bit.ly/SixpenceGroup

Sign up to our newsletter

https://bit.ly/SixpenceNews

Boldwood

Boldwood Books is an award-winning fiction publishing company seeking out the best stories from around the world.

Find out more at www.boldwoodbooks.com

Join our reader community for brilliant books, competitions and offers!

Follow us
@BoldwoodBooks
@TheBoldBookClub

Sign up to our weekly deals newsletter

https://bit.ly/BoldwoodBNewsletter